A love
Lauri Ro
than penning na
and women—who p
riding off into the sunset…or kick them off for
other reasons. Lauri and her husband raised three
sons in their rural Minnesota home, and are
now getting their just rewards by spoiling their
grandchildren. Visit: laurirobinson.blogspot.com,
facebook.com/lauri.robinson1 or twitter.com/LauriR.

Discover more at millsandboon.co.uk.

DIARY OF A WAR BRIDE

Lauri Robinson

MILLS & BOON

First Published in Great Britain 2018
by Mills & Boon, an imprint of HarperCollins*Publishers*
1 London Bridge Street, London, SE1 9GF

© 2018 Lauri Robinson

ISBN: 978-0-263-93296-6

To my uncles, Ralph and Dale.
This one's for you.

Prologue

1st of January, 1943

Dearest Diary,
Little did I know how important you would
become when Charlotte gave you to me.
You've been my confidant in what has
proven to be the greatest journey of my
life, and though I'm saddened that our time
together has come to an end and I shall
never forget the people I wrote about be-
tween your pages, it's a new year and I'm
embarking on a new journey, one of being
a married woman...

Chapter One

26th of April, 1942

Dear Diary,
Our life in the country has been so very different from those who remained in the cities, where bombs have destroyed so much and killed so many, and I fear all that is about to change. Lately, I've insisted that the children sleep holding on to their gas masks, ready to put them on at my command, and wear their clothes to bed so they'll be somewhat warm if we need to run to the bomb shelter. It's so very frightening.

I wrote about the arrival of American troops back in January. How everyone claimed the Americans will help us give the Nazis what they deserve. I can't say *that has happened, but I can tell you this. They built a Bomber Command Station right here in High Wycombe!*

Shortly after the American servicemen arrived, the headmistress of Wycombe Abbey girls' school received an official notice to evacuate all the girls within a fortnight to make room for the United States Army Eighth Air Force. That caused a tremendous influx of students into the small village school. Local children now attend lessons in the mornings and the evacuees in the afternoons, which includes all of the nine children living here with Norman and Charlotte. And, as if that wasn't bad enough, the past week planes started flying in and out of the base like flocks of birds. There is nothing to stop the German bombers from following those planes, intent upon dropping bombs on the base, which would have them flying directly over the farm!

Norman insists Father assured him there is nothing to worry about, that having the base so near should make us feel safer and that air raid sirens would sound if the German planes flew near, but there are no sirens close by us. Furthermore, by the time the sirens sound, it could be too late. That has happened elsewhere. No one can say it hasn't.

When I was evacuated out of London, here to Norman and Charlotte's, I did feel safe and have continued to for the past couple of years, but I truly fear there is no safe place in our country right now. Nowhere that families are safe. I also fear there soon won't be anything left of the country we are all working so hard to protect.

I also wonder why we are expected to put so much faith in the Americans. These aren't their homes. Their families. Their children.

I don't mean to sound so harsh, but I am weary, Dear Diary, and dare only share these thoughts with you. Unlike so many others, I can't put all my faith in the Americans. If they really cared about us, about what has been happening the past two years, they would have arrived long ago. Long before our cities and villages were little more than piles of rubble and long before our children became orphans.

Those planes flying overhead scare me,

almost as if I somehow know one of those
planes will change my life for ever.

The rumble of planes growing nearer sent Kathryn's nerves on edge. She tried to pedal faster, but the road was rutted and wet from the heavy spring rains that had fallen the night before. Her hands and arms, even her legs, shook as the noise overhead grew louder. Afraid to look, but unable to stop herself, she twisted enough to glance towards the sky behind her.

Fear grasped her entire body. Not only was the sound deafening, she'd never seen a plane so close. It was flying right at her, would hit her. Frantic, she tried to steer the bicycle off the road, but it wobbled uncontrollably and then toppled.

She hit the ground so hard, the air was knocked out of her. It was a moment before she could gather the gumption to cover her head as a powerful gust of wind tugged at her scarf and coat.

The noise was so great that her ears were ringing and she felt as if time had stopped, or wondered perhaps if this was how it felt when time ends. Life ends.

It was a moment or two before she realised the noise was fading and another before she concluded the plane hadn't landed on her. That it was still in the sky, flying higher now and away from her.

A sense of relief washed over her, until she saw the contents lying around her. The eggs, cheese and milk that had been in the wicker basket attached to the handlebars of her bicycle. Anger began to coil its way through her system. Every morsel of food was precious right now.

She scrambled on to her knees, reaching for an egg, hoping to salvage at least a few, when a powerful force grasped her from behind and lifted her completely off the ground.

'Miss, are you hurt?'

The egg she'd been about to save tumbled to the ground, cracking and oozing into the muddy gravel.

'Are you hurt?'

A boot, a man's boot, stepped right on the egg she'd been hoping to rescue and a shiver raced over her as her gaze travelled upwards, over the brown trousers tucked into the boots, a waist-length leather jacket and finally a billed hat that sat a bit off-kilter atop a short-cropped head of brown hair.

Twisting, she broke the hold he had on her and stepped aside, trying hard to swallow. 'N-no, I'm not hurt.' He was tall, very tall. She had to swallow again.

'I'm sorry.' He gestured towards the plane disappearing into the horizon. 'Rooster wasn't trying to scare you. He was fooling with us.'

'Fooling?'

He pointed towards an army vehicle. An American one. 'Yes, the pilots do that once in a while, fly low over one of the Jeeps, just as a joke.' The two dimples that formed, one in each cheek as his grin grew wider, showed just how humorous he found the situation. She didn't find anything about any of this funny. Not in the least.

'A joke?' Anger rippled every nerve in her body. 'With an aeroplane?'

He shrugged slightly. 'Yes. I'm really sorry. I'm sure he didn't see you.'

So mad she wanted to scream, Kathryn took a deep breath and glanced towards the ground, trying to gather her wits and nerves into some sort of semblance.

'Are you sure you're all right? Nothing's broken, is it?'

No! She wasn't all right. She'd nearly been scared to death.

He frowned as he gazed to the ground near his feet.

Anger had her hands balling into fists. Disgusted, she snapped, 'What's broken—ruined—is a week's worth of food!'

'That's hardly a week's worth of food,' he said.

She pulled the scarf off her head and used that to wipe some of the dirt off her hands. 'It is when every single egg is rationed.' Mud covered her hands, her coat, everything. A fresh bout of anger joined what was already boiling inside her. Clothes were rationed as tightly as food. 'Oh, you Americans. You're as bad as they say.'

'Who says?' He'd picked up her bike and set the brace so it would stand on its own before bending down to pick up the two crocks of cheese. 'I thought all you Brits were happy we'd arrived.'

Arrogant fool. 'Not all of us.' She snatched the crocks out of his hands. They were unbroken, but mud had saturated the cheese cloth as deeply as it had her coat. She'd known this was how it would be. That the Americans would do more harm than good. 'I assure you. Not all of us are happy in the least.'

He'd picked up the milk bottle, which had lost its cap and now held more mud than cream. 'Why's that?' he asked.

She set the crocks in the basket and took the bottle, setting it between the crocks. A fair amount of straw, which had been on top of the crocks to give the eggs cushioning as she pedalled, was still in the basket. How, she had no idea.

'Are you a spy?'

Not only did he capture her full attention, but she couldn't remember being so insulted, or mad. 'How dare you!'

He cocked his head while looking at her up and down. 'Why else would you hate Americans?'

'Because—' Her mind wasn't working fast enough. 'Oh, you and your stupid planes! How dare you go around scaring people like that! You're—you're rude and pompous and…and accident-prone.' It was the best she could come up with.

His laugh sliced through her, increasing her anger.

'No, we aren't.' He bent down and picked two unbroken eggs out of the mud. 'We are friendly and helpful.' Handing her the eggs, he said, 'See?'

She reached for the eggs, but a mean streak she'd never quite encountered before rose up inside her. Instead of taking the eggs, she squeezed them, cracking the shells. Then as the eggs oozed out over his outstretched palms, she spun about and hopped on to her bike.

Her escape wasn't quick or coordinated and she was hopping mad by the time both wheels managed to reach the grass beside the road where she could pick up a bit of speed. It dawned on her, then, that she was going in the wrong direction. She no longer had anything to deliver to Oscar and Ed, but she kept on pedalling anyway.

Dale Johnson's insides flinched at her departure. The women he'd met since arriving in England had flocked towards American GIs like the soldiers were shaking a feed bag. For the most part the women had been friendly, cute and more than ready to get to know an American soldier. This one certainly hadn't been. She was cute, though, even covered in mud and eggshells and spitting mad.

He did have to admit she had reason. Rooster had flown right over the road.

He waited until her bike rolled along smoothly before he turned about and walked back to the general-purpose vehicle commonly called a Jeep and climbed in the open passenger side. He'd gotten used to not having doors on the topless square-shaped cars. That wasn't the only thing about the Jeeps that reminded him of his father's tractor back home. They went through as much mud and muck as that old tractor had without any troubles. The ride they gave was about as smooth, too.

'Hey, Sarge,' Rusty Sanders said, grinding the gears while trying to hit the right one. 'You ever see that wizard movie? The one with the girl and her dog?'

Every GI had seen the movie. Watching that film ranked right up there with making your own bed. You did it daily and didn't complain. Flinching slightly until the Corporal found the right gear, Dale said, 'Sure have. Why?'

The Jeep sputtered before it took off. With the tyres rolling, Sanders nodded towards the bike rider they were quickly gaining on. 'Remember that scene where the old woman rides off on her bike?'

Dale tried not to laugh, but lost that battle. He lost his next battle, too. The one that told him not to turn around for a final glance after they drove past the rider. And the one that told him not to touch the brim of his hat. Even at this distance, he could feel her glare. Her eyes were as big, round and dark brown as a newborn calf's and her hair as black and shiny as the feathers of a red-winged black bird. Although far more beautiful, the way she was pedalling *did* hold a resemblance to the old witch in the movie Sanders mentioned. This girl was as angry and about as friendly as that old witch had been, too.

He didn't turn around until after she'd brought the bike to a halt by lowering both feet on to the ground and then swiftly manoeuvred it about and started riding back the other direction.

She certainly wasn't like the other women he'd met in England. He'd only been here a few months, but every other person he'd met had gone out of their way to let him know how happy they were that the Americans had arrived to save the day. Other than acknowledging their optimism, he'd kept his thoughts to himself. It would take plenty to stop the Nazis and he was willing to do his part, whatever that might be, but he wasn't willing to let anyone believe the war would soon be over. There was too much unknown for that.

Another thought hit him as the Jeep approached the fork in the road. 'Go left,' Dale told Sanders.

'Why? Where are we going now?' the Corporal asked.

The young man had a lot to learn, but that would happen in time. It always did. Such as learning that orders were followed without question. 'There's a roadhouse up ahead,' Dale replied. Unlike the young Corporal, the army hadn't had to teach him to follow orders. His father had taken care of that years ago.

'I've heard about the roadhouse,' Corporal Sanders said. 'It's called the Village Pub.'

Dale nodded.

'That's where we're going?'

Dale nodded again.

'Why?'

'Reconnaissance,' Dale said.

'Oh.'

Yes, Corporal Sanders had a lot to learn. They, he and Sanders, were mechanics and mechanics didn't usually embark upon reconnaissance missions.

Then again, they hadn't been doing a lot of engineering work up until the past few weeks. Since shortly after arriving in London and being convoyed out here to the country, they'd been building an air force base. You name it, they'd helped build it. Nissen huts, much like the Quonset sheds back home, made out of corrugated iron and built over concrete floors, runways and a number of wooden buildings that were now being used for numerous functions, and tents. Big ones, little ones and those in between. Even with all the buildings they'd erected, a fair number of men would continue to be housed in tents. What had been little more than a field was now almost as big as most of the towns back in North Dakota.

There were several small towns around this area, or villages as the locals called them, and they were only a few miles apart from each other. Back home, people had to drive for miles to reach the next town over. Miles and miles.

He'd caught glimpses of the villages while travelling to and from the base the past couple of months, but stopping at the roadhouse would be a first for both him and Sanders. The planes were finally in the air, flying in and out of the base daily, so today was the first free time they'd had since arriving.

'Looks like this is it,' Sanders said, pulling up next to a cobblestone two-storey building. 'It's hard to tell if they're open with those blackout curtains.'

Dale climbed out of the Jeep. The dark material hung inside every home and business for the same reason they'd covered the outside of the Nissen huts back at the base with black paint. In order to prevent the German bombers from seeing anything as they flew overhead in the darkness of night. 'They're open,' he said. 'The door's open.'

Sanders nodded and then asked, 'Reconnaissance for what?'

'We need to know who that girl is and where she lives before Major Hilts learns about Rooster's flyover.'

'Oh.' Sanders visibly shivered. 'You're right about that, Sarge.'

A short dark-haired man standing behind a long wooden counter waved as they walked in the door. 'Welcome, welcome! Good to see you stopping in. You're from the base, aren't you?'

'Yes, sir,' Sanders replied.

'Been looking forward to you boys patronising our place here,' the man said. 'What can I get you both? A cup of ale?'

'Coffee,' Dale said.

'Same here,' Sanders added.

The man held a finger up in the air. 'I stocked coffee just for you folks. Only take me a minute to get it started.'

Sanders waited until the man walked into the back room before leaning across the table. 'Didn't you read the pamphlet?'

Dale nodded. Every GI was ordered to read several pamphlets, including the one that stated:

The British don't know how to make a good cup of coffee. You don't know how to make a cup of tea. It's an even swap.

'You ordered coffee,' Sanders whispered.

'Because I don't like tea,' Dale said. 'The coffee here can't be any worse than my father's.' For years his father had said strong coffee would put hair on his chest. Both he and his brother, Ralph, had learned that was a wives' tale, but they'd drank the coffee anyway—every Sunday while their mother was at church. For two young boys, it had been an easy trade-off. Dad's coffee won out over Pastor Dunlop's sermons every week. Except for Easter Sunday and Christmas Day. Ma had insisted everyone attend church on those days.

'Coffee will be ready shortly,' the man said, walking back into the room. 'So you boys have been busy on that air base, haven't you? I've not driven out there myself, but I've heard all about it.' Fidgeting with the white apron tied around his portly waist, he walked around the counter. 'Name's Oscar. Oscar Fowler. My brother, Ed, is in the kitchen. The two of us own this pub. We're hoping to get some entertainment in here on Friday and Saturday nights. Just for you boys out there at the base. Hoping you'll feel right at home here.'

'That's kind of you.' Dale chose not to explain that they probably wouldn't have any more time for socialising in the future than they'd had since arriving.

'Least we can do,' Oscar said. 'Ed and I don't think like some others do.'

'Oh,' Dale said. 'About what?'

'Some think the Germans will follow your planes back here,' Oscar said. 'Dropping their bombs.'

'They won't dare come this close to a base,' Sanders answered. 'We've got artillery that will take them down before they could even think about dropping a bomb.'

Dale didn't respond. Although there was some truth in what the Corporal said, there was no telling what the Germans were capable of.

'That's what we think,' Oscar answered while waving a thick arm towards the counter. 'Can I get you something while your coffee brews? A pickled egg, maybe? They're fresh. Ed makes up a new batch every week. We get eggs, cream and cheese from a family up the road every week.'

It had been months since he'd eaten a real egg, yet Dale's mind was more focused on the young girl and the eggs that had broken when her bike toppled rather than eating one.

'My grandmother used to pickle eggs,' Sanders said. 'One year, my cousin and I copped a jar from the cellar and it just so happens the jar hadn't sealed, the eggs had rotted. Haven't been able to eat an egg since.'

There wasn't a lot to be said about the egg powder they ate regularly, except that it had to be better than a rotten pickled egg. Dale couldn't even stomach the thought of that.

'The family has rabbits, too,' Oscar said. 'Got a pot of stew in the kitchen if you'd prefer.'

'The coffee will be fine,' Dale answered. A hint of guilt struck his stomach at what he'd said about her cargo. Food was tightly rationed and what the girl lost wouldn't be replaced easily. 'Would this family have more food to sell? To others besides you?'

Oscar shook his head. 'Not enough to make a dent in what you need at the base, but you can always come here. We don't have to abide by the ration portions for you.'

'We'll remember that,' Dale said.

The brother, Ed, who was as stocky and dark haired as Oscar, but also sported a thick moustache, carried two steaming cups out of the back room and set them on the table while saying, 'Nice to see you boys. We got plenty of coffee, so hope you'll visit regularly.'

The cups were white and the coffee so weak Dale could see the bottom of the cup. The exact opposite of his father's. 'Thanks,' he said. 'Smells great.'

Evidently mid-afternoon was a slow time for the pub. He and Sanders were the only two customers and Ed and Oscar sat down at the table next to them. By the time his coffee cup was empty, Dale knew the girl's name and where she lived. He also knew what he had to do.

After paying for their coffee, he and Sanders climbed back in the Jeep and once again, as they approached the road to the base, he told Sanders to drive past.

'We going to that woman's place now?' Sanders asked.

Dale grasped the top of the windscreen as the rough road jostled the Jeep about. Once the ride smoothed out, he replied, 'Yes, and we're going to pay her for the eggs.'

'Why? We didn't break them on purpose.'

'No, we didn't, but we are going to pay her just the same,' Dale answered. 'Watch for a road to the right, we'll need to take it.'

It turned out to be several miles from the pub to the small house Dale presumed was where Kathryn Harris lived. Like many others, the base of the house was made of stones and the rest wood. The siding went vertical instead of horizontal, which made the two-storey home look taller than it was. There was also a barn and several separate fenced-in areas that housed chickens, rabbits and a large garden. The pen near the barn held a couple of cows and goats. All in all, the site gave him his first real bout of homesickness. Until enlisting, he'd rarely left the farm. Unlike his brother, Ralph, he'd never had a hankering to go elsewhere. Also unlike Ralph, he let his parents know where he was. Another reason he had to make things right with this girl. If headquarters learned about it, they could put a stop to his search for Ralph. His mother had already lost one child. His sister, Judy, had died from dust pneumonia before the war had even started and he'd promised his father that Mother would not lose another one. Not him *or* Ralph.

'This it?'

'Yes,' Dale answered, recognising the bicycle leaning against the barn. 'Pull up next to the house.'

An older, slightly stooped man with a mop of dull grey hair walked out the door before Sanders had cut the engine.

'Hello!' the man shouted. 'Welcome!'

Dale climbed out of the Jeep and walked to the gate, where he waited for the man to walk to the end of the cobblestone walkway.

'Norman Harris,' the man said, holding out one hand while opening the gate with the other. His round face looked jovial and one eye squinted as he talked.

Dale shook the man's hand. 'Dale Johnson and this is Rusty Sanders.' He purposefully left off their ranks. Their uniforms would let the man know they were American GIs.

'Good to meet you,' Norman said as he shook Rusty's hand. 'You part of those boys buzzing overhead all the time?'

'Yes, sir, we are,' Dale said. 'And we're here to apologise for startling your daughter earlier. We hope she's all right.'

The one eye Norman had open took on a sparkle. 'Kathryn's a good girl. Quick to anger, but she gets over it just as fast.' Lowering his voice, he added, 'It's the planes. They frighten her, but don't tell her I told you that.'

Dale had already heard how the planes frightened the locals and chose not to respond to that. 'I understand the incident caused a loss for your family,' he said, pulling his wallet out of his back pocket. 'I would like to reimburse you.'

'Oh, no, no.' Norman shook his head. 'That's not necessary. It was the muddy road. That's all.'

The house door opened, and though Norman might have suggested that Kathryn got over her anger quickly, the way she marched down the steps said that hadn't happened today.

Keeping one eye on her, Dale took out several bills. 'I still feel responsible.'

'No. No. My wife is putting together a basket that I will drive to the pub. Should have done that in the first place. The bicycle doesn't do well in mud.' Glancing over his shoulder, Norman smiled. 'Kathryn, these men came to apologise for the mishap. Wasn't that nice of them?'

Her glare said otherwise and grew in intensity when she settled it on him.

Turning back to the man, Dale said, 'I fully understand the loss of food, the loss of income, and insist upon paying you.' He once again held the bills out towards Norman. 'I'm not familiar with the prices here, so if this isn't enough, just say what is.'

Norman took the bills and counted them. 'This is far too much.'

Her animosity became even clearer as she watched Norman shuffle the bills. 'We cannot take your money. Will not.'

'Because it's American?' he asked. 'I'm sure any bank will—'

'No,' she interrupted, squaring her tiny shoulders. 'Because we all are doing our part in this war and will manage just fine without your assistance.'

He doubted that. 'I insist.'

'So do I,' she said.

For as tiny as she was, the fury in those brown eyes could fall trees.

'Kathryn—'

'Good day, gentlemen,' she said, interrupting Norman. Then with a sideways nod, she said, 'Give him his money back. Please.'

There was an odd plea in her eyes, one the old man recognised because he handed over the bills. 'Thank you for stopping by and for the apology.'

Chapter Two

28th of April, 1942

Dear Diary,
London had been struck again. Buildings I've known my entire life are no longer standing, the beautiful city I called home is becoming little more than rubble. Norman received word from Father that he and Mother are safe, our home remains undamaged. I'm relieved to know that, but so very saddened by all that continues to happen.

I dare say the Americans have yet to help us save the day and I'm not holding my breath. Especially after meeting one. They are dreadful. Nearly hit me with an aeroplane. Yes, an aeroplane. They are arrogant, too, and far too handsome for their own good. They think all they need is a smile and a wallet full of money.

I'm proud to say they did not fool me with either. Andrew taught me a lesson that I will never forget. Of course, I didn't realise that at the time. The war was just beginning then and I thought he wanted to marry me because he loved me, not because he thought marrying me would save him from serving. Mother was right in that sense, that he only wanted to marry me because of who Father is. I may not have before, but I now see the wisdom in her words. If I had married Andrew, I might have been living in one of the buildings that are now little more than rubble back in London. What I do know for certain is that I would never have met Charlotte and Norman and all the wonderful children in their care. I would never have discovered how much I truly enjoy taking care of the children. Of course, I knew nothing about that when I first arrived here. I knew nothing about so many things when I first arrived here, but I do now and I can say with certainty that I will never be fooled again. Not by a handsome smile or a uniform.

Kathryn's nerves had been frazzled since the bicycle accident, but hearing the older boys, George and Edward, bickering as they walked up the road flared a bout of anger inside her. As did the buzz rumbling the skies. The boys had made a contest out of naming the American bomber planes and tallying the number of times they'd seen each one.

The children no longer grabbed their gas masks and ran for the bomb shelter built in the back garden every time they heard a plane—instead, they ran outside unafraid, looking up to see if they could see a pilot.

That was dangerous. There was no other word for it. From the onset of the war, children had been taught to hide from the planes, take shelter, that the rumbling of those large metal birds meant danger.

It still did. Even the American ones. As she'd discovered.

Pulling off her gloves, she left the front garden, making sure the gate was closed tightly, and walked down the cobblestone pathway to open the back garden gate for the children. There was no front garden left to speak of. With everyone doing their part, what had been the front garden now housed rows of vegetables. Having just been planted a short time ago, the green sprouts were tiny and hardly recognisable, but soon there would be potatoes, carrots, cauliflower, parsnips and a few other vegetables that could survive the daily rains and dreary skies of spring. It felt as if it had been years since the sun had shone bright and freely. Almost as if even the weather realised it was wartime.

'Kathryn! Look what we have!' Phillip said, holding something in his hand. 'It's sweets! Chewing gum! I have a piece for you, too.'

The youngest of the boys, Phillip ran towards her, his smile showing the opening left from losing a tooth last week. Despite her melancholy, she couldn't help but smile.

'Chewing gum? Who gave you that?' Sweets of any sort were rare and the smile on all of the faces approaching the gate said Phillip wasn't the only one with a prize.

There were nine children in total who lived with Norman and Charlotte and her. Each one as unique and adorable as the next and each an evacuee who had arrived at some point over the past two years. She'd been the first, arriving nearly three years before at the age of seventeen. Her father had delivered her himself. As an intelligence officer, Father hadn't said *if* the bombing starts, he'd said *when* it starts, and he'd wanted her as far away from London as possible. Her mum had agreed, except for the faraway part. They'd settled for Norman's small farm, little more than an hour outside London.

Since then scores of young people had been evacuated out of the city. And continued to be, finding a temporary and hopefully safe refuge from the war.

'No,' Little George said, arriving a step behind Phillip. They called him Little George because George was already here when Little George had arrived on the same evacuee train as Phillip, Patricia and Doreen. 'A solider gave it to us.'

A shiver raced up Kathryn's spine. 'A solider?'

'The one you met ,' Edward said.

'Yes.' Phillip thrust a wrapped stick of chewing gum towards her. 'He gave me this one for you.'

'He said his name was Sergeant Dale Johnson,' Elizabeth said as she followed in the older boy's wake.

Kathryn's nerves stung. She didn't want a name to put to the face that haunted her, and her fingers wrapped tighter around the gloves in her hand.

'I bet he flies one of the planes we see every day,' George said. 'The one with the blue nose.'

'No, he flies the one with the red nose,' Edward disagreed. 'I've seen the pilot in that one.'

'You have not,' George argued.

'Have to!' Edward said.

'Boys,' Kathryn said, putting a stop to their bickering. There was plenty more she'd like to say, but Elizabeth was handing over an envelope.

'Besides the gum he gave Phillip for you, he asked me to give you this note.' Elizabeth then asked, 'Why didn't you mention meeting him?'

'Because it wasn't worth mentioning,' Kathryn said, taking the envelope, which burned her fingers at the thought of who'd touched it previously. 'Go inside and have your tea, then complete your studies.'

'We don't have any evening studies,' Elizabeth said. 'The soldiers were at school all afternoon, talking to all the children about not going near any pieces of shrapnel, and if we see any, we are to report it right away. I have a letter to give to Charlotte and Norman about it.'

'Is that what this is?' Kathryn asked, ignoring a sense of disappointment.

'I don't think so,' Elizabeth answered. 'Sergeant Johnson asked the teacher which children lived with you and then asked if he could give me that note. That's when he told me he'd met you.'

'Run on in and have your tea,' Kathryn said, turning the envelope over to see her name typed on the front.

'Don't you want your gum?' Phillip asked, following the others through the open gate.

One extra piece was sure to cause a squabble, so she took it. 'Thank you. Run inside now.'

Kathryn waited until each child passed through the front door, then she looked down at the envelope again. She didn't want to be curious, but was. After slipping her gloves and the stick of gum in her pocket, she carefully slid a finger beneath the flap to release the seal and pulled out a single sheet of paper.

It was typed. She'd never received a typed letter before.

> *Dear Miss Harris,*
> *The United States Air Force is presenting you with the enclosed payment for the loss of supplies resulting from a motor vehicle and bicycle incident on the High Wycombe Roadway during the mid-afternoon of April 27th, 1942.*

She unfolded the bottom of the letter and trapped the money against the paper with her thumb while reading the rest of the letter.

> *If you have any questions, please contact Marilyn Miller, secretary for the United States Army Eighth Air Force South Hill Barracks.*

Kathryn flipped the paper over, looking for… she wasn't exactly sure what. Frowning, she turned it over again. The letter was signed by Marilyn Miller. Whoever that was.

Ire rippled her insides as she counted the money. It was the same amount Dale Johnson had attempted to give Norman, but had been converted into shillings and pence. American or English, she would not be keeping this money.

'I really think you should let me drive you,' Norman said a few minutes later while walking towards the barn beside her.

'There's no need to waste the petrol,' Kathryn said. He and Charlotte were worried about the soldiers being in trouble for the mishap. She wasn't. Her concern was more personal. Sergeant Johnson would not get his way. Not with her.

'But after—'

'I'll be far more careful,' she interrupted Norman's response. Feeling guilty about being so discourteous, she added, 'The letter is addressed to me, so I will to be the one to respond.'

'Johnson,' Sam Smith shouted from the doorway. 'You got a visitor!'

Dale wiped his crescent wrench clean and placed it in the metal box among his other tools before tossing the rag aside and walking towards the doorway.

'You're getting to be awfully popular among the Janes.' Smith wiggled both of his brush-black eyebrows. 'The secretary this morning and now a local girl.'

Dale grinned. He'd expected a reaction from the letter he'd had Marilyn type up for him, but hadn't thought it would be this quick. 'Jealous?'

Smith laughed. 'You know it.'

Dale slapped the other man's shoulder as he walked out the door. 'Get used to it, buddy.'

Laughing again, Smith nodded towards the concrete slab outside the main building. 'Say hi for me, will you?'

'Not on your life,' Dale replied as he read-justed his hat.

Her bicycle was standing next to the bench she sat upon, back straight and hands folded in her lap. The base was a busy place, with men meandering in all directions, and every one of them was taking a second look at Kathryn. He couldn't blame them. She was a looker, even with the red scarf hiding her shiny, thick black hair. He'd seen that hair flowing long and loose when she'd pulled a different scarf off her head after taking her tumble. She had on the same shoes as that day and sheer stockings. Riding a bike in those heels had to be close to impossible.

As he walked passed a group of GIs standing stationary longer than necessary, he waved an arm. 'Move on, boys. You're here to fight Germans, not dally with the locals.'

'Ah, Sarge,' one of them said. 'We ain't seen a German since we got here.'

'You will,' he said. 'Now move along.'

They followed orders, heading in the opposite direction as him. A few steps later, he removed his hat prior to stopping in front of the metal bench. 'Miss Harris.'

She lifted her chin as she stood and smoothed her knee-length, sandy-brown coat with one hand while holding out the other one. 'I'm here to return this.'

That wasn't the reaction he'd been hoping for.

Ironically the sun, which hadn't let itself be known very often since he'd arrived, chose that moment to peek out from behind a sky full of grey clouds. 'Would you care to take a walk?' he asked, ignoring the envelope. The Major hadn't learned about the incident and, if Dale had his way, Hilts never would.

Her brows knit together as she barely turned her head while glancing left and right. 'A walk?'

'I've been told there's a garden around the

east side of the building, with a walking pathway the entire length.'

'I'm not here to—'

'I know.' He wasn't one to act impulsively, but convincing her to keep the money would take a bit of finesse. Something that didn't come to him naturally. He'd have to work on it. And her. 'Just a short walk. I've wanted to see the garden but haven't had a reason to walk over there yet.'

She glanced around, this time turning her head fully in each direction. When she faced him again, he wasn't daft enough to think she nodded because of his charm. It was the dozens of other men looking their way.

'I don't have much time,' she said while taking a step.

'Neither do I,' he said. 'But a walk doesn't need to take long.'

'As I said, I'm here to return your money.'

'It's not my money.' That wasn't completely a lie. The money he'd given Marilyn to include with the letter had been American. The secretary had been the one to exchange it for local currency. So far, only he, Sanders and Marilyn knew exactly what had happened and he wanted to keep it that way. 'I'm a farmer, Miss Harris. Or was until I became a soldier. My folks own a farm in North Dakota. Gathering eggs was

my first chore. At least the first one I can remember.' The memories floating back made him
grin. 'That and hauling wood, but my brother,
Ralph, usually did that. He hated chickens and
would haul my share of the wood if I gathered
his share of the eggs.'

He bit the tip of his tongue to stop from sharing other things about himself. She didn't need
to hear his life story, nor want to. 'What I meant
to say is that I know how tough farming can be.
How the loss of even a single egg is felt. Even
more now that the world is at war.'

They'd rounded the building corner and rows
of leafy green bushes, some he might have recognised if he took the time to look closer, edged
the walking path on both sides.

'I can't deny the world is at war, Mr Johnson,'
she said smartly. 'But I can assure you, we do
not need your money. Norman and Charlotte
would not have taken in so many if they did not
have the means to provide for them.'

He'd heard about children being evacuated
out of London and assumed some of the children living with her were part of that. Of the
nine, only two looked similar, as if they might
be siblings. 'Are they all evacuees?'

'Yes.'

Something in her tone, a sadness, had him asking, 'But not you.'

She glanced his way, frowning slightly. 'Yes, me, too.'

'Then how do you have the same last name as Norman. Mr Harris?'

'I don't.'

Not one to usually make assumptions, he searched his mind to recall if one of the Fowler brothers had said she was Norman's daughter. He'd been certain they had. Ed had. He was fairly sure of that.

'You assumed I was Norman and Charlotte's daughter,' she said, with her heels snapping against the stone walkway. 'Just as you assumed we needed to be repaid for the food that was damaged in the mishap. Both assumptions were wrong.' She stopped walking and held out her hand containing the envelope. 'Now if you'd kindly take this, I shall be on my way.'

He ignored the envelope again. 'If it's not Harris, what is your last name?'

She frowned slightly, then shook her head. 'I don't see how that matters one way or the other.'

'It does to me.' He couldn't come up with a solid reason why, so he waved a hand at the trail continuing in front of them. 'It's just as far to walk all the way around as it is to go back the way we came.' With a shrug, he added, 'And once I know your last name, I won't have to assume again.'

When it appeared she might not agree, he added an incentive, 'The sun is shining, Kathryn, I hear that's a rarity this time of year.'

'Winslow,' she said. 'Miss Winslow.'

He'd figured using her first name would goad her into telling him. 'Winslow. Kathryn Winslow. Well, that's a fine name, Miss Winslow,' he said while slowly starting to walk again. 'A mighty fine name. Nothing to be ashamed of.'

'Ashamed of?' She hurried to catch up with him. 'I'm not ashamed of it.'

'You're not?' He gave his head a thoughtful shake. 'Well, I assumed since you didn't want to tell me that—'

'You said if I told you, you wouldn't assume again.'

He nodded. 'I did, didn't I? Well, then, how about the sun? How often does it shine? Just so I don't have to assume again.'

Her sideways glance said he wasn't fooling her, but the hint of a smile she tried to hide gave him hope.

'It shines often enough, but not as much as it rains. Some people don't like our weather. They say it's too dreary. To rainy.'

He almost asked who, but figured that could be two steps backwards. 'I love rain.'

'You do?' There was a hint of disappointment in her voice.

'Back home we had a drought that lasted almost ten years. The worst of it was when I was fifteen. By then, we'd gone so long without rain, it wouldn't have taken much to dry up every last pond. It was so hot the leaves baked right on the trees. Dried up and fell off so it looked like December rather than July. Except for the heat. Nothing could grow and with no plants or moisture to hold the dirt down, it blew everywhere. We had curtains like you do, nailed to the window frames, but they weren't to keep the light from getting out, it was to keep the dirt from getting in.'

Remembering those days had the ability to clog his throat. The windy dry weather was what had given Judy dust pneumonia. 'I prayed so long and hard for rain, that, even now, almost ten years later, I still love it. Will love rain for as long as I live.'

'How did you survive?' she asked. 'Your family. Being farmers.'

'We were lucky in some ways,' he said. 'There's a fair-sized lake that's spring fed on our property. That year we thought it might dry up, but it didn't so we had water for the animals and some crops.' There was a row of tiny purple flowers beside the path and he stopped long enough to pluck one and hand it to her. 'Much like you, we shared what we could with others. Any neighbour who had a way to haul water was welcome to do so.'

She took the flower and sniffed it while twirling the tiny stem between her finger and thumb. 'That was kind of you.'

Some didn't think so. They'd claimed his family should be hauling water to those who didn't have a way to get it. His family couldn't have afforded to do that any more than the next. And they'd had other things happening. Judy dying. Letting that thought go, he asked, 'What kind of flower is that?'

'It's a columbine.'

'Do they grow wild here?'

'Yes. When I first arrived here, I dug up several that were growing among the hedgerows at Charlotte and Norman's and gave them to my mum to plant in the flower beds at our house in London.'

She pinched her lips together then and started walking again, obviously not happy about sharing even that little memory with him. Accepting that, he took the subject off her.

'Did all the children living with the Harrises arrive at the same time as you?'

'No. George, Elizabeth and Jennifer arrived several months after I did. They are siblings. Then Phillip, Little George, Patricia and Doreen arrived the following spring. They aren't related, but were all on the same train. That summer, a billeting officer brought Edward and Audrey to the house late one night. They aren't siblings either, but had been on the same train and the officer explained no other host family was able to take them.' Her tone was soft and she'd smiled while saying each child's name.

'How old are they?' he asked, mainly just to keep her talking.

Still twirling the flower, she said, 'George is twelve and Edward is eleven. Little George is eight and Phillip seven. Elizabeth is fourteen, Audrey thirteen, Jennifer nine, and Doreen and Patricia are both six.'

'That's a houseful.'

Her face lit up as and her eyes literally shone. 'It is, but they mind well, are very helpful and get along with one another for the most part.'

'Even the siblings?'

'Yes, why?'

'Just curious,' he answered. 'My brother and

I fought when we were young. He's two years older than me.'

'Do you have any sisters?'

'One.' He bit his tongue. Even after all these years he couldn't get used to saying he didn't have a sister. He'd had one for thirteen years and would never forget it. Judy had been two years younger than him and her death had left a hole in his family. Especially in his mother's heart. She'd said it wasn't right for a parent to bury a child and he didn't want her to go through that ever again. Not wanting to explain more, he asked, 'What about you?'

She frowned slightly while glancing his way. 'I'm an only child, but I have a cousin.'

Not sure why her frown turned into a scowl while she pinched her lips tight and started walking faster, he asked, 'Do their families know where they are? The children, that is?'

She blinked and kept her eyes closed for some time before saying, 'If they still have families, yes, they know where they are.'

A shiver rippled the hairs on his arms. 'Their homes have been bombed?'

Marching forward, she said, 'Most of London has been hit by bombs. Most of England.'

Dale didn't have a response for that. Couldn't have said the bombing was over either. If Hitler had his way, it wouldn't be over until there was nothing left of London. Of England. Of most of the world.

They had rounded the building again. While woods had been the backdrop of the garden on the other two sides, this side showed the Nissen huts, tents and other structures of the base. For a moment he'd almost forgotten they'd been walking around the huge headquarter building. A few months ago, it had been an all girls' school. The transformation had taken place, but it still seemed odd to imagine that not so long ago, rather than hundreds of soldiers, the grounds had been covered with giggling girls.

News of the war had filled the papers and airways back home, but until he'd arrived, seen the destruction firsthand, he'd been detached from the actual tragedy that was taking place in certain spots of the world. Those over here, like Kathryn, hadn't been. They'd been living it. Still were.

They walked in silence along that side of the building, all the way to the corner and then around the front towards where her bicycle stood.

A B-25 was coming in for a landing, the one he'd worked on earlier and sent the pilot out to put it to the test. New equipment and instructions arrived regularly and it was his job to try out new ideas on various planes, report to others what worked and what didn't. Most of it had to do with conserving fuel. The planes needed to fly a considerable distance and back, and every drop of fuel counted.

The ground beneath them rumbled. He was used to that and the noise, but to others, the roar of those engines was considered deafening.

Although she'd tucked her chin to her chest and was cringing at the noise, Kathryn watched as the bomber touched down and then rolled up the runway.

'That's the same plane that—'

'Yes, it is,' he admitted.

She lifted her chin. 'Do you fly those?'

'Mainly, I work on them,' he answered. 'But that also means I'll fly them when I have to. The pilot flying that one is Rooster Robins. He was at the school with me today.' He left out the part that Rooster had been flying it the other day, too, and that the pilot knew nothing about the mishap.

'Passing out chewing gum.' The pinch of her lips was back, saying she didn't approve.

'We hoped it would make the kids listen. Our Commander received word of Air Raid Wardens in London catching children, mainly young boys, collecting shrapnel, shell caps and fins, and all sorts of other pieces of bombs. One report said a pair of brothers had a complete incendiary bomb hidden in their outhouse. Groups of us went out to all of the schools within a thirty-mile radius today to warn the children to stay away from any shrapnel. That every piece is dangerous. We sent warning letters home with all of the students, instructing every adult to use caution, too.'

'And you sent this home,' she said, once again handing him the envelope.

He'd had Marilyn type up the letter, thinking if it looked official, Kathryn, or at least Norman, would accept the money. A good sort, and always willing to help, Marilyn was also trying to locate Ralph for him.

'I can't take it, Miss Winslow,' he said. 'I've already told you that. Buy the children some more chewing gum with it, or other candy, they were excited with the pieces we passed out.'

Kathryn squeezed the envelope harder. He had to take it. She didn't want his money. Didn't want anything to do with him. She was flustered, too. Both by her behaviour—walking the garden path with him should not have happened—and by his actions. Asking all those questions about her and the children. She shouldn't have answered those questions. And he shouldn't have told her about loving rain. No one loves rain. Furthermore, it was easier not to like him when she knew nothing about him, other than he was just a man. One of many.

Pulling her thoughts back to where they belonged, she said, 'There are no other sweets to be purchased, Mr Johnson. The only people with such luxuries are you American soldiers.'

'Then buy something else they need. There has to be something—'

He stopped in order to turn around at someone shouting, 'Sarge!'

'Excuse me,' he said, turning to her before turning about again and jogging over to meet the man running towards them. The same one who'd been driving the Jeep the other day.

Warning bells went off inside her as she noted other men quickly gathering around Dale. He pointed in several directions, as if giving orders before he and the man she recognised started walking towards her.

'Corporal Sanders will give you a ride—'

'What's happened?' Kathryn interrupted.

'Nothing for you to worry about,' he said. 'Corporal, get her bike.'

Her heart was in her throat. 'Is it the Germans?'

'No, Miss Winslow, it's not the Germans, it has nothing to do with them, but I need to go.' He gestured towards the other man already wheeling her bike across the pavement. 'Corporal Sanders will give you a ride home.' He then touched the brim of his hat. 'Good day.'

She didn't have time to say more, he was already running towards another car park that held several Jeeps and lorries. Others were running, too, jumping in the vehicles.

Before she had time to contemplate what she should do, a Jeep pulled up next to her. She shook her head. 'I don't need a ride.'

'Sarge said to give you a ride home and I can't disobey a direct order. Name's Rusty Sanders. Corporal Rusty Sanders. Go ahead and climb in, I already have your bike in the back.'

The young man had found a way to make her bicycle fit behind the seats. Sort of. The front tyre hung halfway out of the Jeep, but it appeared secure enough not to fall out.

She tucked the envelope she was still clutching into her pocket while nodding towards a line of vehicles already exiting the base. 'What's happening?'

'Rooster, that's one of the pilots,' Corporal

Sanders said, 'saw a barn on fire when he was coming in for landing.'

'A barn? Near here?' She climbed into the Jeep. 'Whose?'

'Don't know. It's not too far away. Sarge is taking a unit out to help put it out.' Pointing towards the vehicles, Sanders said, 'Those are water-tank trucks. They are always ready to go put out a fire.'

'Why?'

'In case a plane crashes or a bomb goes off.'

Pressing a hand against her racing heart, she asked, 'Was the barn bombed?'

'No, there haven't been any bombs dropped around here. Won't be either.'

She grasped the edge of the Jeep when he shifted into gear and speeded up, and held on with all her might until the jerking motions smoothed out and allowed her to relax a bit.

'Where is it? The barn the pilot saw on fire?'

'Sounds like it must be over by the pub.'

Her heart leaped to her throat. Widow Whitcomb's barn was near Oscar and Ed's pub. Two billeted children were currently staying with her. Brothers who were close to Little George and Phillip's ages. 'Take me there.'

'Ma'am, miss, I couldn't—'

'Yes, you can.' Recalling how he'd said Dale

had ordered him to take her home, she said, 'It's an order. Follow the others.'

'I can't do that. Sarge will—'

'Then stop right here so I can get my bicycle out.'

He glanced her way and then, after scratching the side of his head, said, 'I'm going to be in trouble either way.'

'No, you won't be, I'll see to that.' She had no idea how she'd go about doing that, but she had to see if the billeted children living with Mrs Whitcomb needed help. The widow hadn't been happy about being required to take in children and had already sent away several others for misbehaviour.

Upon arriving at the pub, Kathryn wasn't worried about Corporal Sanders being in trouble, it was the two boys she saw being put in another Jeep. She climbed over the edge of Jeep and ran towards them. 'Are they hurt?'

'Sarge says the burns aren't bad, but the old woman refused for them to be seen by a doctor, so I'm taking them to be checked out by a medic at the base,' a soldier said.

The barn, still on fire, was in the field behind the pub. Mrs Whitcomb was standing near one of the lorries, clearly yelling at the man who stood on top of it spraying water on the ground. Dale stood next to her, shaking his head, also clearly telling the man spraying the ground to listen to him, not her. Until Corporal Sanders stepped up beside them, then Dale spun around and though he was a distance away, Kathryn felt the moment his eyes landed on her.

She turned back and stepped closer to the Jeep in order to examine the boys. They were both dark with soot and their hands had red welts.

'We tried to put out the fire,' the younger boy said solemnly.

'I can tell,' she answered while reaching into her pocket for a handkerchief. After wrapping it around one of the largest blisters on the older boy's hand, she said, 'That was very brave of you.'

'Mrs Whitcomb didn't think so,' the younger one said. 'She said we can't come back.'

'We don't want to go back,' the older boy said.

Kathryn offered them each a reassuring smile. 'Don't worry about any of that,' she said, making a mental note to call the billeting officer.

'Excuse me,' the soldier now behind the wheel of the Jeep said, 'but Sarge told me to hurry.'

A quick glance over her shoulder said the 'Sarge' was walking towards her. Along with

Corporal Sanders. 'Then go.' Slipping her hand into her pocket again, this time she withdrew the envelope she'd felt while pulling out the handkerchief. 'Please deliver this to the base as well.'

The solider took the envelope and drove away, and Kathryn drew a deep breath before turning about. Without waiting for Dale to comment on Corporal Sanders bringing her here, she said, 'Why aren't you putting out the fire? You're just spraying the ground.'

'It was already too far gone by the time we arrived,' Dale replied. 'We'll keep the fire from spreading and then clean up the debris. Corporal Sanders will now give you a ride home.'

She hadn't followed his last order and wouldn't this time either. 'I do not need a ride. When I'm ready to return home, I shall ride my bike.' Head up, she spun around and walked towards the pub to call the billeting officer.

Chapter Three

21st of May, 1942

Dear Diary,
I heard the boys' burns are healing fine
and that they are doing well now living
with the Butlers. No one knows how Mrs
Whitcomb's barn caught fire, but every-
one is talking about how the fire would
have spread if not for the soldiers. Espe-
cially Sergeant Johnson. I am thankful the
soldiers were able to keep the fire from
spreading and that the young brothers are
no longer with Mrs Whitcomb, but I'm not
singing praise. I find I have a great desire
to remind the locals that we took care of
each other before the Americans built the
base and will do so again after they leave,
but have managed to keep it to myself. No

matter how difficult it may be, I must re-main diplomatic.

However, I do find satisfaction in the fact I won when it came Sergeant Johnson and his money. I dare say I'm a bit sur-prised he gave in so easily and have con-cluded he must be angered that he didn't get his way this time because I have not seen him since the day of the fire. Which of course is fine. I have no desire to see him again.

On her knees, pulling tiny weeds just poking out of the ground, Kathryn couldn't stop herself from glancing up when the sky rumbled. Not one, but five planes were coming towards them. How could something so large glide through the sky? It seemed impossible. So impossible, she couldn't stop thinking about them. Some things did that. Stuck in her brain, making her try to figure out what it was about them that she dis-liked. She made no mention of them, though. Under no circumstance did she want to appear interested in anything associated with the base. Not even to satisfy her own curiosity.

It was a Saturday, so the girls were helping in the garden and the boys were seeing to the ani-mals. They'd all stopped to stare up at the planes growing closer. Just as Kathryn was about to instruct them to return to their chores, the first plane flew directly over the farm. At first, she'd thought she was seeing things, until a moment later, when she realised something was dropping from the sky. She couldn't recognise what the tiny specks were, but they were falling directly at them.

Fear overtook her so quickly, she momentarily froze. Then, hooking Doreen around the waist with one hand, she grabbed Patricia's hand with the other. 'Run! Run for the bomb shelter!'

Fumbling with the gate as the planes continued to fly overhead, she screeched as something hit her head. It didn't hurt, but fearing the next one, she gathered Doreen and Patricia close and crouched over the top of both of them, trying to protect them. Save them.

When nothing else hit her, she grabbed both girls and hurried though the gate. The other girls were on the path, as was Charlotte.

'Hurry,' Kathryn shouted as terror still raced over her. 'Run!'

'Why?' Charlotte asked.

With her heart pounding, Kathryn attempted to usher them all towards the house. It would be shorter going through it than around it to the shelter. 'The planes!' Not exactly sure how to describe the dangers, she said, 'The—the shrapnel, the—the things falling from the sky. Bombs.'

'There aren't any bombs,' Charlotte said. 'Those were American planes.'

Frustrated and scared, Kathryn couldn't stop from shouting, 'There are things falling from them! Shrapnel!'

'That's not shrapnel!'

'It's sweets!'

She wasn't sure who said what, but spun to where the boys were running around the house.

'They dropped sweets for us! Lots of it!'

Kathryn's heart was still pounding, but an icy shiver had her lowering both Doreen and Patricia on to the porch. Her arms ached from holding the girls, but it was the fear that had encompassed her that had her trembling. The children were running about, picking up things.

'Stop! Don't touch anything!'

'Kathryn, dear—'

'Didn't you read the letter they brought home?' she interrupted Charlotte. 'Anything falling from the sky is dangerous.'

'Of course I read that letter. But as I said, those were American planes. Not German ones.' Charlotte took something from one of the children and held it out. 'It's just sweets. Truly it is.'

Kathryn's fear turned into anger as she

plucked the single piece of gum, wrapped in shiny foil. 'Chewing gum?' Her mind seemed to turn a complete somersault. 'Gum!'

'Other sweets, too,' Little George said, holding out a grubby palm full of colourfully wrapped sweets.

'We can keep it, can't we?' Phillip asked.

'Of course you can,' Charlotte replied.

With squeals of delight, the children, including Doreen and Patricia, ran throughout the garden, searching for sweets.

'Be careful of the plants!' Charlotte yelled before quietly saying, 'Now, wasn't that nice? Dropping sweets for the children?'

'Nice?' The fury ripping across Kathryn was as hot as it was cold. 'No, it wasn't nice. It was the most deceitful, nasty trick anyone has ever played.'

'Trick?' Charlotte asked. 'What are you talking about?'

'Not what.' Kathryn was so mad she wanted to scream. *'Who.'* Spinning about, she marched into the house. 'Sergeant Dale Johnson. He'll pay for this one.'

She walked straight through the house to the scullery, where she washed her hands and removed her apron. After tying a scarf around her hair, she headed out the back door and rode away on the bicycle before anyone had the chance to try to stop her.

This had gone too far. Scaring the daylights out of people was not funny and would not be tolerated.

The harder she pedalled, the madder she became. She should have known Dale wouldn't have given up that easy. Men didn't stop until they got what they wanted. Andrew hadn't. When her father had said she was too young to marry, especially a soldier who was going off to war with no certainty of what the future might bring, Andrew hadn't given up. No, he'd gone ahead and got married. Not to her, but to the youngest daughter of Sir Russell Childs, a Commander in the Royal Navy. Andrew got exactly what he didn't want. He was now serving in the Navy, on a ship somewhere. She didn't know. Or care.

When she'd first arrived at Charlotte and Norman's, she'd written to Andrew, several times, and had been hurt when there had been no response. Broken-hearted for months, until Mum had told her about his marriage. She'd grown angry then. As she was now. Dale would get exactly what he deserved, too.

Kathryn forced herself to concentrate on the road. It hadn't rained for a few days, so there was no mud to contend with, but the previous water fall had left the road rutted, forcing her to continuously ride from edge to edge, utilising the smoothest sections and, at times, the grass along the road when cars approached from either direction.

Each time she heard one, her insides clenched and she kept her gaze forward, not willing to look in case it was Norman coming to stop her or Corporal Sanders driving someone around. Particularly Sergeant Johnson. That was exactly who she was going to see, but wanted it to be on her terms. She would not be surprised by him again.

Upon turning on to the road leading to the base, the much smoother surface allowed her to travel faster and she wheeled up to the main building. Last time, she'd gone through the front doors and a nice older woman sitting there had sent someone to find Dale. Assuming it would be that way again, she stationed her bicycle beside the bench and hurried up the steps. The older woman wasn't behind the desk today. A pretty younger one, with short blond hair, was sitting there, wearing the same green uniform as the older woman had been.

'May I help you?' she asked.

'I would like to see Sergeant Dale Johnson, please,' Kathryn responded.

The younger woman's smile increased as she shook her head. 'I'm sorry, he's not available. Could someone else help you?'

Kathryn's stomach hardened with a sickening sensation. Almost four weeks had passed since she'd given that money to the soldier. She'd thought that had been the end of it. That Dale had accepted he'd failed and she'd won, but maybe he'd been transferred. The sickening sensation inside her grew. 'May I wait until he is available?'

The woman's face softened. 'I'm not sure when he'll be back. You can leave a message and I'll see he receives it upon his return. It should be some time this evening.'

Relief filled her that he was still stationed here. 'Thank you, there's no message.'

'I'm sure he'll be available tomorrow if you want to come back.'

Kathryn nodded even as a great sense of disappointment seemed to drain her. She sincerely had wanted to see him today, while her anger had driven her. By tomorrow, it might not be as strong. 'I'll consider that. Thank you again.'

She had been so focused on seeing Dale that she hadn't noticed the other soldiers on the way in. The way out was different. She could feel their eyes and hear their whispers as she climbed on her bike and rode away. Whether she'd left a message or not, he'd know about her visit.

Dale hadn't considered what he'd say upon arrival until he slowed the Jeep down to take the road that led to Kathryn's house. The entire base knew she'd been there to see him and knew who she was. Brigadier Winslow's daughter. The head of British Intelligence. There was no denying he'd wondered if her father couldn't assist in his search for Ralph, but Major Hilts had ordered him to find out why she'd been at the base and to make sure she got whatever it was she needed. Hilts hadn't said it better not be anything personal, but Dale got the message just the same.

He also knew why she'd been there. The candy dropping had to have surprised her and, knowing her as he already did, most likely irritated the pants right off her. He couldn't say why that made him smile, except for the fact he hadn't had this much fun teasing someone in a long time. He'd teased Judy plenty. Being close in age, they'd picked on each other almost as much as he and Ralph. His throat swelled slightly. Certain memories did that to him. Made him miss Judy all over again and reminded him of the reason he was here.

As his thoughts returned to the present, he let out a sigh.

He couldn't afford to have Kathryn mad. Not for his sake. If it was just him, he'd 'fess up to the Major about the plane scaring her off her bike, but couldn't because of Ralph. They hadn't heard from him in two years, so he'd enlisted and been willing to do whatever he had to in order to find his brother.

Pulling into the garden, he glanced around. The place looked vacant. Back home, on a sunny afternoon like this, no one could have kept him or any of his siblings inside. Even during the drought years.

While parking the Jeep, Dale kept one eye on the front door, expecting it to open. There was the possibility that no one was home. Norman had mentioned a car before. It was nowhere in sight, but it hadn't been on his last visit either. The bicycle, however, was leaning against the barn.

The door opened and Norman appeared while Dale was climbing over the side of the Jeep.

'Hello, Sergeant Johnson.' Norman waved as he came down the steps. 'Good to see you. The children were beside themselves with the goodies you dropped from the sky yesterday.'

Dale met Norman near the fence that surrounded the garden and, glad the other man had brought up the subject, he replied, 'I didn't drop the candy, but did ask the pilots to.'

'The children were still searching the ground come nightfall.' Once again, only one eye stayed open while Norman spoke and the wrinkles around both eyes grew deeper as he laughed. 'They hadn't had that much fun in a long, long time. I'd be remiss if I didn't thank you for that.'

'No thanks necessary,' Dale said. 'Miss Winslow refused to take the money, so I bought candy with it instead. Lots of it. If you don't mind, I'll have the pilots make a drop every so often.'

'That will tickle them pink.' Norman's lips pinched and his eyes grew a bit serious. 'Except for Kathryn.'

Dale nodded. 'I assumed as much. Could I speak to her? Explain my reasons?'

When Norman's thoughtful expression grew deeper yet, Dale said, 'This war has already been going on for a long time and I predict it won't be over any time soon. I've heard stories of the evacuees, met a couple. There's not much I can do for any of them, except pass out a few pieces of candy, hoping in some small way it will brighten their days.'

'It does,' Norman said, nodding and smiling. 'It surely does. Kathryn's up in the field with Charlotte and the children picking berries in the hedgerow.' While speaking Norman had opened the gate. 'This way, I'll show you.'

Norman asked about the Jeep as they walked past it and Dale answered his questions while scanning the fields beyond the barn. They were good-sized and a lot to manage for an old man, two women and a bunch of young kids. He couldn't help but wonder why she was here. The daughter of a Brigadier.

'They are on the other side of that far end.' Norman pointed past the fence that housed goats. 'There's a pass to get through the hedgerow near the corner. You'll hear the kids before you see them. I imagine those boys will be doing more playing than picking.'

'My brother and I would have been,' Dale said.

'Me and mine, too.' After a good-hearted laugh, Norman waved towards the house. 'Leave yourself time to stop in the house. Charlotte's been itching for a chance to try out that coffee-making pot she bought. You won't want to let her down.'

'Thank you,' Dale replied, not able to promise coffee could happen. That would depend upon Kathryn.

The vegetables that must have been planted only a short time ago looked like potatoes and, not wanting to damage any, Dale walked along the edge of the field. The hedgerows that grew along all the fields in the area intrigued him and he recognised some familiar plants among the various other bushes and weeds. Or maybe they weren't considered weeds here. There were plenty of flowers blooming along the edge.

Norman was right, he'd yet to come to the corner when he heard children squealing and laughing. Someone else was laughing, too, and he'd bet the chocolate bar in his pocket who that was.

The opening Norman told him about was hidden. If he hadn't been looking for it, he'd have walked right past it. Ducking beneath the vines, he entered the bushes, but, seeing the sights on the other side, he paused to watch.

Kathryn was playing with the children and looked almost as young and carefree as the rest of them as they tagged each other and ran, trying not to get tagged back. She had on a red-and-white short-sleeved dress, sheer stockings and those same shoes she rode her bike in. Running in them couldn't be any easier than bike riding. However, they did make her look, well, elegant, even while chasing the children around. Overall, she looked too refined for the life she was currently living.

The odd sense of being watched had him glancing around. It was hard to say if the elderly woman who must be Charlotte was able to see him or not, but she was walking towards the bushes and squinting.

Dale pushed through the bushes, standing up when completely clear of the vines. Besides the older woman, Kathryn was the first to notice him. At least the first to react. She stopped dead in her tracks, bumping into a little girl as she stared at him.

'Hello,' the older woman said. 'I'm Charlotte and you must be the sweet Sergeant.' Giggling softly, she explained, 'That's what the children call you. They found a few pieces out here today, which led to their game of tag rather than picking berries.'

She'd gestured to the basket in her hand and, noting the small amount, he said, 'Well, then, I better get to work.'

'Oh, no, that's not what I meant.'

He held out a hand. 'If you don't mind. I haven't picked berries in years, but when I did, I was excellent at it.'

'Were you?' Her ageing blue eyes took on a shimmer as she handed him the basket. 'My boys used to eat more than they picked.'

Her grey curls and softly wrinkled skin reminded him of his grandmother, who used to make jam that he and Ralph ate by the spoon. 'I may have been known to do that a time or so myself,' he admitted. 'But today I will fill this basket to the rim before giving it back.'

'Excuse me?'

The sun was too bright for him to be chilled by Kathryn's cold tone. 'Good afternoon, Miss Winslow.' He gave a slight bow. 'I'm sorry I missed you yesterday and do hope you weren't too put out by my absence.'

'Not at all, as I wouldn't be right now either.'

He grinned. 'I'm sure you wouldn't.' Nodding towards Charlotte, he said, 'But Mrs Harris might be. I promised her a full basket of berries, so if you will excuse *me*?'

The shocked look on her face was more than enough to make him smile, as was the welcome he received from the children. A total of nine, all speaking at once, and all thanking him for the candy that had dropped from the sky. Four of the children were almost as tall as Kathryn— two boys and two girls. Then another girl and two other boys were a bit shorter, about up to the older ones' shoulders, and then two little girls that came up to Kathryn's waist. Right where a wide white belt encircled her, hugging the white-and-red-striped dress.

Looking up and catching the glare that once again had settled in her eyes, he said, 'I didn't drop the candy, the pilots did, and don't eat it all at once.'

'I assure you, they won't,' she said. 'It would not only ruin their appetite, it would rot their teeth.'

'Nonsense,' Charlotte said. Without waiting for a response, she waved for the children. 'Bring your baskets. We need to get some berries before Norman comes looking for us.' Smiling at him, she added, 'Kathryn, please show Sergeant Johnson which berries to pick and which to leave behind?'

She wanted to say no and did so with her eyes. He'd bet the only reason she didn't voice exactly what she thought was because of the children.

'I'll show him,' one of the children said.

'*I'll* show him,' Kathryn said. 'You go help Charlotte.'

She certainly wasn't happy, but Dale was. However, he was smart enough to keep his smile hidden inside where it tickled him as much as a feather did a sleeping man's nose. He'd never claim to be a charming man, but he sure planned on trying to be one today. Her father being the head of the British intelligence might be exactly what he needed to find Ralph. Without anyone knowing, of course.

'This way,' she said, spinning about.

He glanced over his shoulder at Charlotte pairing off the children and sending them towards the bushes. Dale took several long strides to catch up with Kathryn. 'They sure do mind well.'

Kathryn kept her eyes straight ahead and marched forward like a soldier doing drills.

'The children,' he said. 'They mind well.'

She still didn't respond.

'Charlotte reminds me of my grandmother. We, my brother and younger sister, used to go berry picking with her. And for the most part, we minded her. Our dad had said she knew how to use a switch and we never wanted to find out if he was telling the truth or not.'

Although she clearly hadn't wanted him to notice, he'd seen the way she looked at him out of the corners of her eyes.

No longer trying to hide his smile, he continued, 'And she made the best jam. Ralph and I never waited for bread, we ate it right out of the jar.' He chuckled while recalling an incident he hadn't thought of in years. 'She had a bunch of grapes that grew along the fence around her garden. Sour grapes. But she made the best jelly out of them. One time, she'd boiled down the grapes and seined the juice out, but must have run out of time or something, because there was this big jar of the juice on the counter. Thinking it would taste as good as her jelly, I sneaked a big swallow.'

His entire being shuddered at how bad that juice had tasted. 'She hadn't added any sugar yet. My first reaction had been to spit it out, but she'd walked into the kitchen just then so I couldn't.' Laughing, he said, 'I'll never forget how hard it was to swallow that mouthful of juice.'

That story did more than he'd been able to. She not only smiled, she covered her mouth to smother a giggle.

'I don't think I ate grape jelly for a good five years after that,' he said. 'Just couldn't bring myself to eat it.'

'I know the feeling,' she said softly.

'You drank raw grape juice, too?'

She nodded. 'Our housekeeper was making wine.'

He had to shake in order to get rid of the shudder rippling over him. His grandfather had made wine once. It had been bad. The morning after had been downright miserable. Being fifteen might have had something to do with it. 'That had to be worse,' he admitted aloud.

Her cheeks had turned pink. 'It certainly was awful.' With a sigh, she added, 'And like you, I had to swallow it or get caught.'

Curious, he asked, 'So do you drink wine now?'

'Not if I don't have to,' she answered.

The laugh they shared lightened the air between them. Hoping it stayed that way, but not wanting to put too much into it, he asked, 'So which berries are we picking?' The berries in the basket he'd taken from Charlotte were green and hairy. And more unappetising than any he'd ever seen.

She stepped near the bushes and pointed out a small cluster of berries. 'Gooseberries.'

'They're supposed to be green?'

'Yes.'

'And hairy?'

She tried but couldn't smother another giggle, even with her hand. 'Yes.'

'Most of the green berries I've seen haven't been ripe, and hair, I associate that with mould.'

'Well, you're not in America, Sergeant Johnson.'

'You don't say?'

Her brief glance showed the shine was disappearing from her eyes.

Not wanting that, he asked, 'Can I eat one?'

She shrugged. 'Yes.'

'You aren't trying to poison me, are you?'

The shine returned to her eyes, turning them a thoughtful, shimmering brown. If he wasn't careful, he could get lost in those eyes. Except he couldn't look away because he knew what she was thinking.

'You hadn't thought about poisoning me?' Coaxing, he added, 'Come on. I know you did.'

'No, I didn't.'

'But you are now.'

She laughed and handed him a berry she'd plucked. 'Go ahead and eat one.'

He took it and ate it, puckering the entire time because his first reaction had been to spit it out. Swallowing twice to get it to go down, he shook his head. 'That's as bitter as Grandma's grape juice had been.'

Hiding a smile, she continued picking berries and dropping them into her basket. 'They'll be sweeter later in the year.'

'Then why don't you wait until later to pick them?'

'Because the more we pick now, the more we'll have later.' She held up one of the green berries. 'They may taste bitter by themselves, but you'd be amazed by how good they are in a bread and butter pudding.'

He waited for her to pop the berry in her mouth, but when she dropped it in the basket instead, he shook his head. 'I find that very hard to believe considering you won't eat one.'

A hint of dog-eared determination crossed her face as she plucked another berry and popped it in her mouth. Her expression remained un-changed, except for a hint of a pinch to her lips as she swallowed.

'Satisfied?' she asked after swallowing again.

With her lips pinched tight, pink cheeks and the sunshine making her black hair shimmer, she was cute. Really cute. His mind shifted. 'Why don't you like Americans?'

He wanted to kick himself at how her face fell and she blinked slowly, as if trying to hide something. She bit her bottom lip before turn-ing back to the berries.

'That was a terrible trick you played,' she said.

'What trick?'

She cast him a scathing look while saying, 'What trick? Have you ever been hit on the top of the head by a sweet? Well, I have and it hurts.'

Now he really wanted to kick himself. He hadn't thought of that. 'I'm sorry, I—'

'Didn't think of that? You only thought of a way to mock me. To get me to take your money?'

'I wasn't mocking you,' he answered. 'I wouldn't do that.' Noting there was more she was trying to hide, he shook his head. 'Honestly, and I wasn't trying to scare you either.'

She reached for another clump of berries, but stopped and balled her hand into a fist instead. 'Are you trying to say it wasn't another one of your jokes? Like the plane?'

'Yes, or no, I'm not sure which is right. Yes, that's what I'm saying, no, it wasn't a joke.'

She eyed him critically.

'I truly didn't think about the candy hitting someone or that it would scare you.' He huffed out a breath. Those were things he should have thought about, but hadn't. These people had been taught—hell, the entire world was being taught to run and hide, protect themselves, from anything and everything falling from the sky. He'd talked to the school children about that very issue. 'I'm sorry.' Shaking his head, he admitted, 'I'm not sure what else to say.' He dug in his pocket and pulled out the candy bar. 'I brought a peace offering.'

'I don't want a peace offering.'

'Will you accept an apology?'

She looked around, not necessarily at anything in particular, just anywhere but at him.

They stood there for a stilled moment. Not sure what more to say or do, he didn't as much as breathe.

She moved first, spun around and started picking berries again. 'I still won't take your money.'

'That's good.' He dropped the candy bar into his basket and picked several berries before adding, 'Because I spent it.'

'It was yours to spend.' She'd taken several steps away, clearing the berries off the bushes with remarkable speed.

He took a couple of long steps to catch up with her. 'I bought candy with the money. Lots of candy. Ten, maybe twenty times more than what was dropped.'

Turning to face him slowly, she asked, 'Why?'

He shrugged. 'You said it was rationed and hard to come by. We, the GIs, get it with our food packs. A wide variety. Some men like it, others don't. So I bought up all I could. Figured I'd pass it out to the children and, being short on time, I came up with the idea of the pilots dropping it as they flew overhead.'

Her frown increased, but so did the thoughtfulness of her gaze. 'Did you drop it other places?'

'No, I guess you could call this my test run.' Flashing her a smile that showed the guilt inside him, he added, 'I guess I'll have to rethink the delivery.'

She turned completely around, pausing briefly to look off at each of the children picking berries at different places in the long hedgerows encircling the field. 'They certainly were excited yesterday and again today when they found a few more pieces.'

'I suspect there are more children like those two boys who'd lived with Mrs Whitcomb.' He glanced at the children picking berries. 'Those boys had been miserable there.'

'Yes, they had been and are much better off with the Butlers.'

He stepped up beside her. 'You gave me the idea. When you said there wasn't any candy. I knew where there was an abundance of that and sharing it seemed appropriate.'

Her shoulders slumped slightly. 'It appears your benevolence was in the right place, it was just your delivery that was lacking.'

Taking advantage of her acknowledgement, he asked, 'Would you be willing to help me work on that? The delivery?'

Her frown included a gaze that said he'd either lost his mind, or that she thought he was teasing her.

He laid a hand on her arm. 'I'm serious, Kathryn. I can't imagine how these children must feel, being taken away from their families, but you can. You've seen them brought to the house, scared and alone, and are helping them adjust.' He glanced towards the children and a hard lump formed in his throat. 'My sister, Judy, died when she was young, thirteen, and a day doesn't go by that I don't miss her.'

Her expression grew so soft, so tender, he had a hard time swallowing.

'I'm sorry for your loss. I truly am.'

Somewhat shocked that he'd told her that, he shook his head. 'I— Thank you, but I didn't say that for sympathy, I was thinking of the children. War is tough all the way around, but it has to be worse for them.'

She followed his gaze towards the children. 'I agree, and not all children are treated as well or have fared as well as the ones placed with Norman and Charlotte.'

'I've witnessed that myself.' The two boys from the fires had told him that they hadn't been allowed out of the bedroom except to go to school and that the only food they got to eat was what Oscar and Ed left outside the pub for them grab on their way to and from school. That's what they'd been doing in the barn, eating, and had found an old lantern they decided to try to light. 'I know it's not much, but the candy could be a small consolation for them.'

'It certainly thrilled these children and I'm sure it would others.'

Before he could stop himself, he asked, 'Why are you here?'

She started picking berries again. 'My father sent me here three years ago, when many of the girls my age were joining the Auxiliary Territorial Service. He's a British Intelligence Officer and knew many of the ATS members would be sent to France and Germany. He didn't want that for me.' Glancing his way, she added, 'And my mum didn't want me anywhere near soldiers, including the American ones.'

'Why?'

'She has her reasons.'

Considering how outspoken and stubborn Kathryn was, he questioned if she'd merely obeyed what her parents wanted. 'Do you?'

Without missing a berry, she said, 'Yes. The same reason as my mum.'

'What's that?'

The way she eyed him, from head to toe for

a silent moment, he questioned if she'd answer and, for a reason he wasn't willing to investigate, he discovered he was holding his breath.

Turning back to the bush, she said, 'This isn't the first war to bring American soldiers on to our soil.'

The air left his chest as relief washed over him. A simple reason, really, yet to her it must be more. 'No, it's not.'

'They come and leave again, go wherever the army sends them with no concern to those they leave behind.'

The bitterness in her tone was colder than a North Dakota winter and chilled him just as deeply. Not sure he should, but still had to, he asked, 'That happened to your mother?'

'No, my aunt.' With an even colder tone, she added, 'And her son, my cousin.'

'What about after his tour of duty?'

As she turned back to her berry picking, she snapped, 'He'd forgotten all about them by then.'

World War I, as it was now being called, had provided many men with foreign brides, just as he had no doubt that this war would. For those foolish enough to go down that lane. He wasn't. He also wasn't foolish enough to continue a conversation that clearly disturbed her. However, what he had learned was all the more reason to befriend her. If the Brigadier disliked Americans as much as Kathryn did, he wouldn't be any more interested in helping him find Ralph than the army was, unless his daughter asked him to.

Stepping up beside her to pluck a few more berries, he asked, 'So, back to my original question—will you help me figure out a better way to distribute the candy to the children? I know it's not much, but...' nodding towards the children, he continued '...it could mean a lot to them.'

'It would need to include other children as well,' she said.

'Of course. As many children as possible, which is another reason I need your help.'

Tucking several strands of her long black hair behind one ear, she said, 'You are persistent, aren't you?'

The smile she attempted to hide gave him hope. 'I've been called worse.' Lifting the candy bar out of his basket, he held it out to her. 'Truce?' When it appeared she wasn't going to give in, he added, 'Think of the children. How much it would mean to them.'

Her smile included a hint of pink covering both cheeks as she shook her head and took the candy bar. 'Truce.'

'That's made by the Hershey candy company,' he said, hoping to keep the smile on her lips. 'It comes from Hershey, Pennsylvania, where the world's largest chocolate factory is.'

When she eyed him critically he held up a hand.

'Honest. They make all sorts of candy.' He had no idea if his next statement was 100 per cent true, but wanted to get her further on his side. 'They even make a candy bar named after Babe Ruth, the greatest baseball player in the world.'

'Baseball?'

'You've never played baseball? Well, let me tell you about that.'

Chapter Four

11th of June, 1942

Dear Diary,
The warmer days have arrived, with plenty of sunshine, which seems contradictory with all that's happening in the world. The war continues to rage on and it would be far more fitting for the skies to be cloudy and grey. I feel as if I should be that way, too, and I'm a bit ashamed of myself for feeling so happy at times.

I tell myself that it's not my own happiness as much as it is the children's that I'm feeling. Dale has visited us at the house three times during the past two weeks. His visits aren't long, but he brings the children treats. Today, it was a full-sized chocolate bar for each of them. They enjoy his

*visits immensely because he tells them silly
stories about America, like baseball games
and rodeos.*

*His storytelling is rather captivating
and I find myself wondering about America, if all the things he says are true. It
sounds quite amazing, then again, any
place not ravaged by war would be quite
amazing right now and that is why I find
myself thankful that he's able to make the
children forget, for a small amount of time,
the uncertain world we are living in right
now.*

Kathryn's insides grew as warm as the sun
overhead when she spied the Jeep parked in
front of the pub. She'd seen many of those Jeeps,
so this one didn't mean that Dale was inside. But
the prospect that he might be had her pedalling
a bit faster, and once the bike was parked she
nearly spilled the contents of her basket by un-
hooking it so quickly.

After assuring no eggs had been broken by
her clumsiness, she took a deep breath and approached the pathway with what she hoped appeared to be a calm and steady stride, the exact
opposite of her insides. She also told herself she

shouldn't care if it was him or not, but despite all, she was hoping he was inside.

Oscar met her near the door. 'Good day, Kathryn.'

Extremely friendly, Oscar was also a large man. It was impossible to see around him without making it obvious, so she smiled and handed him the basket. 'Hello, Oscar, how are you today?'

'Fair to middling,' he replied.

'That's nice,' she answered, still waiting for him to step aside so she could see the tables. The room was quiet, so there couldn't be many people sitting at them. 'And how is Ed?'

'Fair to middling,' Oscar replied with a wink. 'May I get you a refreshment on this sunny day?'

'I think she'd like a cup of coffee.'

Kathryn's heart skipped a beat at the sound of Dale's voice. Peering around Oscar's wide shoulder, she said, 'I don't drink coffee, Mr Johnson.' His grin made not smiling in return rather impossible. 'I drink tea.'

'Which I have tried.' He stood up and tipped the brim of his flat hat. 'Therefore, you should try coffee. Oscar has learned how to make it just the way I like it.'

'I have,' Oscar said. 'The Sergeant says mine is the best for miles around.'

'Does he?' She was still looking at Dale, who was pulling a second chair out from beneath his table. As usual, he was wearing his brown flight jacket with a white scarf tied around his neck and his brimmed flat hat. Only lately had she allowed herself to admit he looked properly dashing dressed that way. She'd also admitted, only to herself, that the twinkle in his sky-blue eyes always made her want to smile.

'I do.' The twinkle in his eyes right now shone even brighter in the darkened room. 'But, Oscar, put two sugar cubes and a splash of cream in her cup.'

'Coming right up,' Oscar said as he moved towards the kitchen.

She crossed the room and sat in the chair Dale stood behind. It was rather bold of her, but he was the only customer. Furthermore, there was no reason for her not to sit with him for a moment. The ride had been warm today and a rest was in order. She found herself justifying things more often than not lately and couldn't muster up the ability to curb that.

'I was hoping to see you today,' Dale said.

She'd managed to keep the way her heart leaped inside her chest hidden while asking, 'Oh, and why is that?'

He sat back down in the chair adjacent to her.

'I'm curious to know if you've come up with a better plan for the candy deliveries?'

She had given that considerable thought, but had to shake her head. 'No, I'm afraid I haven't.' Untying her scarf, she removed it and placed it on her lap. 'Other than to distribute it at school like you had before.'

'That's too boring,' he said. 'It has to be fun and exciting.'

'Like falling from the sky?'

His grin was charming, so was the way he cocked his head and shrugged.

'Need I remind you that was also scary and dangerous?'

'No, I recall you saying that.'

And she recalled how much fun the children had had picking the sweets up off the ground. They'd been excited for days afterwards, continuously searching for a piece they might have missed. She considered mentioning that, but Oscar arrived and set a cup before her. Looking at her expectantly, Oscar crossed his arms and waited.

'Thank you,' she said while picking up the cup. 'It smells wonderful.' Charlotte had made coffee during Dale's visits and it filled the house with an amazing aroma that remained long after he left. The scent would remind her of him for ever.

'Quit stalling,' Dale said with a grin. 'Taste it.'

'I'm not stalling,' she argued. 'I'm just taking my time.'

'At this rate, it'll be Christmas before you taste it,' he responded.

She had to stop herself from taking the sip she'd been about to because the giggle making its way forward was sure to cause her to choke.

'Come on, miss,' Oscar said. 'Give it a go.'

Finally able, she took a sip and was a bit surprised. It wasn't nearly as bitter as she'd heard. That could be because of the cream and sugar, but even beyond that, the taste was rich. 'Hmmm.' She tried to sound thoughtful.

'Hmmm what?' Oscar asked with raised brows. 'Hmmm good, or hmmm bad?'

'Good,' she said, taking another sip.

Oscar clapped his hands while Dale picked up his cup and held it out to clank against hers.

As their cups met over the table, he said, 'Cheers!'

Being able to laugh was so refreshing and his good humour made not laughing impossible. After another sip, she set her cup down. 'It really is good.'

'I'm glad you like it.' He gave a nod and took

a long swallow off his cup. 'I do believe Oscar has got it down pat. I've been looking forward to a cup of his joe all morning.'

From conversations they'd had before, she knew he rarely had free time. That and the fact she'd never run into him while making one of her deliveries instilled a bit of apprehension. 'What's that?'

He laid a hand on a manila folder sitting on the table that she'd gestured towards.

Her insides grew jittery. She wasn't sure how things worked for the Americans, but knew British servicemen didn't stay in one spot too long. There was a war happening, which meant there wasn't time for guessing about one of the things she'd grown to worry about. 'Are you being transferred?'

He frowned, then glanced at the folder. 'No. Not yet anyway.'

She'd only known him a short time and, for reasons she chose not to explore, didn't want it to end yet. 'But you will be?'

He shrugged. 'I assume so.'

'When?'

'Don't know.' He shrugged. 'Whenever the army decides. And I'm sure that won't be a meeting I'm privy to.'

She had to agree with his answer, but still

questioned, 'So why are you here, in the middle of the day?'

'I just left a briefing on reserving fuel. Making every drop count.'

'But everyone is already conserving petrol,' she said. 'No one uses a motor car unless absolutely necessary.'

'I know, but another US oil tanker bound for Britain was torpedoed by a German U-boat. Those submarines are everywhere and threatening to cut off all of the shiploads being sent to England. Without fuel, our planes aren't worth anything.'

The despondency in his tone reminded her the world was at war and there was little to be happy about. 'Is there anything more we can do to help?' Frustration filled her as he shook his head. 'There are times I wish Father hadn't sent me away from London. I feel as if I'm not doing anything to help.'

'But you are,' he said. 'You take care of evacuees every day, you've turned nearly every inch of Norman's property into gardens to help feed the masses, you deliver blackout curtains wherever needed and help hang them, you deliver food supplies and news and—'

'How do you know all that?'

His grin was a bit sheepish as he glanced towards the door to the kitchen where a clatter or rumble from Oscar and Ed could occasionally be heard.

She didn't mind that he'd asked, nor did she mind that Oscar and Ed had shared the information. Prior to the war, she'd never had to know how to grow food, or take care of children, or gather eggs, or milk cows and goats, make cheese, butcher rabbits and chickens, and even though she did know how to do all those things now, it didn't seem like much. Though, in truth, she didn't have much say in any of it. Last year, when Parliament had called for all unmarried women between the ages of twenty and thirty to join one of the auxiliary services, Father had enrolled her in the Women's Land Army, stating by helping Norman on his small farm, she was doing her part. Her family's past was not of the working class, and Kathryn knew that gave her special privileges during this time of war. She had it far better than many others. Because of her, so did Norman, Charlotte and the children they'd taken into their home.

Dale's hand was still on the folder and something about that folder still pulled at her attention. 'Is that about conserving petrol?'

'No, it's of a personal matter.'

His tone had become deep and troubled,

which had her insides churning. 'Is something wrong?'

'I don't know, but can't seem to find out.'

Frowning, she asked, 'What do you mean?'

He slid the folder towards her.

She waited, but when he didn't say more, she clenched her hands for a moment to stall the shaking and then folded back the cover. There was an official-looking paper with the word 'denied' stamped in red across the front and a picture. Glancing up, she picked up the picture.

'That's me and my brother, Ralph,' he said. 'It was taken two years ago at my grandfather's funeral. Funny how people always think they need to take pictures at funerals.'

'I see the resemblance between the two of you.' Her attention was mainly on Dale. His hair had been longer, but otherwise he looked exactly as he did sitting across from her. Except in the picture he was laughing and had an arm around his brother, who was also laughing.

'Yeah, we're both Johnsons. That's for sure.' He let out a sigh. 'Ralph joined the army shortly after that picture was taken and, except for one phone call, we haven't heard from him.' After taking another sip of coffee, he said, 'It's not like we expect him to write every day, but...' He shook his head as a pained expression covered his face. 'I told you that my sister died several years ago.'

She nodded.

'My mother says that not knowing is worse than knowing.'

Compassion washed over her. 'You think something happened to him?'

'Don't know.'

'You haven't heard anything?' She shook her head, fully prepared to explain not hearing was often better than hearing.

He held up a hand. 'I know that's considered good during wartime, but that pertains to official notices. Ma hasn't gotten any of those either.' He shook his head while taking another sip of coffee. 'I see boys penning letters home every chance they get, so I know Ralph has had the time. He'd know how worried Ma is about him and it's not like him not to let her know where he's at. Right after boot camp I started looking for information as to where Ralph could be, but haven't found so much as a clue to take me further. When I ran out of ideas as to where to look next, I asked Marilyn to write this.'

Kathryn set down the picture to pick up the typed sheet of paper with the word 'denied' stamped on it.

'It's a missing-in-action report,' Dale said,

'which was denied because I can't report some-one missing who's not in my division.'

She set the paper and the picture down. 'What division is he in?'

'If I knew that, I'd have a clue. Marilyn's ac-quired every roster and list she can get her hands on and, though there are Johnsons on every one of them, there isn't a Ralph John Johnson, at least not one from North Dakota born in 1915.' He closed the file. 'I can't help but think he's been captured by the Germans.'

Real concern filled her. Stories of German prison camps filled the newspapers, which claimed they were hell on earth. Worse even. She laid a hand on his arm. 'There has to be a way for you to find out.'

Dale had hit so many dead ends, his hope was waning, especially after today's report. He'd promised his mother he'd find out where Ralph was, so she'd at least know that much, but he'd promised himself he'd find Ralph alive and bring him home so she wouldn't know the pain of losing another child. Dead end after dead end had not fulfilling that promise eating at him night and day.

Marilyn had given him the denied request upon his arrival back to the base no more than an hour ago. After sending Sanders off on a task of which he couldn't even remember, he'd climbed back in the Jeep and driven here, hoping the change of scenery would help him clear his mind and consider his next steps. When Kathryn had walked through the door, it had been like a burst of sun on a gloomy day.

'Norman's an amateur ham radio operator and collects names of all soldiers that have become prisoners by the Germans,' she said. 'I can ask him to look for Ralph's name. If that will help.'

Dale took a moment to consider her offer. She was already doing so much for so many others and he could end up in serious trouble if his Major learned he'd asked her for help. A day didn't go by when the entire base wasn't warned about becoming too friendly with the locals. He wanted to find Ralph, and would, but there were things he couldn't risk. Mainly her.

Laying a hand atop hers, he said, 'You can help by thinking up a way to deliver candy to the children. The pilots run a constant schedule of missions, bombing missions, and dropping that candy made them feel good. They keep asking when they can do it again.' That was true and Major Hilts hadn't minded candy being shared with the local children, said it was good for morale.

She gradually slipped her hand out from between his and he felt a bit awkward for not having thought her hand sandwiched between his might make her uncomfortable.

With a gentle smile, she picked up her coffee and took a sip. 'I have been thinking about that. A lot, but I can't think of a way— Oops,' she said, while bending over to pick up the scarf that had fallen off her lap.

He reached for the scarf, too. They both got a hold of it at the same time and then, realising the other had it, let go at the same time, causing the scarf to float back down to the ground.

'I'll get it,' she said.

Dale, somewhat amazed by what he'd seen, said, 'No, let me.'

He picked the scarf up by the centre and, contemplating if what he was imagining would work, he brought it up as high as the table top, then dropped it again.

The way the scarf floated to the ground excited him. 'Did you see that?'

'I've seen it fall to the floor three times so far.'

He held up a finger. 'Watch.' Bending down,

he picked the scarf up again, lifted it table high and dropped it.

'Amazing,' she said. 'Something dropped, falls to the floor. Hmm. Never knew that.'

He chuckled at her wit while picking the scarf up again. This time he laid it on the table. 'The candy. We can tie pieces on to squares of material like this. They'll look like little paratroopers falling out of the sky. The children will know not to fear them and the miniature parachutes will keep the candy from falling too fast to hurt anyone.'

'Parachutes?'

Her confused frown made his grin grow. 'You've never seen a parachute, have you?'

She shook her head. 'Sort of like how you'd never seen gooseberries.'

Since the first time he'd met her, she'd put a permanent grin on his face. After picking berries that day, he'd stayed for coffee, then for supper that had included the bread and butter pudding she'd told him about. In his opinion, those berries might be edible, but they weren't something he'd look forward to eating again. 'Sort of.'

Her face literally shone as she laughed aloud. 'You can admit you don't like gooseberries. I won't be offended.'

'They weren't that bad.'

She laughed again. 'Spring berries are sour, the summer ones will be better.'

'I think I'll just take your word for that.'

Shaking her head, she took another sip of coffee before asking, 'What kind of berries do you like?'

'Most of them, strawberries, raspberries, but blueberries are my favourite. My mother makes a blueberry pie that makes my mouth water just thinking about it. Have you ever had blueberries?'

'No.'

He let out a low whistle. 'I don't mean to sound rude, but they put your gooseberries to shame.'

'Much like our coffee?'

She was hitting below the belt. 'Oscar has learned to make a great cup. You said so yourself.'

She picked up her cup again. 'It is good.' With a sassy grin, she added, 'Unlike you, I can admit when I like or don't like something.'

It was amazing how carefree she made him feel. Much like the candy-drop idea, she was good for morale. His. 'I can admit when I like something. I just didn't want to hurt your feelings.'

'That's very gallant of you, but saying you don't like gooseberries wouldn't hurt my feelings.'

'All right, then, I don't like gooseberries.'

The both laughed, then she touched her scarf. 'So, will it work? Your parachute idea?'

He glanced at the scarf. 'In theory, yes.' While in the midst of envisioning how to construct miniature parachutes, a rumble stole his attention. He listened to plane engines every day and knew when one was in distress. 'Excuse me.' Pushing away from the table, he rushed towards the door.

Dread filled him at the sight of the B-17 leaving a trail of black smoke as it lost altitude. With the speed it was descending, it would never make it to the base.

'It's going to crash.'

Dale spun around and, though his first instinct was to tell her no, he couldn't lie, nor could he think of anything to say except, 'I have to go.'

He ran for the Jeep in order to head in the direction of the plane. They'd been lucky so far, hadn't lost a plane or a man, and he didn't want that to change.

As the engine engaged, he shifted into Reverse and twisted, about to back up. Catching sight of Kathryn's bicycle, he remembered the last time he'd had to cut their visiting short. He twisted the steering wheel and backed the Jeep up next to where she stood.

A hard knot formed in his throat at the anguish in her eyes as she met his gaze. Swallowing hard, he said, 'Don't follow me, Kathryn.'

She shook her head. 'I won't. But be careful, please, just be careful.'

He drove off then and the sickening feeling growing stronger inside him had as much to do with her as it did the plane going down. She was too soft and gentle for war. Her father should have known that and sent her further away, much further away.

Kathryn's heart sat heavy inside her as she watched Dale drive away. The plane was no longer visible, but there was a large cloud of black smoke billowing up into the sky.

'That doesn't look good.'

She turned and shook her head in agreement with Oscar. 'No, it doesn't.'

'I brought you your basket,' Oscar said, handing it to her. 'And Dale left his folder on the table.'

Her heart sank a little lower at the thought of Dale's brother being lost, or missing, or… She let out a sigh as her gaze went to the cloud of smoke. There was a very good chance something bad had happened to Ralph. There was a good chance something would happen to every man and woman serving in this war.

'I'll take that,' she told Oscar. 'I'll drop it off at the base.'

He handed her the folder. She tucked it in her basket while bidding him farewell and then climbed on her bicycle.

There was a large amount of traffic coming out of the base, including the water lorries. Kathryn stayed clear of the vehicles by riding in the grass on the opposite side of the road, wondering the entire time if anyone could survive a plane crash. It seemed highly unlikely and that both scared and saddened her.

The blonde woman was sitting behind the desk and, though she stood and smiled as Kathryn walked in, there was sorrow on her face.

'May I help you?'

Kathryn held out the file. 'I'd like to drop this off for Sergeant Johnson. He left it at the Village Pub.'

The woman set the file on her desk. 'Did he see the plane?' She bit her lips together for a second before saying, 'It's the first plane we've lost here. I'm praying the crew survived.'

'I am, too,' Kathryn answered softly. 'Dale—Sergeant Johnson drove off in that direction. Quickly. That's how he left this behind.'

The woman laid her hand on the file. 'I feel so bad for him. He's tried so hard to find Ralph. Tried everything.'

'You must be the Marilyn he mentioned.' Kathryn had caught the name when Dale said Marilyn was helping him and assumed it was the same one who'd written her the letter concerning the money.

'Yes, forgive me, I'm Marilyn Miller.' With a genuine smile, she added, 'And you're Kathryn.'

'Yes.'

Marilyn smiled sheepishly. 'I'm assuming everything was settled over the mishap that happened with your bicycle.'

Kathryn ignored the heat that penetrated her cheeks. 'Yes.' Then, attempting to come up with an excuse to have seen Dale today, she added, 'I was talking with Sergeant Johnson about delivering the sweets to the children.'

Marilyn nodded. 'Everyone's excited about that. Especially the pilots.'

A thick silence surrounded them for a moment, before Marilyn asked, 'Did you come up with a plan?'

Although the conversation had ended abruptly,

Kathryn nodded. 'Dale is considering the idea of tying the sweets to scarves to create miniature parachutes.'

'Oh, that would be amazing,' Marilyn said. 'I haven't been able to help him find Ralph, but I know I can acquire some cloth for the scarves.'

'I'm sure he'd appreciate that,' Kathryn replied. Then a strange need to be of some help had her adding, 'And I know someone who will be checking on any word of Ralph.'

'You do? Oh, my, that's wonderful,' Marilyn said. 'After today…' She stopped and shook her head.

Kathryn couldn't think of anything to say, of any comfort she could offer.

'Mrs Miller…' a man appeared in the doorway '… Major Hilts would like to see you.'

'Thank you, Lieutenant,' Marilyn answered.

There was a stretch of silence before the man walked away from the door and Kathryn shivered slightly at the way he'd stared at her.

Marilyn then picked up a notebook and pen. 'I'll see that Dale gets the file, Kathryn. Thank you for bringing it over.'

Kathryn left and, as she pedalled home, found herself wishing that there was more she could do besides ask Norman to check his lists. The idea of asking her father formed, but she couldn't do that. Mum would never understand.

Chapter Five

25th of July, 1942

Dear Diary,
Norman continues to check every name that comes over the radio, but Ralph's hasn't been included. I haven't mentioned that to Dale, I don't want him to get his hopes up needlessly. The news on the radio continuously reminds me of how many lives are being lost. Much like the men who had been on that plane. None had survived, and though I didn't know them, others did, and I feel for their families and friends.

I also wonder about the other servicemen. Not just here, but elsewhere. How none of us has any control over this war. I also wonder if it will ever end. And what our world will be like when it does.

On a much happier note, there was another sweet drop the other day. Dale had delivered more cloth and Charlotte and I once again spent an afternoon stitching strings to all four corners. They are amazing to see and it's fun to watch the children running after the little parachutes falling from the sky. The entire countryside is talking about them. In the past, there were times that I'd wished Father hadn't sent me out here, but now I find myself happy that he did.

I can only admit to you that Dale is the reason. I've never known someone as kind and caring as him. Every moment I spend in his company is so delightful. He is so gracious. And handsome. You would agree if you could meet him. I am very conscious of my feelings, though, for I know he could be transferred at any time, or worse, and I don't want to think about that. Which is another reason I will never allow myself to care that much about a man again. I can't. I promised myself I wouldn't.

The warm and bright morning sun had the upstairs bedroom balmy as Kathryn helped the girls comb and braid their hair. None of them mentioned the heat. They were too excited about the upcoming day's events. She was, too, and that excitement had her all fingers and thumbs.

'Give me the brush again, please, Jennifer, I can't seem to get these curls right today,' Kathryn said. Patricia's thick blond hair was fighting to be braided, but leaving it loose would mean an hour's worth of brushing tonight.

'Will Sergeant Johnson be there today?' Patricia asked, sitting very patiently.

'Of course he will,' Elizabeth answered while tying pink ribbons to the ends of Jennifer's long black braids. 'He lives at the base.'

'Will he have sweets for us?' Doreen was still working on getting her shoes tied, a task she hadn't fully mastered because the shoes Charlotte had purchased for all the children last week were Doreen's first set of shoes with laces.

'I think you're acquiring a sweet tooth from all the treats he's already given you,' Kathryn said.

'What's that?' Patricia asked.

'It means you like sweets,' Kathryn answered, leaning around the side of Patricia's head in order to tap the end of her tiny nose.

'Doesn't everyone?' Doreen asked.

'I suspect most people do.' The children certainly did, but more than that, they enjoyed the act of receiving each piece. After tying off the final braid, Kathryn patted the top of Patricia's head. 'Done.' Glancing from girl to girl, she asked, 'Is everyone ready?'

Excited squeals of 'yes' filled the room— even Doreen had responded because, with assistance from Audrey, her shoes were tied in perfect bows.

'Then let's go see if everyone else is.' Kathryn was having a hard time not acting as excited as the girls. The day was sure to be full of fun. The army base was hosting a picnic for the entire countryside.

They'd barely made it downstairs when the boys outside started shouting. Along with the girls, Kathryn hurried to the door. The sight of two Jeeps pulling into the farm yard surprised her. Seeing Dale driving one of those Jeeps sent her heart into a flutter.

'Didn't know if you'd all fit in Norman's car,' he shouted while waving a hand over the windscreen.

Biting her lip to keep her smile from growing too large, she walked down the pathway as the Jeeps rolled up next to the fence. 'The children and I planned on walking while Charlotte and Norman brought the food in the car.'

Swinging one leg over the short side, he

climbed out of the Jeep and, though it was too warm for his jacket today, he looked as dashing as ever as he walked to the fence. His swagger was confident, even a bit intimidating, until you saw his smile. Kathryn had to tell herself to breathe as she arrived at the other side of the fence. Just the sight of him practically stole her breath away now.

'They can still bring the car, but the children can ride in the Jeeps,' he said with a cheeky grin that displayed his dimples. 'You, too, if you want.'

While she was still trying not to put so much thought behind his every action, the squeals behind her said each and every child had heard him and was overly excited at the idea.

'I think you're spoiling them.' She tried to sound stern, but failed.

He laughed and winked. 'Just being neighbourly.'

She shook her head to keep from laughing aloud. 'It'll be a few minutes before we're ready. We still have to load the car.'

'We'll help.' He unhitched the gate and opened it with one hand while waving towards the other Jeep. 'Sanders, come help get everything loaded.'

'Yes, sir!' The Corporal climbed out of the other Jeep and hurried forward.

Though they were always willing to help, the children rushed to load things into Norman's small car. In mere minutes, everyone was situated in one of the vehicles and on their way to the picnic. The four younger children seated behind her, Little George, Phillip, Doreen and Patricia, giggled happily as they waved to the five older children riding with Corporal Sanders in the Jeep behind them. Charlotte and Norman followed in their car.

'This was very thoughtful of you,' Kathryn said, holding on to the side of the windscreen with one hand. Riding in the Jeeps, with no roof overhead, was freeing in a way. Sort of like spending time with him. It was hard to explain, but lately, she felt like a different person than the one she'd always been.

'It's a long walk,' Dale said. 'They'll need their energy for all the games that have been set up for them to play.'

'I'm sure they would still have the energy, even after walking that far. They've been looking forward to this all week.' The children had hardly spoken of anything else ever since hearing about the picnic. Charlotte and Norman were almost as bad. Having a base built so close might have intensified the war on some days, but it had brightened other ones. Norman often was the first to hear of the whereabouts of local soldiers and shared any pertinent information with families whenever possible. That was also how they heard about blackout enforcements. Whenever that happened, or other news that needed to be spread, she wrote up notices and posted them at the pub for anyone who might not have heard. Lately, the news she was spreading had been good, touting the success the American and British armies were having concerning keeping the Germans at bay.

'So has everyone at the base,' Dale replied.

Even though they hadn't seen each other that often over the past couple of months, talking with him had become easy. He was smiling and appeared to be happy, but something was different. Concerned, she asked, 'Have you had any news about Ralph?'

He gave a slight shake of his head and she understood his desire not to discuss the subject. She kept quiet, too. The children didn't. As Dale answered questions from the children that went from enquiries about the Jeep to what sort of games they would play, Kathryn found herself wondering what her parents would think of

Dale. They were set against her marrying a soldier. At least Mum was. Soldiers and Americans.

'You didn't, did you?'

Caught not listening, Kathryn searched her mind for a moment before responding to Dale's question. 'Didn't what?'

'Bring a gooseberry pie?'

She laughed and laid a hand on his arm while turning about to cast a pretend scowl at the children. 'Who let out my secret?'

'I didn't know it was a secret,' Little George said.

'It's not.' Giving her a teasing glare, Dale continued, 'Unless it's made with gooseberries in order to trick someone.'

She turned back and smoothed her cream-coloured skirt over her knees. 'I wasn't planning on tricking anyone. I planned on letting everyone know it was a gooseberry tart'

'When? While I was choking?'

Laughter bubbled up her throat. 'Of course not.' Glancing his way, she added, 'Choking can be dangerous.'

'You're dangerous.'

Happiness fluttered inside her at his teasing. She had made the tart just for him and was certain he'd like it. The berries were much sweeter now and the entire time she and the children were picking them, she'd been thinking about making a tart for him, one that would rival all others he'd eaten. Pride and glee had filled her at how perfect the tart had looked as she'd taken it out of the oven the night before. She'd had a hard time falling to sleep afterwards thinking about how much he was going to like it. At least she hoped he'd like it. Lately, she found herself hoping for things and a good number of them had to do with him.

Like others, due to him, the day was certain to be one that she'd remember for ever and the children would, too. Tables had been set up in the garden that she and Dale had walked through, and while half of the tables were ladlen with food the army had prepared, the other half overflowed with dishes locals had brought to share.

Among other things, there were three-legged and gunny-sack races, as well as a baseball game that young and old took part in. The air sang with laughter and swirled with goodwill. Dale introduced her to a number of people from the base and she was surprised to learn how many British servicemen were in attendance.

When Dale suggested they fill some plates and find a place to sit down, she was more than willing. He pointed out things that she might like from the American foods and she did the same for him from the English ones—including a piece of her gooseberry tart.

'I'm trusting you on this,' he said, while scooping a piece on to his plate.

'And I'm trusting you on all this,' she said, gesturing towards her plate that held more food than she normally ate in an entire day.

'This way.' He led her around the side of the big main building to a set of steps that weren't occupied. Rather than choosing to sit on the bottom one, he climbed all the way to the top.

She followed and sat down on the top step of the wide stairs. Although she'd only taken a small amount of each of the food items he'd suggested, the abundance on her plate was overwhelming. She didn't know where to poke her fork first. 'I shouldn't have taken so much.'

'You don't have to eat it all.'

'That would be a waste.'

'Considering how frugal you've been for years, I don't think it will hurt anyone for you to be slightly wasteful this one time.'

Although she'd never known it before the war, the scarcity of things had been fully embedded in her life the past few years. 'Perhaps, but I would feel guilty.'

He grasped her hand holding her fork and

poked it in the small piece of ham she'd taken and then held it near her mouth. 'Worry about that once your stomach is full.'

There was something true about his words, as always. She pulled the fork out of his hold and ate the ham, which was flavourful and moist. With a nod, he began eating the food on his plate. He asked about some foods, both before and after tasting them, commenting on how they reminded him of things back home.

'Besides blueberry pie, what's your favourite food?' she asked after noticing her plate was almost empty and she'd yet to take a bite that she hadn't liked.

'I don't know. Around my house we ate whatever was put in front of us or we went hungry. I suppose there are things I favour over others. Fried chicken is good, but so is roast beef, and ham, and bacon. Pork chops are always good, and sausage, and venison and fish. And everyone likes turkey.'

Shaking her head at the items he'd named, she asked, 'Do you eat anything besides meat?'

He held up his fork that held the last piece of her tart. 'Yes, pie.'

She glanced at his plate, which was empty. Not wanting to get her hopes up, but unable to keep them from rising, she asked, 'And?'

'And, there are only two kinds of pie I like.'

Her shoulders felt as if they'd fallen to her elbows. The gooseberries were much sweeter now and she'd truly hoped he'd like them. 'Oh.'

'Warm and cold.'

'Excuse me?'

'The only two kinds of pie I like are warm and cold.' He slid the fork in his mouth, chewed and swallowed, before saying, 'You were right. Those berries are much better this time of year. Much, much better. I'd say they rival blueberries closely. Might even surpass them.'

'You aren't just saying that?'

'No, I'm not. If there's any left, I'll have another piece of that gooseberry pie before the day is over. I'd have some right now, but I'm stuffed.' While rubbing his stomach, he nodded towards her plate. 'How about you? Getting full?'

'Very,' she admitted. 'I can't believe I ate so much.'

'It wasn't that much,' he said while taking her plate and stacking it atop his empty one.

Earlier she'd sensed something different about him and that was back again. There was a seriousness to him that hadn't been there before. She also sensed it had to do with his brother. Though she had asked before, she asked again, 'Have you heard something about Ralph?'

* * *

Dale had options: not fully answering her question was one, fibbing the truth was the other. Neither appealed to him. Something he hadn't wanted to happen, had happened. He'd been told his search for Ralph had involved too many people. Mainly one too many persons. Her. His orders had been given. Make sure she has a fun time at the picnic and then leave her alone. Don't ask her to help in his search for his brother and don't involve her in the candy drops. Which were to continue because they showed good will.

This morning, shortly after Major Hilts had given his talk to the GIs, Lieutenant Banks had called him aside and given him the orders to leave Kathryn alone. Once the anger that had flashed forward inside him settled, he'd had to silently admit that he'd seemed to find a reason or excuse to visit her at the farm or the pub more often than he should have.

He also thought about her more often than not. That could cause trouble and trouble was the one thing he'd stayed clear of most of his adult life—his younger years didn't count. Boys were notorious for finding trouble around every corner.

He'd come to England for three reasons—to

serve his country to the best of his abilities, to find out where Ralph was stationed and to return home in one piece.

'Dale?' she asked with a voice so soft it nearly melted his insides. 'Did you hear something?'

'No.' It might have been fate, or merely a coincidence, that when he looked towards the crowd of people, Lieutenant Banks was looking their way. Long before this morning, he'd concluded Banks was the kind of man who let the insignias on his arm go to his head. He didn't want to think that way about a superior, but Banks made it easy. Everyone at the base thought the same way. Still, the Lieutenant outranked him and, like it or not, an order was an order. 'And I'm done looking.'

'You're what?'

'I'm done looking.'

'Why?' She laid a hand on his arm. 'I don't understand.'

He pushed the dishes further away, mainly because it gave him an excuse to shift enough so her hand fell off his arm. They had become friendlier than they should have and that was his fault. Giving her something she could understand, he said, 'The bombing in Germany is in full tilt.'

'Are you being shipped out?'

'No.' That might be easier. He tossed that thought aside because deep down that was not how he felt. 'I may some day, but haven't been told anything along those lines. What is happening is more planes have arrived. That means we need more men to fly them. My first duties are to the mechanics of the planes. Keeping them in top flying shape.' He didn't want to sound as though he was tooting his own horn, but did want her to understand the position he was in. 'As a mechanic, I know more about those planes than the men who fly them.'

She was nodding, but also frowning.

'Every B-17 that leaves this airfield has ten men aboard. The pilot, co-pilot, navigator, bombardier, flight engineer, radio operator, and four other gunners. Everyone except the pilot and co-pilot are also gunners. They've all been trained for their positions, but that training happened fast, with information tossed at them from all directions, and now that they are in action, they rely on me more and more to fill in any of the blanks they have missed. Especially the engineers. They need to know more about that plane than the pilots. Their main focus is on flying, but the success of the mission falls on the flight engineer. He oversees everything about the plane—the engines, the equipment, fuel consumption, the radio equipment, the transmitters and receivers. He needs to know and understand the reasons behind every piece of equipment on the plane. And he needs to know the ins and out of the weapons. He has to be able to strip, clean and reassemble the guns and how to cock, lock and load the bombs.'

He was over-explaining things, but had to in order to convince himself this was the right step to take.

'In every type of emergency, the engineer is the first one everyone turns to. The lives of the crew are in his hands.'

'Why are you telling me all this?'

'Because you asked. Bottom line is I don't have time to look for Ralph.'

There were few things he was afraid of and looking into her eyes right now was one of them. She couldn't help how pretty she was, how much care and empathy filled her eyes even when she tried not to let it show. What scared him was her insight. How she might be able to tell he wasn't being completely honest. What he'd said about engineers earlier was that he was training them. In the air. During combat missions. Every time he'd climbed into a plane the past two weeks, she'd been on his mind. Each mission came with the chance that he wouldn't return. He had enough people back home who were holding their breaths, waiting for his return, and he didn't need another one. Her family had already experienced other Americans being here and leaving people behind. He couldn't do that. She didn't deserve that.

'I'll look for you,' she said. 'Norman—'

'No. I don't want you looking.' Guilt-stricken for snapping at her, he continued, 'Ralph will eventually let us know where he's at.' That was a lie. Deep inside he knew there was a reason Ralph hadn't written and, despite all he'd said, he had to know what that reason was. He just couldn't involve her in it.

'I'm sure he will, but there would be no harm in looking.'

'No good would come from it,' he replied. 'In fact, no good would come from you being involved in any way with an American soldier. Remember your aunt? Your cousin?'

'Of course I remember them, but this has nothing to do with them. The situations aren't even remotely close.'

He rose to his feet and walked to the railing. The garden was before them, a plethora of colours. The grass, trees and bushes were varying shades of green, and he'd have a hard time finding a colour that wasn't represented by all the flowers. It was a lovely sight, but all he had to do was walk around the building to see the real world. The Nissen huts, the tents, the planes. 'You're right, they aren't.'

The picnic was still going strong, laughter and gaiety filled the air, yet there was none of that inside him. Turning about, he said, 'The entire world is at war. People are dying every day. Ralph could already be dead and maybe I'm better off not knowing that.'

'Don't say that.'

Leaning against the railing, he crossed his arms. The stance wasn't much protection, but it would keep him from reaching out to touch her as she stood and stepped closer. 'We lost two planes this week. Twenty men who won't be returning to their families. To their mothers, their wives, their children.' Knowing the men who'd lost their lives had affected him deeper than he'd expected. It was war and he'd known there would be casualities, had already experienced that before last week, but the loss of Rooster Robins yesterday had thunderstruck him. Rooster had been one of the best pilots out there—if the Germans could shoot him down, they could shoot anyone down.

Compassion filled Kathryn's face as she took

another step closer. 'Oh, Dale, I'm so sorry. I hadn't heard that.'

He had to move before she touched him. Climbing down a couple more steps, he said, 'There's no reason for you to know. No reason for you to be involved in this war. Your father should have sent you further away.' Spinning around, he said, 'As far away as possible.'

He'd read all the pamphlets every man had been commissioned to read, including the ones Major Hilts had referred to at roll call this morning, right before passing out copies of an armed-forces magazine article entitled *Don't Promise Her Anything—Marriage Outside the US is Out*. Perhaps because of their recent losses, the deaths of two full crews, Hilts had taken the opportunity this morning to remind them all that any romance was a distraction from the job they'd been sent here to do. Right after that was when Lieutenant Banks had called him aside and pointed out how any American GI would be frowned upon for forging a relationship with a British Brigadier's daughter. Though it goaded him to use Banks's words, Dale did. 'Relationships forged during wartimes never last.' And though it hurt worse than he'd ever imagined, he also said, 'You know that from your aunt. I think it's best that we end our friendship.'

* * *

Kathryn's heart stopped beating right then and there, and became so full of pain the air wouldn't leave her lungs. 'What? End—' She couldn't get any more out. It hurt too much. So did the look on Dale's face. There was no twinkle in his blue eyes. No sadness either.

Unable to get past that, she bolted down the steps. She was around the corner before her senses kicked in enough for her to realise there were others present. Plenty of others, and she certainly didn't want to make a spectacle of herself.

Glancing around, she held her breath while hoping to no one had witnessed her running away from Dale. Others all seemed preoccupied by their own activities, including the children who were playing a game of tag with several soldiers.

As she watched them run to avoid getting tagged, her mind found a moment to catch up. It didn't make sense. Dale didn't make sense. Why would he stop looking for Ralph? Why would he no longer want to be her friend?

Yes, they were at war. Yes, tragedies were happening every day, but they had been since his arrival. No one was immune to them. They were all just trying to do the best they could in a situation where they had very little control.

She understood that so well. Control was something she'd never had. In a sense, being sent here had given her more control than she'd ever known. She loved her parents, loved them dearly, but they had dictated her life, including sending her here.

Some of it had been necessary. Children needed rules. She'd learned the importance of that since arriving at Charlotte and Norman's. Adults needed rules, too, people in general, and had accepted all those that had been laid down during this wartime, even some she didn't agree with.

Dale knew that, too, that there were rules to follow, but their friendship hadn't broken any.

'Excuse me, Miss Winslow, but are you all right?'

She glanced at the man beside her. Tall, with short dark hair and dressed in an American uniform, he looked vaguely familiar, but she'd been introduced to many soldiers today, they all looked vaguely familiar. Drawing a deep breath, she nodded and then, mainly because saying it aloud might help her believe it herself, she said, 'Yes, I'm fine, thank you.'

'I saw you running around the corner and thought something was wrong.'

Pulling up the first excuse that came to mind, she gestured towards the children. 'I thought one of the children had gotten hurt, but they'd only taken a tumble while running and are fine.' Still needing to believe, she added, 'Just fine.'

'I'm Lieutenant Willis Banks. You may not remember me, but I remember you. I saw you in Mrs Miller's office.'

Kathryn really didn't care where she'd met him before, but did recall he'd been the soldier who had lingered in the doorway after telling Marilyn she was needed elsewhere the day Dale had left his file about Ralph at the pub. What she cared about was Dale and what had happened that had changed him so much. Something must have.

'I hope you are enjoying the day.'

She had been, but no longer was, therefore, she merely nodded.

'Did Sergeant Johnson say or do something that upset you? I am one of his superiors and will reprimand him for such behaviours.'

She might be upset with Dale, but not to the point she'd want to see him in trouble. Furthermore, the Lieutenant's suggestion of reprimand fully irritated her. 'No, Lieutenant, Sergeant

Johnson did not,' she said pointedly. 'I already told you I saw one of the children stumble.'

'All right, then,' he said.

She waited for him to bid farewell and when he didn't, she was about to say hers when he spoke again.

'I only asked because I'm sure he's upset that your father wouldn't assist in finding his brother.'

A sickening ball formed in her stomach and she had to ball her hands into fists to keep them from shaking.

'Even if Sergeant Johnson doesn't, I assure you,' the Lieutenant continued, 'I fully understand that the British Intelligence units are far too busy to be concerned about one American soldier. I apologise that Sergeant Johnson attempted to take advantage of you being the Brigadier's daughter.'

Too stunned, and instantly reliving too many memories that involved Andrew's reaction when her father wouldn't fulfil his requests, Kathryn was too overwhelmed to respond. She had no idea where she got the fortitude to say, 'Excuse me, it's time for me to collect the children. We have chores to see to at home.'

Chapter Six

❧⸻❧

21st of August, 1942

Dear Diary,
Once again, as the night closes in, I find myself thinking of Dale. I have not heard from him, nor do I expect to. But I can't help but worry every time I hear a plane overhead if he's in it. I try to count them as they leave and again as they return, praying it will be the same amount. I have no way of knowing if he's in one or not, but do know for a fact that he is training in others, which means he must often be in one of those planes. Lieutenant Banks affirmed that when he stopped by to ask the children about the latest candy drop.

I really don't care for that man. He is far too nosy. Norman agrees. In fact, the

Lieutenant asked so many questions on his first visit to the house that Norman asked Father about him. The Lieutenant isn't a spy, but I still don't care for him. Perhaps because he talks so highly of himself and so lowly of others. You should have heard him the other day, he spoke as if the candy drops were his idea.

He certainly is nothing like Dale. I've thought long and hard about certain things and find it difficult to believe that Dale would end our friendship or stop looking for Ralph because Father wouldn't help him. I can't believe that Dale would have gone behind my back to approach Father, but I truly see no other reason for Dale to have ended our friendship. I had struggled to believe that Andrew only wanted to marry me so that Father would advance him in the ranks without time served. Although Andrew was far more selfish than Dale, he would never have thought of others the way Dale did, would never have rushed to put out a fire or search for ways to deliver sweets, I can't deny the facts.

I guess I never fully understood what being my father's daughter meant. Mum told me long ago that our status also *brings expectations and consequences. I know that Charlotte and Norman are able to care for so many children because I'm here. Because Father compensates whatever monies they need and I'm grateful for that. Grateful I can help others, but I'm also sad because it means I'll never be able to do enough. There will always be people who expect more, whether I have any influence in the situation or not.*

I guess I could say that's unfair, but I know others will say it's unfair that I had so much to begin with. Therefore, I guess life isn't fair. Not on any level and that's something I just need to get used to.

The heat was stifling, had been for the past two weeks, and the sweat trickling down Kathryn's back added to her overall crossness. Digging potatoes was back-breaking work, but she didn't mind how it made every muscle in her body ache, how it made her forget the hollowness inside her. The emptiness that was there when she woke up and still there when she went to bed. She tried to overlook it, hide it, forget about it, get used to it, but nothing seemed to work.

'Kathryn!'

Sticking the blade of the shovel into the ground,

she turned around at the sound of Charlotte's shout and used a hand to shield the sun from her eyes.

Waving a tea towel in the air, Charlotte shouted again from the edge of the field. 'Kathryn! Come quick and bring the children!'

'What's the matter?' Elizabeth asked.

'I have no idea,' Kathryn replied. 'Gather the girls, I'll get the boys, and hurry.' There were any number of war-related events that could have happened, but the hollowness inside her prevented her from reacting overly much. Whatever it was, they'd follow an order that had been issued, hunker down in the shelter, deliver news or simply sit by the radio and listen to the announcer talk about things there wasn't a single thing anyone could do anything about.

Leaving the shovel sticking in the dirt, she ran towards the far end of the field, where she gathered the boys and then hurried back towards the house. George and Edward ran ahead. Holding on to the hands of both Little George and Phillip, she kept her pace even with their shorter legs. There were no German fighter planes filling the sky, yet she encouraged the boys to run as fast as possible, knowing those planes could swoop over the horizon at any moment.

She'd noticed how that happened more closely lately, while wondering if Dale was aboard each one that flew overhead. During the weeks that had passed since the day of the picnic, thinking about him had filled her with anger, hurt, sadness and a mixture of other things she couldn't begin to describe. All of them had led to where she was now. Empty. It was as if she no longer had feelings, no longer cared one way or the other.

The only time a hint of emotions came to life was when she delivered supplies to the pub. Oscar or Ed, whoever met her at the door, usually always mentioned that they'd seen Dale, that he'd enquired about her and asked them to give her his best. At first that had irritated her. If he no longer wanted to be her friend, he shouldn't enquire about her, or have others pass along the fact that he had.

Eventually, though, she'd come to understand that she couldn't help who she was, who her father was or what people expected, so she asked Oscar and Ed to give him her best in return. There was solace in knowing Dale stopped by the pub. There would only be two reasons for those visits to stop. He'd either have been shipped out, or worse, and she wasn't prepared to think about that either.

The older boys and the girls were already entering the house when she, Little George and

Phillip arrived. 'Stomp the mud off your boots,' she reminded, close to being breathless from the long run. 'But hurry and get inside.'

She stomped her boots off, too, and then rushed through the scullery and into the front room where everyone was gathering. No crackling from the radio split the air as she followed Phillip into the room, but he did let out a squeal.

'Mummy!' Phillip shouted. 'Mummy!'

A tiny woman with short dark hair knelt down in the centre of the room and held her arms out. 'Phillip. My baby.' Tears fell from her eyes as she gathered Phillip into an embrace. 'Oh, my baby, how you've grown!'

Most of the children had received letters or small packages from family members, but not one of them had received a visit. As a cold tingle crept up Kathryn's spine, she turned to glance at Charlotte, who was dabbing her eyes with the tea towel as Norman stood next to her, hugging her close with one arm around her shoulders.

Nodding her way, Norman cleared his throat before saying, 'This is Phillip's mother, Mrs Newman. She's here to take Phillip home with her.'

Kathryn might have thought she was hollow inside, but at that moment knew differently. She had to press a hand to her lips to keep a painful gasp from escaping. The room had gone silent and every set of little eyes, including Phillip's, had turned towards her.

Drawing a breath and willing her voice not to crack, she said, 'Oh, isn't that wonderful.'

Phillip had stepped out of his mum's arms. With a deep frown, he turned back to his mum. 'But we don't have a home,' he said. 'Remember? That's why I had to come here to live. And I like it here.'

With a gentle smile, his mum said, 'Oh, darling, we will soon have a new home. A wonderful new home. It will be in America.'

'America?' It was a moment before Kathryn realised she'd spoken. Shaking her head, she controlled the volume of her voice to ask, 'You're moving to America?'

As Mrs Newman rose, she ran a hand along the straight lines of her olive-green dress. It was fashionable, and new, and from the looks of it would have taken an entire year's worth of rationing coupons. 'Yes. I've married an American soldier and the army are going to provide Phillip and me transportation to America. They do that regularly, ship brides to America.'

'They do?' Kathryn found herself biting the tip of her tongue for a moment before asking, 'Along with your husband?'

'No, my husband has been shipped to Africa, where he will complete his tour, but he has family in Georgia who will help Phillip and me until his return to America.' Mrs Newman once again knelt down in front of Phillip. 'I know you will miss all your friends here, but we need to hurry. There is a car waiting outside that will drive us back to London.'

Norman once again cleared his throat. 'Charlotte's already packed his bag and I carried it out to the car. You children need to say goodbye to Phillip.'

Tears hit her eyes so hard and fast, Kathryn could barely stop them from trickling out. Stepping forward, once again because all the children were looking at her, she nodded. 'Norman is right. It's time to say goodbye.'

One by one, led by Elizabeth, the children moved towards Phillip, offering hugs and saying goodbye.

Except for Jennifer. Of all of them, she was the quietest and the most caring. With tears running down her cheeks, she whispered, 'We'll never see him again, will we?'

Kathryn didn't like the idea, but had to be honest. 'Most likely not.'

Closing her eyes, Jennifer scrunched her face up and wiped the tears off her cheeks before she said, 'I'll be right back, don't let him leave until I say goodbye.'

Kathryn didn't have time to ask Jennifer where she was going. The girl was already racing up the stairs.

The others had just completed their farewells when Jennifer returned. As she stepped up to say goodbye, she held out her hand to Phillip. 'I know this is your favourite treat,' she said. 'And I want you to have the parachute, too, so you'll always remember us.'

Kathryn covered her mouth with one hand. It was a stick of gum, still tied to one of the little squares of soft white cloth used for the sweet drops.

'Thank you, Jennifer,' Phillip said. 'But I thought we had to give all the parachutes back to Sergeant Johnson.'

With her heart clenching at his leaving and the mention of Dale, Kathryn stepped forward and knelt down in front of Phillip. 'All except for this one,' she said, touching the one in his hand. 'It is yours and, just as Jennifer said, every time you look at it, you can remember all of us and how much we loved having you live here with us.'

He nodded and held on to the parachute a bit tighter. 'I will, Kathryn, I will.'

She wrapped her arms around him and, while holding him close, fought to keep the tears at bay all over again. The idea of not saying goodnight to him, of not answering the dozens of questions he asked about nearly everything, of not knowing he was safe and close by was enough to make those tears rush forward. Holding him a bit tighter, she kissed the top of his curly brown hair.

'We really must be going.'

Kathryn nodded at Mrs Newman's words and, after one other kiss atop his head, she released Phillip. 'Please send a letter, telling us that you made it safely to America.'

'I will,' Mrs Newman said. 'I do appreciate how well you took care of him. You'll be in my prayers for ever because of that.'

'As you will ours,' Charlotte said. 'He was a darling to have live with us. A complete darling.'

The older woman had stepped up beside her and, seeing her red-rimmed eyes, Kathryn hooked her arm though Charlotte's.

They all followed Mrs Newman and Phillip out the door and, when the time came for the car to drive off, they all waved and shouted goodbye. Kathryn felt as if a part of her drove away in that car, a part she would never get back and, despite the fact she'd tried hard not to remember the words Dale had spoken that fateful day of the picnic, they came back to her. *Relationships forged during wartime never last*, he'd said, and at that moment she knew the truth of it with all her heart.

Standing there watching Phillip drive away wasn't going to make his leaving any easier, only time would do that, so she turned about and laid a hand on George's shoulder. 'We still have a lot of potatoes to pick yet today.'

He nodded. 'The lorry will be here before dark.'

'We best get back at it,' Edward said.

'Yes, we should,' Elizabeth agreed, rounding the younger girls before her.

No one had ever been excited about picking potatoes and, as they walked back towards the field, the solemnness could have been cut with a knife.

'Moving to America,' Edward said. 'Who'd have thought it?'

'I am going to miss him,' Little George said.

'We all are,' George replied, laying an arm across Little George's shoulders.

'I wonder what it's like in America,' Doreen said. With a serious frown, she asked, 'Phillip won't be cold over there, will he, Kathryn?'

'I'm sure his mother will have a jacket for him on the colder days,' she answered.

'Is it cold over there all the time?' Patricia asked.

'I don't believe so,' Kathryn said.

'Sergeant Johnson said it snows a lot,' George said.

'Enough to build snow forts and have snow-ball fights,' Edward said.

Not in the mood, or the condition, to talk about Dale, Kathryn gestured towards the vegetables in the field they'd just entered. 'Time to start digging potatoes, again.'

The boys started towards the end of the field they'd been working on earlier, but stopped when a rumble sounded overhead. Kathryn tried to stop herself, but it was no use. A full dozen of American planes flew overhead. They were headed away from the base, not towards it, and once again, Kathryn wondered if Dale was in one of them.

Her wondering was answered a moment later.

'It's Sergeant Johnson,' George shouted, raising both arms into the air. 'He's waving at us!'

Kathryn put a hand over her mouth to once again smother a gasp as her insides fluttered. One of the planes tilted one way and then the other as if it was waving. Dale had done that before, during a sweet drop. She'd waved back that day, but today, she clasped her hands together and said a prayer for his safe return.

Dale gestured towards Tony Snow, the pilot who'd tipped the wings of the B-17 towards the group below. From this distance, the people were unrecognisable, but it was Norman's farm and therefore that had to be the children and Kathryn below. He'd done what he'd needed to do, stopped spending any amount of time with her, but that didn't mean he'd stopped thinking about her. It also didn't mean he liked what he'd done.

He'd enjoyed spending time with her, having her as a friend, and those feelings hadn't just gone away because he'd been ordered to stop seeing her. However, he could understand the army's reasoning. He could get shipped out at any time and never return to this region, or worse, and it wasn't right to subject her to all of that just because he enjoyed her friendship. He had to keep telling himself that.

The B-17 hit cruising altitude and that shifted Dale's train of thoughts to his job duties. Jefferson Kidd was a new engineer, as green as they came. This was only his second flight, meaning Dale had to stay focused and oversee Jefferson's every move. The engineer would have to survive twenty-three more flight missions before completing his tour, and, if he was lucky, wouldn't be called up to fly another twenty-five. Even luckier would be that he'd be able to out-manoeuvre the Luftwaffe the entire time. Every serviceman knew one lucky strike from the German Air Force or flak from the ground guns ended flying careers as quickly as they started.

'This gal is running in tip-top shape!' Jefferson's excitement came across clearly even as his words crackled over the interphone.

'What's the speed and elevation?' Dale asked, focused on keeping the newbie's attention on the tasks at hand.

'*The Dream Bomber* is running at two hundred and seventy-three miles an hour at twenty-four thousand feet...'

The crackling drowned some of Jefferson's report, but because he was tracking the instruments himself, Dale knew exactly what the man was saying. He took a moment to pull up the collar of his heavy flight jacket to keep the cold wind from blowing down the back of his neck. For a moment, his mind shifted to how warm the summer sun would be for Kathryn and the children in the field. It was the opposite for him. The temperature at this altitude was cold no matter what time of year it was and, for as big as the flying bomb was, the conditions were cramped. Each of them had their own space, albeit he and Jefferson shared the area dedicated to the engineer, sitting with their backs to the pilots.

Rather than the fresh country air below, gas fumes spewed from the engines and the cold thin air had the vapours hanging heavy inside the plane because every window was open for the eleven machine guns. The roaring from all four engines also made it harder to hear through the interphone, but Dale still requested, 'Report in!'

One by one, the pilots and crew members responded and Dale mentally checked each one off his list, watching that Jefferson was doing the same while checking the instrument panel. The onboard oxygen system had to be in top working order and reach every man.

There was a bit of good humour as the men answered, as usual. This was their last chance for any joking around before everyone began to silently prepare themselves to enter the heavily guarded Nazi-occupied territory.

Once again Kathryn formed in Dale's mind. He felt awful about how things had ended between them and wished he'd been able to do things differently. But, ultimately, he was an enlisted man—when he was ordered to jump, he couldn't even ask how high.

The static crackling in his ears brought his attention back around and he gave a thumbs up to the plane gliding into formation beside them. The full dozen of planes that had left the base would form a combat box that would result in tighter bombing when the time came.

As one of the three front planes, *The Dream Bomber* had a plane on each side, a formation of three more directly behind her tail and formations of three more flying on each side behind her wings. All twelve planes roared forward, crossing landmarks that were the gateway to the line of no return. Not until every last bomb they were sitting on had been dropped.

'Lock and load!' was ordered through the interphone and, moments later, the battle began.

The armour plating of the B-17s could soak up a lot of bullets and *The Dream Bomber* held her own, until German artillery took out the number two engine. The explosion had been massive and a direct hit. Scanning the instruments, Dale confirmed Jefferson's report and added, 'Number four's damaged, too!' With only two of the four engines working, he laid out the truth. 'We can't maintain speed!'

Having flown several missions, Snow understood exactly what that meant and responded immediately. 'Watch your fire, boys!' the pilot ordered. 'We're dropping out of formation.'

There was plenty of danger in that, sur-rounded by other B-17s firing guns and drop-ping bombs, they could easily be hit by their own comrades, taking them out if not careful.

Falling behind made them an easy target and the German aircrafts took advantage of that. Bullets pelted the plane and every crew mem-ber fired back. Urgency, the reality of life or death, filled the plane. Sweat poured off Dale and the shaking of the powerful gun racked his entire body. While keeping his gun firing at the Germans he continued instructing Jefferson to report the plane's condition.

'The oxygen system's been knocked out! And the hydraulics,' Jefferson reported.

'Johnson?' Snow shouted.

The damage they'd already sustained was im-mense and Snow was asking his opinion as to their next move. With two engines now gone, the plane was vibrating so hard a chunk of armour plate came loose, catching the tip of a wing as it flew past. Dale had already assessed the situa-tion and knew their chances were slim to none. 'Turn about, send out an SOS and have your parachutes handy!'

'Our radio has been taken out,' Bill Fredrickson, the radio operator said.

An SOS wasn't going to get them any assistance in their current position, so the loss of their radio was of little consequence.

'Should I kick out the emergency door?' Jefferson asked.

'Not yet,' Dale responded. 'There's full ground artillery under us.' Addressing the pilot, he added, 'We have to make the English Channel before barrelling.'

'Roger!' Snow responded. 'It's going to be rough, boys, but I'm not telling you anything you don't already know!'

'I got us covered!' Randy Myers, the ball-turret gunner, responded from his position below the wings. 'Got full fire power and won't let up!'

There were other shouts, check in's and remarks that were meant to be encouraging for all. Every man knew this could be their last moments, but weren't willing to admit that, not even among themselves, yet wanted to say something as they strapped on their parachutes.

Dale listened, but remained silent as Kathryn filled his mind. The plane listed and vibrated so hard he lost hold of his gun. Grabbing the edge of the open window, he tucked his chin against his chest as the plane went into a full spiral and plummeted towards the earth.

Kathryn flashed before his eyes and the idea of never seeing her again filled him with such loss, such anger, he pulled up his head and fought the spinning forces to examine the instruments before him. They were still high enough to do something. 'Pull up!' he shouted into the mouthpiece. 'Pull up now!'

There was no response from Snow, but that didn't stop Dale from shouting instructions to fully engage the two engines they still had. 'Snow! We've got the power! Use it! Now!' He didn't bother to say before it was too late, because it might already be. He just had to believe it wasn't. Had to believe.

What happened next was somewhat of a blur. The spinning slowed just above the tops of trees that seemed as if they were rising up to meet them. Dodging one and then the other, *The Dream Bomber* slowly climbed higher and higher. The plane was finally flying level again, but they were only at two thousand feet.

'Check in!' Dale ordered.

'Lost my bubble, but I'm still with you,' Skye Miller said, referring to the Plexiglas nose protection of his bombardier station.

'Newton took a bullet to the shoulder,' B. F.

John said. He was a waist gunner, along with Pete Reynolds. Newton was the tail gunner.

Dale spun around. The guns in their stations hung useless, but B.F. gave the thumbs-up sign as he said, 'Reynolds and I are with him. He's doing all right.'

Not ready to count any of them as casualities, Dale hoped no one else had been hit as he listened to each one check in. All accounted for, he said, 'The Germans must have thought we crashed and burned.'

'All right, boys,' Snow said, 'Now we just have to get this heap back to England.'

'If anyone can do it, you can,' Dale said. He was confident in Snow's ability, but the plane had been hit hard and was losing power with every mile she flew.

Other than crackles and pops, the interphone remained silent as the plane loped mile after mile. When the English Channel flowed beneath them, Dale considered ordering all to take positions for a water landing. They were flying so low the parachutes might not have time to open fully. Yet, both remaining engines, though overworked, were still roaring, so he did the next best thing and silently encouraged the flying fortress to live out her reputation and get them as close to the airbase as possible.

The grey that came before darkness had filled the sky by the time they flew over Norman's farm, and Dale knew the windows in the house must be rattling loud enough to scare every occupant. The plane was little more than three hundred feet in the air. Almost as close to the ground as Rooster had flown the day he scared Kathryn off her bicycle.

The interphone had remained silent ever since they'd left Germany and, as Dale's mind once again filled with thoughts of Kathryn, he said, 'We're almost home, boys.'

'Never thought I'd be this glad to see that base again,' Skye Miller said.

'Roger that,' Snow replied.

Others agreed, and a short time later, rattling and smoking, *The Dream Bomber* touched down. The old girl might have been on her last leg, but she hadn't let them down and that alone filled the entire plane with exuberance. Until the roar of the engines completely died.

Exhausted and weak, crawling out would have been easier, but not a one of them was willing to display any form of defeat, not even Frank Newton. With one arm hanging at his side, he stepped on to the ground and waved aside the gurney two men had carried towards the plane.

The Dream Bomber was a little more than a

pile of shredded metal. Bullet holes, and larger, gaping cavities in her fuselage, stared back at them like a wrinkled old woman with teeth missing. The only place not damaged was the mural painted below the cockpit. It was of a smiling red-headed woman carrying an American flag and winking one eye.

They stood there, all ten of the crew members, staring at the plane for a few silent minutes. Dale had no idea what the others were thinking. They might be silently cursing the Germans or thanking their lucky stars, but his mind was once again on Kathryn and, more specifically, what he was going to do about her.

'When will she be ready to hit the sky again?'

Dale turned to Snow and shrugged. 'I can rebuild her engines, but the rest of her might be commissioned to scrap.'

Snow shook his head. 'Any lady who can live through that deserves to fly again.'

Dale slapped Snow's shoulder. 'Any pilot who brought his crew home in a mess like that deserves praise.'

'I didn't do it alone,' Snow said.

Dale slapped the shoulder of Jefferson, who stood on his other side. 'None of us did,' he said.

Some silent, some aloud, they all agreed and once again looked at the plane.

Their moment of reflection ended as men gathered around, including commanding officers. Standing at attention until at ease permission was granted, Dale then shook hands with anyone who offered and listened to the news of what had happened to the other eleven planes that had left the base with them earlier in the day.

His stomach fell at the news that two of the planes would not be returning, ever, or the crews that had flown on them. The reports of the German planes that went down excited some, but he couldn't agree with their sentiments. The Germans were no different than any of them standing around their downed plane. They had homes full of families waiting for them to return just as much as everyone else did.

'Sergeant Johnson.'

Dale turned about and gave a salute as Major Hilts approached.

'At ease, Sergeant,' Hilts said upon arrival. 'I'll expect a full report of how this plane was able to return in this condition. I've never seen one this battered and bruised. It took skill to keep her from hitting ground or sinking in the Channel. Snow claimed it wasn't his flying abilities, it was the leadership on board.'

'It took the entire crew, sir,' Dale responded. 'I'll have a report ready by tomorrow morning.'

Hilts nodded before saying, 'You have a visitor. I'll walk you over to headquarters.'

The battle that raged inside him was more ferocious than the one he'd experienced in the air. 'Yes, sir,' Dale replied, falling in step beside the Major. He tried to convince himself his visitor wasn't Kathryn, but his heart refused to believe that and it was fighting hard to make the rest of him as excited at the prospect of seeing her as it was. His brain, even though fully exhausted from the day's mission, was on high alert and warning him that seeing her would be dangerous. Not only to him, but to his career as a serviceman.

The tight-lipped expression on the Major's face never changed as he said, 'You've done a lot when it comes to building a healthy rapport, Johnson, not only with your crew, but the locals.'

Some of Dale's excitement faded fast.

'I appreciate that, Sergeant.'

Dale held in his sigh of relief, realising Hilts was referring to the candy drops. Word of them had travelled fast even before the picnic, but since then, Hilts had reported that the base had received a positive citation from his superiors for the display of benevolence.

'Thank you, sir,' Dale said.

'We wouldn't want to have any of them change their thoughts towards us now,' Hilts said.

'No, sir, we wouldn't.'

'Rules are put in place for a reason, Sergeant Johnson,' Hilts said. 'That reason is to protect us and others from potentially harmful situations.'

Dale hadn't set out to break any rules and so far hadn't completely broken a single one, but each step he took towards headquarters had him wondering if he was going to be strong enough to remain that way. 'Yes, sir.'

'As long as a man knows where the boundaries are, no harm's done.'

Dale wasn't certain how to take that comment, but still replied, 'Yes, sir,' mainly because a response was required.

Although the base was lit up by outdoor lights attached to the Nissen huts, tents, mess hall and other buildings, night had completely fallen and Norman's car parked near the front entrance of the main headquarters building was impossible to miss. Dale kept any reaction to seeing it well hidden—to any onlooker. Inside he was as torn up as *The Dream Bomber.*

'I'll expect your report on my desk tomorrow,' Hilts said, stopping near the bench Kathryn had sat upon the day she'd tried to return his money.

'I'll have it to you, sir,' Dale said, giving a salute.

After saluting in return, Hilts said, 'Your company is inside.' The Major then spun on one heel and walked away.

Dale drew a long, deep breath, and held it as he started up the steps. Telling Kathryn she shouldn't be here wasn't going to be easy. Truth was, he wanted to see her. She'd been the reason he hadn't given completely in and accepted fate while the plane had been spinning towards the ground.

The door creaked as he opened it and his boot heels echoed off the empty hallway as he started towards the waiting area. The desk there would be empty this time of night and he wondered if that would make seeing Kathryn worse or better. With an onlooker, it would be easier to remain aloof.

Approaching the doorway, he took another deep breath, then turned left to enter the waiting area.

The sight of Norman sitting there jolted his insides. 'Where's—?' Stopping himself from enquiring about Kathryn's whereabouts, Dale asked, 'Is everything all right?'

Norman stood. 'She wouldn't wait until morning, like I suggested. George insisted the plane flying close to the ground and leaving a trail of black smoke was the same plane that had waved at them earlier today and that you had to be on it. She had to know that you're all right.'

Fully understanding Norman was referring to Kathryn, Dale asked, 'Where is she?'

'Outside, in the car,' Norman replied. 'She was afraid you wouldn't see her, but wouldn't stay home either.'

Dale exited the building twice as fast as he'd entered it, leaping down the steps two at a time. He tried to see through the car windows. It appeared to be empty and *was* empty, he concluded upon opening the passenger's door. Spinning about, he was prepared to run back up the steps when movement near the side of the building caught his eye.

It was her, standing in the shadows on the walkway that led through the garden. Relief washed over him, as did a wave of something so powerful his knees trembled slightly.

He kept his movements slow and steady as he walked towards her, wishing, while telling himself he shouldn't, that he could see her more clearly. Know what she was thinking in order to prepare himself for her reaction to seeing him.

'You were in that plane,' she said quietly, 'the one that looked as if it would drop out of the sky at any moment, weren't you?'

'Yes,' he admitted, stopping within a few feet of her. She was still cloaked in the shadows, preventing him from making out the expression on her face. 'But it landed just fine. We're all fine.'

'The children will be very relieved to hear that. They were worried.'

He let the breath release from his lungs, and tried to think of a response. He'd thought of her friendship, but hadn't thought of the children, which was odd because, in a sense, it was a complete package. Whether it was what the army wanted or not, he'd made friends with all of them and merely staying away wasn't going to change that.

'They've had a hard day, and…' Her voice was shaky and she'd covered her mouth with one hand, smoothing a hiccup.

'Why? What happened for them to have a hard day?' She had to be referring to something other than work. They all worked hard every day—she and the children. He'd witnessed it, knew all they did to survive and to provide for others.

'Phillip's mother collected him today, took

him back to London with her.' Her voice was barely a whisper.

'For good?'

'Yes.'

Dale's heart nearly melted at the amount of sorrow that must be filling her over Phillip's departure and, without further thought, he stepped into the shadows and wrapped his arms around her. 'I'm sorry, Kathryn,' he whispered while pulling her close. 'I know how much you care about each and every one of the children.'

She was trembling and her breathing was uneven as she buried her face against the thick leather of his flight jacket.

'I had to know if you were gone for ever, too.'

He stepped forward, aligning his body so the entire length of hers could lean against him. 'I'm fine,' he said. 'And I'm glad you came. I've missed you.'

Her arms wrapped around his waist as she said, 'I've missed you, too.'

They stood like that for some time, holding on to one another until she stopped trembling and they were both breathing normally—well, as normal as he could be breathing considering the circumstances. Holding her had awakened his entire system, even the parts of him that had been exhausted to the core a short time ago.

She released her hold first and he eased his as she took a step back.

'I'm sorry,' she said. 'I do remember what you said and—'

'There's a bench over here,' he said, indicating one built of stone and nestled among the bushes a short distance up the pathway. 'Let's go sit for a moment.'

She agreed with a silent nod and he took her hand as they walked to the bench. His mind ran amuck with what he should say, should do, but nothing settled. Whatever he said right now would be said because he was going to let his heart, not his mind, oversee things.

Once seated, he kept a hold of her hand as his mind tossed about where to start, what to say.

'I wish you would have asked me instead of him. I might have found a way for Father to help you find Ralph.'

Utterly confused, he asked, 'What are you talking about?'

'You assuming because I'm his daughter, my father would help you find Ralph.'

'I never assumed that…' He might have considered the notion, but hadn't followed through on it because he hadn't wanted to use her like that. To expect something like that from their friendship. 'I've never met your father. Never talked to him about anything. Why would you think I have?'

'Lieutenant Banks told me.'

Anger was coiling up Dale's spine like a rattlesnake preparing to strike. Banks. He hadn't liked the Lieutenant before, but now…

'I could call Father and—'

'Kathryn, no.' He squeezed her hand. 'I don't want, nor would I ever expect, you to be in the middle of my search for Ralph.' Glancing around the base, he continued, 'I don't want you to be in the middle of any of this.' He didn't want Banks in the middle of it either. In the middle of anything. 'I don't know why Banks would have said that, or how he knows about Ralph, but I have never spoken to your father and—'

'Oh, no,' she whispered.

'What?' He held her hand tighter. 'What is it?'

'Lieutenant Banks must have overhead Marilyn and me talking, the day I delivered the folder to your office.' She shook her head. 'He was standing in the doorway.'

Dale held the air he wanted to huff out. That explained how Hilts found out about it.

'I'm so sorry, I—'

'You have no reason to be sorry. I'll find Ralph. So please, don't worry about it. Don't concern yourself over it.' Needing to change the subject so his anger would ease, he referred to the news she'd given him about Phillip. 'You have enough going on. I wish you only had to worry about picking gooseberries and—'

'It's over.'

For a split second, his heart stopped beating.

'Gooseberry season is over,' she said.

She was something and the thoughts of never seeing her again that had raged through his mind earlier had him leaning closer to her. He shouldn't, but almost seeing his maker wouldn't allow him to stop either.

The first touch of her lips sent a fiery blaze through his system like nothing he'd ever known, and the next moment, when she released a tiny sigh, did even more. He had to be careful, his life had already been spared once today, and he was pretty certain he didn't have nine of them.

He kept the kiss soft and gentle, and savoured every moment of it.

The smile on her face as their lips separated filled him with a satisfaction he'd never known. 'So, what berries are ripe now?'

She giggled slightly. 'I'm not sure, I'd have to walk the hedgerows to check.'

After the flight today, the entire crew would

be given a furlough, it was mandated. Others would look forward to spending that time in London, especially the West End, and return with colourful stories about being propositioned. Some might think it strange, but to him picking berries sounded far more desirable. 'I'll have some time later this week, maybe I could go check with you.' With excitement humming inside him, he asked, 'If that would work for you?'

'Yes, it will. The last of the potatoes will be picked up tomorrow.'

Lorries had been rolling around the countryside the past few weeks. After the crops were gathered from the small farms, they were delivered to a central collection point for the government to divvy out.

'All right, then,' he said. 'I'll let you know what day and, if it's all right with you, I'll plan on spending the entire day picking whatever berries are ripe enough to pick.'

'That would be nice.'

The shine on her face, the sparkle in her eyes, were downright irresistible, which was why he stood up and helped her stand as well. 'We best get you back to the car. Norman has to be worried about you.'

'He was worried about you, too,' she said, falling in step beside him. 'We all were.'

'Truth be, I was worried about all of you, too.' No rule book could change certain things, especially inside things. No rule book would stop him from seeing Banks minded his own business either.

Two days later, when Kathryn opened the door and saw Dale standing there, she had to force herself to keep from jumping with joy. He'd been on her mind non-stop, especially the way he'd kissed her. It hadn't been demanding or insistent, as if he expected more. Andrew's kisses had been like that. He'd pressed her to take things further, several times. Dale's kiss hadn't unnerved her like that. In fact, his kiss had been perfect and filled her with a wonderful sense of fulfilment every time she thought of it.

'I was wondering if you'd have time to check the hedgerows today,' he said, grinning so that both of his dimples showed. 'For berries.' Both eyes sparked as he added, 'Preferably not green ones.'

The ability to stop herself from giggling wasn't there, yet she tried to contain her excitement. 'I may have an hour or so before the children return from picking potatoes.'

'If we can't find any berries in an hour, then I'd guess there aren't any,' he said.

She nodded and gestured for him to enter the house. 'I'll need to get some baskets and let Charlotte know.' As he stepped into the house, she said, 'She'll probably want to make you some coffee.'

He gave her a wink and whispered, 'And I'll gladly drink it.'

Charlotte did make coffee and Dale drank it, while conversing with Norman on a variety of subjects. He made sure to include Kathryn and Charlotte in on the conversation, which, by the time the two of them walked out the back door, had Kathryn's insides churning.

'I'm truly sorry,' she said as they walked towards the barn.

'For what?'

Guilt made her cheeks burn. 'Listening to Lieutenant Banks, assuming you only wanted my father's help in finding Ralph.'

He took hold of her hand and held it tightly as they walked. 'You have nothing to apologise for. Banks should never have been listening at Marilyn's door, nor should he have assumed I'd ask your father for help. That's not the job of the British Intelligence.' He sighed, but was also smiling. 'I'll find Ralph. Have to. Not only for my parents, but for myself. It's my duty to take care of my family, of those I love, but that doesn't mean I can shirk other duties while doing so. To ask the British Intelligence would be against army rules. I won't do that.'

His sincerity increased her desire to help him. 'Perhaps—'

He stopped walking and tugged on her hand so she faced him. 'I appreciate your kindness and your willingness to help, but I don't want you involved. Don't want you to even worry about it. I'd rather spend my time with you doing fun things. Things we both enjoy.'

He had the ability to make her smile, and to forget, forget there was a war going on or that the world wasn't a perfect place, and that was refreshing. 'Like picking berries?'

With a nod, he started walking again, urging her along beside him with a slight tug on her hand. 'Yes.'

As they walked, she couldn't help but compare him to Andrew and the way he made her feel compared to how Andrew had. He'd always made her feel as if she owed him something for being her friend. Dale didn't. That was a first. In the past everyone had always expected something from her.

'And playing baseball,' he said.

'Baseball?'

'I brought along a bat and ball for when the children are finished their chores.'

'You did? They'll love that.'

'Good, because I have all weekend and I can't think of a place I'd rather spend it.'

That made her extremely happy. Not wanting to appear too overeager, she asked, 'Even though Charlotte's coffee isn't as good as Oscar's?' It wasn't. She'd tasted it.

He laughed. 'Even if it makes me learn to like tea, there's no place I'd rather be.' He bumped her shoulder while saying, 'Didn't know I was a poet, did you?' Laughing harder, he added, 'Neither did I.'

Chapter Seven

4th of September, 1942

Dear Diary,
Some evenings when I think about the
events of the day, I tell myself I should
write about every moment, but then I fear
if I do, some day I may read what I wrote
and long for it all to happen all over again.
I'm of course speaking about Dale. The
wonderful days we spend together, talking,
laughing or, at times, just sitting quietly.
Those days have grown and I'm enjoying
them very much, but there is a part of me
that knows they can't continue and that
saddens me. For I know there will come a
day when he returns to America.

I then wonder if he'll ever see Phillip,
even though I know that's a silly notion.

America is very large and North Dakota is nowhere close to Georgia. We are still awaiting word from Phillip's mother. The children continue to save specific pieces of sweets so they can mail them to Phillip when we acquire an address.

I am happy to report that Dale is no longer flying combat runs. He's never told me what brought about the change and I've never asked. I'm just happy that Lieutenant Banks no longer comes to the house.

Kathryn set the pen down and stared at the words she'd just written. Despite the serenity that at times surrounded her, especially while spending time with Dale, there was a tense and distressing sensation inside her that she couldn't escape. Nor could she blame it all on the war. This was more about her, something inside her wasn't quite right and, though she didn't know what, she sensed it was a forewarning. Yet that wasn't quite it either. It was more complex than that. Something she couldn't explain even enough to jot it in her diary.

Those thoughts weighed heavy as she tucked away the little book and went downstairs to listen to the radio. That was how they always ended their day, listening for any new reports.

Norman was in the process of turning off the radio when she entered the front room. 'Some days are so much like the one before, I'm not completely sure if another day has passed or not,' he said.

'Come now, dear,' Charlotte said. 'There is something to be thankful for in each and every day.' Winking at Doreen, Charlotte added, 'Like losing a tooth.'

'That is correct,' Norman said, his tone growing merrier. 'Don't forget to put that tooth under your pillow tonight.'

'I won't,' Doreen replied. 'Phillip got two pennies when he did that.'

'Yes, he did,' Kathryn replied, happy that they all could speak of Phillip without sadness overcoming them. 'But he'd also lost two teeth that day.' Nodding towards the others still sitting on the rug in the centre of the room, she said, 'It's bedtime for all of you.'

'I wish school hadn't started up again,' Edward said, dragging himself to his feet.

'I'd think you'd rather sit in school than spend the day in the fields,' Kathryn supplied.

Edward shook his head. 'I like being outside, even if it's working, it beats sitting around staring at four walls.'

'You shouldn't be staring at the walls,' she

said as he walked past. 'You should be doing your assignments.'

'I tried that.' Now walking up the steps, he added, 'The four walls are more interesting.'

Having had conversations with his teachers last year and this year, Kathryn knew Edward was a good student and made a note to visit his class in order to see about assignments that might challenge him, or at least pique his interest.

Patricia's little hand wrapped around Kathryn's as the child asked, 'When will I lose a tooth?'

Although she'd turned seven last month, Patricia was still as tiny as a peanut. Kathryn picked her up and settled her on her hip while turning towards the stairway. 'I'm sure it will be soon,' she replied. 'I'll help you check for any loose ones after brushing out your hair.'

There were no loose teeth for Patricia, but the tooth fairy did exchange Doreen's tooth for a penny. How she might possibly spend that penny was the talk of the house during breakfast, and it continued as Kathryn walked the children to school. After taking a moment to speak with Edward's teacher, Kathryn started for home.

With Dale always on her mind—fully aware

of how close he'd come to perishing made her want to see him as often as possible—she was wondering if she might see him at the pub this afternoon when a horn honked behind her. Even though it didn't have the distinct low note of the army Jeeps, she couldn't help but smile as she glanced over her shoulder.

The big black Hillman Minx reminded her of the one her father always rode in, which made her stumble slightly. When the back window rolled down and her mum's head appeared, Kathryn nearly fell over.

'Mum! What are you doing here?'

The car rolled up next to her. 'I'm here to give you a ride,' Mum said. 'I expected to find you at the Harris home.'

'I wanted to talk to Edward's teacher,' Kathryn explained. It was odd, a part of her was very happy to see her mum, for it had been over a year since they'd seen each other, yet she wasn't sure how to respond. She wasn't a little girl so couldn't jump in Mum's arms for a hug, but she wanted that connection. 'It is so good to see you,' she said, stepping forward to touch her mum's hand, hoping the contact would settle the unease inside her. With her black hair neatly styled, and her lips bright red, Mum looked as lovely as ever.

'It's good to see you, too, darling,' Mum said, patting her hand. 'Come around and climb in the other side.'

Kathryn did so and, upon closing the door, asked, 'How is Father?'

'Fine, busy as always.'

'And you? How have you been?' Her mind shot off in several directions then. 'And Aunt Melody? Is she doing well? Has there been any news about Allen lately?'

'Melody and Allen? I should have known you'd ask about them,' Mum replied coldly.

'Of course I'd ask about them.' With her stomach sinking, she asked, 'Has something happened? Is that why you are here?'

Mum's face softened. 'No, they're fine, darling.' Patting her hand, she said, 'We'll speak of my visit in private.'

Kathryn nodded and caught the sheepish grin coming from James, the driver. He'd been driving her parents around for longer than Kathryn had been alive and knew everything there was to know about their entire family, including every distant relative.

'Hello, Mr Duncan,' Kathryn said. James had driven her to school for years and she'd been given permission to call him by his given name, but only when Mum wasn't near. 'I hope you have been well.'

'I have, Miss Kathryn,' he replied. 'Thank you for asking.'

'And Mrs Duncan?' Kathryn enquired. Annie, his wife, had been housekeeping for her family as long as James had been driving them.

'She's doing well and sends her love.'

'Please tell her hello from me,' Kathryn said. When she'd first arrived at Charlotte and Norman's, she'd missed James and Annie as much as she had her own parents. That had eased over the months that had now become years. When the time came and she moved back to London, it would be the opposite. She'd miss Charlotte and Norman dearly. And the children. She didn't even want to think of being separated from all of them. It had grown easier to talk about Phillip, but her heart still ached over not seeing him regularly.

'I will,' he said. 'Princess misses you, too.'

Princess! She hadn't thought about her cat in years. Then again, it wasn't truly her cat. Mum didn't like it roaming the house, so it lived above the carriage house with James and Annie.

'That cat is too fat and lazy to miss anyone,' Mum snapped.

Kathryn nodded and bit her lip to stop from

responding. If one of the children had spoken so unkindly about another, even an animal, she would have quietly spoken to them about minding their manners, but she couldn't do that with her mother. No one could.

Thankfully, the ride home didn't take long. However, upon entering the house and having Mum demand Charlotte leave the two of them alone, Kathryn was too ashamed to remain quiet. 'Mum—'

'I was just heading out to the garden,' Charlotte said with one of her gentle and understanding smiles. 'There's a fresh pot of tea on the table.'

Charlotte hadn't been heading out to the garden any more than Kathryn might have been, but she knew better than to argue with Mum. 'Thank you, Charlotte,' she said. 'We won't be long.'

'No, we won't be,' Mum agreed.

As Charlotte hurried through the scullery, Kathryn asked, 'Would you like a cup of tea?'

With an exaggerated huff, Mum sat down. 'No, I'll have some while you're packing. We need to speak first.'

Kathryn put both hands on the table. 'Packing what?'

'Your things.' With a scowl, Mum eyed her up and down. 'I do hope that's not your best dress.'

Kathryn closed her eyes. The white blouse and green skirt she had on were completely presentable, but that wasn't the point. She had forgotten just how controlling Mum was, how set in her ways and how pretentious society allowed her to be. Moving here had been freeing in a sense, which was why she'd accepted it so completely, so easily. Up until this moment, she hadn't fully understood that. Letting the breath out of her lungs, she said, 'No, it's not my best dress.' Taking a seat, she asked, 'Has something happened? Is that what we need to talk about? Why do I need to pack a few things?'

'I expected more from you, Kathryn. You were always a good child. Always listened. Always behaved.'

Because she hadn't had a choice not to. Mum, at times with little more than a glance, had always communicated her expectations of toeing the line.

'Can you even imagine how embarrassed I was when I learned of your conduct?'

Utterly confused, Kathryn shook her head. 'My conduct? What conduct?'

The anger that snapped in Mum's dark eyes was beyond any she'd seen.

'Don't try to hide it from me. You father tried that, but eventually, he had to confirm that you've been consorting with an American serviceman.'

Kathryn's heart sank clear to her toes. Further than that. It went past her toes, hit the floor and was rolling across the room.

'There I was, hosting a dinner party, listening to an American general talk about *candy* falling out of airplanes to the children below. Fully unaware, I asked where this had happened and was shocked to hear him say High Wycombe. Then, as he continued, and talked about a *local* young woman who had made the miniature parachutes for the pilots, I knew in my heart it was you. How could you do that to me? Don't you remember what happened to Melody?'

Kathryn had thought about Aunt Melody more times than she could count the past few months and, without her mum's influence, her opinions on several things concerning Melody's particular situation had changed. However, that was not the issue right now.

'Yes,' Kathryn said. 'I sewed the miniature parachutes and the entire countryside has been uplifted by the amount of joy the sweet drops have brought the children. Such acts of kindness and goodwill should not upset you.'

'That's not what I'm so upset about and you know it.'

Kathryn drew a deep breath to calm the anger flaring inside her. Hoping to de-escalate the situation before anger got the best of either of them, she said, 'Mum, everyone has made friends with some of the men at the base.' She refused to indicate any one person. Dale's name was the last information Mum needed right now. 'They are good people, and they are here on our behalf.' Needing her mum to understand she was no longer the easily influenced seventeen-year-old she had been when she was first sent out here, but a full-grown woman who'd learned to think for herself and take care of others, she continued, 'Now stop acting as though I'm walking the streets in London's West End.'

Mum's eyes grew wide as she pressed a hand to her chest.

Kathryn flinched slightly, for she'd never spoken to Mum that way, but she'd never had a reason to. Needing a piece of optimism, of loyalty, she asked, 'Does Father know you're here?'

'Of course he does.' Patting her face with a flowered kerchief, Mum then said, 'Now go pack your bags so James can drive us home.' Now waving her kerchief before her face, she added, 'And get that cup of tea, please.'

Kathryn retrieved the tea because they both needed a moment to consider the tension filling the room. Adding two lumps of sugar, she thought of Dale and how he always made sure Oscar or Ed provided sugar when she joined him for a cup of coffee at the pub. Providing a spoon to stir the tea, she carried it to the table and sat back down.

After a few quiet moments, where they both seemed to be calmer, she quietly said, 'I can't leave here, Mum. Charlotte and Norman need me to help with the children and the chores.' Her parents understood that beyond most, they sent a goodly sum to Norman regularly.

'They'll have to find someone else to help.'

'It's not as easy as that. There is no one to help,' she explained. 'Furthermore, I'm stationed here as a member of the Women's Land Army under the National Service Act and I can't leave without permission.'

'Your father can see to that. He can arrange for you to be stationed anywhere, as a member of anything.' Mum's cup rattled as she set it on the saucer. 'He never even told me they'd built a base out here.'

'They've built bases everywhere,' Kathryn replied. Then, needing a bit of an alliance, of sustenance, she laid a hand atop her mother's.

'Don't you trust me? Don't you have enough belief in me to know I'm old enough, smart enough, to know what I'm doing?'

The lack of understanding on Mum's face hurt as much as her accusations had.

Leaning back in her chair, Kathryn searched for inner solace. It was all she could hope for. 'I've grown since coming here and learned so many things. I now know how to cook and clean and sew, how to grow and harvest food, how to take care of children and animals, and—'

'I don't want you to know how to do all those things. I don't want you to *have* to know how to do all those things.' Mum's tone had softened and held a hint of grief. 'You're my little girl. You're supposed to wear pretty dresses and…' She let out a small growl. 'Oh, this damn war.'

Once again laying her hand upon her mum's, Kathryn said, 'I can't be your little girl for ever—even without the war, that would have changed.'

Lifting her chin, Mum drew in a deep breath. 'That may be true, but I won't have you marrying an American.'

Kathryn chose her words carefully because they were too close for comfort. 'You have an alliance in that. The American armed forces.

They warn every serviceman against building relationships with locals.'

'Oh, darling.' Mum shook her head. 'Warnings mean little. Don't you remember what happened with Andrew? How as soon as he didn't get what he wanted, he married someone else?'

'Yes, I do and I'm grateful for that.' Squeezing Mum's arm, she continued, 'And I'm grateful that you and Father forbade me from marrying him. He would never have made me happy. He was too selfish and too controlling.'

Mum once again had a shocked look on her face as she whispered, 'Oh, my, you have grown up.'

Dale checked his watch several times. Kathryn was late. Oscar and Ed had confirmed today was an egg delivery day and, from his calculations, she should have been here over an hour ago. Concerned, because that wasn't like her, he paid for his coffee and left the pub. He had been inside so long, the sun stung his eyes and he blinked several times, hoping to speed up the adjustment to the brightness.

He was in the Jeep, ready to start the engine, when a car rattled up the road. Turning about to glance over his shoulder, he pulled the key from the ignition. He was standing next to the passenger side of his Jeep when Norman pulled in.

'Is Kathryn all right?' Dale asked.

'Yes, her mum came to visit her today so I brought the delivery.'

'I see,' Dale said. He hadn't heard of her mother coming to visit her before and that instantly installed a rare form of fear.

'Just a visit, mind you,' Norman said. 'She won't be taking her home. The Brigadier would never stand for that.'

Dale wasn't sure if that relieved him or not. 'Is that everything?' he asked, pointing towards the crate on the passenger seat.

'Yes,' Norman said, opening the driver's door now that he'd stepped back.

'I'll get it for you,' Dale offered, walking around the car. 'No one's inside, I'm sure Oscar and Ed wouldn't mind a visit.'

'I wouldn't mind that either,' Norman said.

'Is Mrs Winslow nice?' Dale asked while lifting the box out of the car.

'She didn't say more than two words to me,' Norman replied. 'But James, the man who drove her out from London is a good chap. He's worked for the Winslows for years.'

Not wanting to probe, but wanting to know more, Dale contemplated his next question. He

knew enough about Kathryn's family to know
her mother was where her hatred of Americans
had come from. And the fact she had servants
said he'd have very little in common with her
no matter where he was from. 'How long is Mrs
Winslow staying?'

'I suspect she'll be gone by the time I get
home,' Norman said.

With the way Norman, Oscar and Ed liked to
talk, that could be hours. Dale had to get back to
the base well before then. 'I may have a couple
of free hours this evening,' he said. 'Mind if I
stop by the house?'

'Not at all.' Norman held the door open for
him to enter the roadhouse. 'If there's a big black
Hillman Minx in the driveway, Mrs Winslow
is still there.'

'Thanks.' Dale set the box on the counter and
tipped his hat to Norman, who was already making himself comfortable at the counter.

The afternoon lingered. He was rebuilding
two engines, but waiting on parts, as he had
been for the last several days, which meant any
other mechanical duty had already been taken
care of. He wrote a letter home, took it to headquarters to be posted, hung around talking to
Marilyn who, unfortunately, mentioned the list

she'd uncovered that did have an enlisted man named Ralph Johnson was not the one he was looking for.

'I'll keep trying,' she said.

'I know you will.' She'd become as obsessed with finding Ralph as he was and he appreciated that. He wondered if it had to do with the fact that Lieutenant Banks had read the folder about Ralph that Kathryn had delivered to Marilyn last summer. Banks had admitted to Major Hilts that he'd looked in the folder and had made his own conclusion. The admission had come behind closed doors, with only him, Major Hilts and Lieutenant Banks present. Dale had assured Hilts that he had not requested help from the British Intelligence or from Kathryn and had been satisfied that Banks had been transferred. It seemed Banks had tried to stir trouble for others and Hilts was glad to have a reason to request the transfer.

He gave the corner of Marilyn's desk a pat before heading towards the door. 'See you.'

'Wait a minute,' she said. 'I brought you something back from London.'

She'd gone on a furlough last week and met up with her husband who had been granted one as well. He was in the Navy and docked there for a short time. Although she was never cross,

Marilyn had returned happier than she'd been in some time.

'Why would you bring something back for me?' he asked, returning to her desk while she pulled open a bottom drawer.

'It's not necessarily for you,' she said while handing him a small brown bag. 'Bruce bought me some of this. It's hand lotion. It smells and feels wonderful, and I thought it might be something that you'd like to give to Kathryn.'

Her smile was sincere, yet his insides churned a bit and the bag felt as if it was burning his hand. 'Why would I—?'

'Stop right there, Dale Johnson,' she said rather sternly. 'I've spent more time with you than anyone else on this base except maybe Corporal Sanders and you can't hide how you feel about Kathryn from me.' Picking up a pen while flipping open a report on her desk, she added, 'Furthermore, that secret is as safe with me as the one concerning all the extra paperwork I keep requesting concerning Ralph.'

His feelings for Kathryn went deep, all the way to a depth he wasn't ready to explore. And wouldn't be for some time. Not even with Marilyn, whom he thought of almost as a sister. Nodding and then shaking his head, he headed for the door again. 'Bruce is a lucky man.'

'I know,' she said, with a confident grin. 'And so does he.' As he reached the door, she added, 'And so are you.'

Knowing his secret was safe with her, he laughed before saying, 'I'll be off base for a few hours.'

'I know,' she said. 'Rounding up parts is time consuming.'

He headed straight for the Jeep and leaped over the side. About halfway to Norman's place, he wondered if he should have taken the time to grab a few pieces of candy for the children. That would make it easier to give Kathryn the hand lotion. At least more justifiable.

To whom? He didn't need to justify his actions, especially something no one would ever know about. Except himself. All Major Hilts had said following the meeting with Banks was to point out that some boundaries were not to be crossed.

Dale knew what the Major meant and had been careful not to overstep any boundaries, not to make promises or talk about the future in any way with Kathryn, yet giving the lotion might be looked upon that way. He wouldn't give it to her. That's all there was to it. Things might be different, he might be willing to take a few more chances, if he knew where Ralph

was. Hilts hadn't said anything about that either, and Dale couldn't take the risk of another
Banks entering the picture and getting things
blown out of proportion again. He had to think
about Marilyn in that instance, too. Angering
the wrong person had consequences. A good
number of the documents Marilyn had managed
to acquire for his search for Ralph were classi-
fied and someone upset with him would look at
things far deeper than Major Hilts had.

His mind was still chasing those thoughts
around when he pulled up to Norman's house.
Relieved to see there was no other vehicle in the
farmyard, Dale left the brown paper bag sitting
on the seat, climbed out of the Jeep and headed
up the walkway.

It was the oldest boy, George, who opened
the door even before Dale had opened the gate
of the fence around the garden.

'Hey, Sergeant Johnson,' George said, waving
an arm. 'We just sat down to eat and Charlotte
says to hurry in while it's still hot.'

He'd eaten with the family several times before, but usually brought a contribution, even if
it was just candy or sodas from the base. Feeling empty-handed, he was about to shake his
head when Kathryn appeared in the doorway.

She quietly sent George back inside as she

stepped on to the porch. 'There's plenty,' she said. 'My mum brought a few things down from London today that have to be used up. Do join us.'

He wasn't certain if the pleading came from her or his insides. 'I don't want to impose.'

'You aren't,' she said.

She sounded sincere and there was a smile on her face, but she was hiding something, something that pained her.

'Did you have a nice visit with your mother?'

'No,' she said. 'But it was good to see her.'

And that was just one of the things he liked about her. There was very little beating around the bush when it came to Kathryn. He doubted she even knew what a white lie was, for she certainly would never consider lying about anything. After a moment of searching his brain, he shrugged. 'I don't even know what to say to that.'

'Say you'll join us for supper.'

'All right, I'll join you for supper.'

The meal was an assortment of English foods that he couldn't say were bad, they were just different. It wasn't as if they made him homesick, but sitting around the table, listening to the children prattle, and arguing a pinch, did. As did the laughter.

When everyone had eaten their fill—actually when the food was gone, for he imagined George and Edward could have eaten plenty more had it been available—Norman pointed a finger his way.

'I'm glad you stopped by, Sergeant,' Norman said. 'Oscar mentioned he could use a few more supplies today. Kathryn has them bundled up. Would you mind giving her a ride? I don't like her riding that bike after dark and it would save her a trip tomorrow morning.'

Dale glanced her way and, noting her smile, which said she wasn't opposed to the idea, he agreed. 'No, I don't mind. That is, if she doesn't.'

A faint blush covered her cheeks as she collected a few plates. 'Of course I don't mind. I'll be ready as soon as I help Charlotte with the dishes.'

'The girls and I can handle the dishes,' Charlotte said, collecting other empty dishes. 'You two run along.'

'Can I ride with you, Kathryn?' Little George, who was as opposite-looking from the other George as two boys could get, asked.

He was of course much smaller, but had carrot-red hair and a round face full of freckles while the older George was dark-haired and as lean as a fence post and tall. He must have grown a good three inches since the first time Dale had met him.

'It'll be past your bedtime before they get home,' Norman said, 'and you promised me a game of draughts this evening. Did you forget that?'

Little George shook his head.

'I'll get my coat,' Kathryn whispered.

Dale rose from his chair and removed his jacket from where he'd draped it over the back. 'While I get the supplies,' he whispered in response.

Charlotte showed him where the box was in the back room they called a scullery, but looked like an extension of a kitchen that also included the things his mother kept in their back porch. That was where Kathryn collected her coat from.

It was a fair-sized box and, as he lifted it up, she opened a door.

'We can go out this way and walk around the house,' she said. 'It will save you from seven other requests to ride with us.'

'It's up to you if you want any of them to tag along,' he offered. They weren't alone very often and, at times, he felt as if that was how she wanted it.

'If I wanted them to tag along, I would have suggested it,' she said, closing the door behind them.

That was true. 'Need an escape?' he asked.

She looked at him, studied him rather intensely as they took several steps before nodding. 'Yes, I do.' Glancing around, she added, 'Not necessarily from the children...' She sighed heavily. 'Just from everything for a few moments.'

'I know that feeling,' he admitted. 'Sometimes I walk into the woods behind the base and pretend I'm back home, sitting in the woods and waiting for a big buck to walk past.'

'A big buck?'

'A stag. Deer hunting.'

She nodded. 'You miss your home.'

It wasn't a question, but he responded as if it was. 'Yes. Don't you?'

They'd arrived at the Jeep and she stood beside him as he lowered the box into the back. 'I should. Sometimes I think I do, but then I remember it's not the same London I grew up in and probably will never be the same again.'

He held her elbow as she lifted a leg over the Jeep's side bar. As soon as she sat down, she rose up again and reached beneath her.

Knowing what she'd found, he walked around the Jeep and climbed in.

'I'm sorry,' she said, holding out the brown paper bag. 'I sat on this.'

He started the Jeep before saying, 'Hope you didn't break it, because it's yours.'

'Mine?'

'Yes, open it up while you can still see.' Dusk was setting in, but there was still plenty of light.

As the paper crinkled while she opened the bag, he tried to pretend he was concentrating on backing the Jeep up, even though there wasn't anything he had to worry about hitting.

'Rose-scented hand lotion?' She sniffed loudly. 'How did you know that was my favourite?'

'I didn't,' he admitted while shifting the Jeep into first. 'Marilyn picked it up while she was in London.'

'For me? Why? I mean, it was very nice of her, but...'

He was feeling more squeamish than a worm at how, well, worm-like the entire thing was. He huffed out a breath. 'She went to London on furlough last week, met her husband there and he bought her some of that lotion. She said that she liked it so much, she picked up a container for me to give to you, thinking that if I'd gone to London on furlough, I might have wanted to buy you some.'

The scent of roses filled his nostrils as she rubbed her hands together. 'Would you have?'

'I don't know. I've never bought a girl a present before.'

'You haven't?'

Dang, sometimes it felt as if he had to dig deep in order to stay honest when it came to her. 'None other than my sister, for her birthday or Christmas, or now and again when I had spare cash. But if I had gone to London and you'd told me you wanted some, I'd have searched until I found it.'

'Thank you,' she said. 'And thank Marilyn for me, I haven't had any store-bought hand lotion in a very long time.'

Now he wished he'd simply said it was from him. He shifted the Jeep into neutral at the crossroad and looked her way. 'I will tell her that and you're welcome.'

Her nose was buried deep into the triangle her hands made. Turning his way slowly, she grinned and lowered them. Then, she held one out. 'Want to smell it? It's wonderful.'

Even though he could already smell the rose scent, he leaned over to sniff her proffered hands. More focused on her eyes, the way she was looking at him, it was a moment before he thought to say, 'It smells nice.'

'Yes, it does,' she said, smiling. 'And this is nice. Thank you for offering to give me a ride this evening.' She leaned her head back against the seat and closed her eyes. 'This is very nice.'

'So what other things do you like?' he asked while pulling out on to the road.

'I don't know. I'd forgotten about store-bought hand lotion until I saw it.' With a sigh, she said, 'I'm sure if I thought hard enough, I'd remember some things, but nothing comes to mind. Nothing seems important enough.'

'But it was before the war?'

'I'm not sure about that either,' she said. 'I imagine some things I once thought were important would have changed even without the war.'

'That's true.' It was that way with many things.

'The war might have accelerated some things, then again, it might have just made everyone take a closer look at what really matters.'

That was true, too. 'Did that little container bring on all this philosophical thinking?'

She laughed softly. 'No.'

Not entirely sure he should bring up the subject, yet unable not to, he asked, 'Did your mother's visit?'

'Yes.'

She'd answered so quickly he hadn't had time to regret asking the question.

'At least the reason for her visit did,' she said.

'And what was her reason?'

Her silence had him glancing her way. She was looking out the side of the Jeep and had four fingers pressed to her lips. Turning back to the road, he noted a side road coming up and slowed enough to make the corner. A walk in the woods might help her as much as it did him at times.

'Where are we going?' she asked.

'I don't know,' he said. 'What's down this road?'

'The Wainwrights live about four miles down it, other than that, there's a stream just a short way from here that Norman goes fishing in when the water is high enough.'

A bridge appeared almost instantly and he downshifted in order to pull over in a gravelled area next to the road that suggested more people than Norman must fish here. Once parked, he turned off the engine. 'Want to go for a walk?'

She shrugged. 'All right.'

They climbed out at the same time and met in front of the Jeep. A dirt path led down the gently sloping embankment to where the water slowly flowed over several boulders. He took her hand and held it firmly as they followed the path to the water and then walked along the stream to where several logs had been purposefully laid to make a sitting bench, or perhaps a headrest for a fisherman to take an afternoon nap.

Once they were both seated, he purposefully left out exactly what he was referring to while saying, 'You don't have to tell me if you don't want to, but if it'll help to talk about it, I'll listen.'

She picked a tiny pebble up off the ground and tossed it in the water. 'About Mum's visit?'

He didn't need to confirm it, so didn't. Nor did he press it harder. But he did like the way she said 'Mum.' The way she talked. Had since meeting her.

After tossing in another rock, she said, 'She wants me to go back to London.'

'Why?' Although it had slowed considerably, London was still being bombed.

She twisted slightly in order to look at him, study him the way she had when they'd walked out of the back door back at Norman's. He had no idea what she expected to see and that worried him in a way he'd never worried before.

A hint of a grin curled the corners of her mouth as she said, 'Because she doesn't want me consorting with an American.'

He couldn't say her response surprised him, but it did put a solid lump of dread in his stomach. The desire to stretch an arm around her shoulders struck him, but he planted both palms on his knees to prevent that from happening. 'I'm sorry.'

She chuckled slightly, which struck him as odd until she said, 'There's no reason for you to be sorry.'

'I don't want to cause a rift between you and your family.'

'My family, at least those who live in London, don't even know you. The family I have here, the ones I've come to care about as much as the ones back in London, thinks you're absolutely wonderful.'

A part of him, a large part, had to know her thoughts. 'What do you think?'

She smiled and gently bumped his shoulder with hers. 'What do *you* think?'

Not entirely sure how to proceed, he considered several aspects before admitting, 'I think we're both walking on some shaky ground.'

Turning to face the water, she nodded.

Needing to explain his answer, and hoping he wouldn't blunder things as badly as he had during the picnic, he said, 'There's a war happening, one that's brought us together in a unique way, but one that will also separate us. We don't know when, or how, but we know it will happen.

We aren't sure what to do about that because we both have commitments we need to fulfil.'

'That's true,' she said. 'But there's more to it than that.'

He held his breath for a moment, not sure how to answer. Not sure what he'd say if she admitted to having feelings for him, ones that went deeper than friendship.

'When I first came here, to the countryside, the impending war wasn't the only reason Father sent me away from London. A boy had asked me to marry him.'

The air was now stuck in Dale's lungs.

'I'd said yes, but that he had to ask my father, who said no.'

Smothering a cough at how fast the air left his lungs, he asked, 'Why?'

'Because the government had called all men between the ages of eighteen and forty-one to serve. Andrew didn't want to serve. He considered himself a scholar and wanted to continue his studies of astronomy. So he asked me to marry him and upon asking my father for my hand, asked that he receive a pardon for serving.'

Dale could imagine how a Brigadier might feel about that, but still asked, 'Your father wasn't happy about that?'

'My father was angered that Andrew would use me to get what he wanted.'

Dale didn't comment, mainly because his mind went to when he'd considered the notion of asking for her father's assistance in finding Ralph.

'Mother was even more furious and forbade me from ever marrying a serviceman.'

'But your father is a serviceman.'

'Exactly.' She shrugged then. 'Mother probably would have agreed to me marrying Andrew if he'd gone about things differently. Requested a pardon from someone other than my father.' She tossed another pebble into the water. 'Which is exactly what Andrew did. He requested one from a Naval Commander.'

Curious, Dale asked, 'Did he get it?'

'Well, he married the Commander's daughter, but last I heard he was on a ship in the Indian Ocean.'

In his mind, Andrew got exactly what he deserved, but Dale was more concerned about Kathryn. 'How do you feel about that? About all of it?'

She leaned her head against his shoulder. 'When the whispers of war first started, it was like, I don't know, a secret. You couldn't talk about it because that might make it happen. I felt that way about Andrew's proposal, then I was angry when my parents forbade it, because I thought I was old enough to make my own decisions. I was sent here, to live with Norman and Charlotte, a few weeks later and I felt as if I was being punished, as if it was their way of showing me I was still a child.'

She lifted her head and let out a long sigh. 'Then I grew up. I went from being a somewhat spoiled girl living a pampered life to a woman who had several others she was now responsible for. The war changed a lot of things, including me.'

He patted her knee. 'I like who you are.'

She smiled. 'I like who you are, too, but I'm not sure who I'll become.'

'What do you mean?'

'Norman and Charlotte, and the children, need me, will continue to need me for I don't know how long. They depend upon me for many things, including the funds to live on. Father pays Norman a sum every month for me to live here—without that money...' she shrugged '... I don't know what they'd do.'

He wrapped an arm around her and held her to his side as they sat in silence, pondering all she'd admitted. Things he had to believe she hadn't shared with anyone else. His thoughts took corners and rolled about hills and valleys he didn't know existed inside his head until they all ended up in the same spot—nowhere. He felt as if he was trapped in a time and place as foreign as England had been when he'd first arrived and he wasn't sure how to navigate around it all.

Unable to think of anything else to say, he asked, 'Who do you want to become?'

'I don't know that either,' she said. 'But I know one thing, I'm not going to let this war dictate who I am.'

Her determination alone was enough to make him smile. 'I'm sure you won't.'

She wrapped both arms around his waist and held on tightly. 'I've never had a friend like you, Dale.'

A flashback of *The Dream Bomber* spiralling out of control raced across his mind and the reaction he'd had that day erupted inside him again. The idea of never seeing her again, the loss, the pain, had him twisting about and wrapping both arms around her. His movements were so fast, so intense, her head jolted upright, meeting his gaze.

He hadn't kissed her since that day, but had thought about it. A lot. He didn't want her to become a spinster like Mrs Shakes back home, but couldn't stop his growing fondness for her either.

Her eyes dropped to his mouth, as his did to hers, and the next moment, as if they both knew this was their only chance, the only moment in time they might ever have, their lips met with a fiery intensity that grew. And grew. And grew.

Chapter Eight

5th of September, 1942

Dear Diary,
I must relieve some of the burden inside
me. Mum came to see me today, wanted me
to return to London, but I can't. Then, this
evening, Dale came to visit and we went
to the pub to deliver supplies. We stopped
along the way and talked. Other than you,
I've never confided to anyone the way I did
to him tonight. Once I started, I couldn't
seem to stop. I couldn't seem to stop kissing him either. Which frightens me a bit.
Kissing him was so amazing. Words can't
begin to describe how I felt inside. And I'm
afraid I'm more confused than ever before. I can't wish the war had never happened, because then I would never have

*met him, nor can I wish the war would end,
because he will then return to the States.
I can't wish he'd forgo returning home to
live in England for the rest of his life because that would be as unfair to him as
wishing that I could go to America. That
could never happen. For the pure fact I'm
not that brave. Not courageous enough to
leave all I've ever known, to completely
embark in an entirely new life.*

*In fact, I'm so cowardly that I won-
der if I should tell Dale that I can't see
him again. Because each time I do, it gets
harder to say goodbye. Even writing that
brings tears to my eyes. Which tells me
I'm too much of a coward to do that, too.*

Kathryn's heart leaped at the sound of the
army Jeep coming up the drive. No other vehicle sounded like the Jeeps did. She hadn't seen
Dale for three days, ever since the night they'd
kissed. A memory that left her insides glowing
and made it impossible to erase the smile that
formed on her lips, even as she told herself it
shouldn't. They had stayed by the stream until
it had been completely dark, then had delivered
the box to the pub and returned home, where
Dale had kissed her goodnight on the pathway.

The wondrous memories filled her so fully, the sigh that seeped out was full of happiness and contentment.

Setting aside the spade because the rattling of the Jeep was closer, Kathryn walked around the side of the house to watch the Jeep pull up next to the front garden. Disappointment, along with a bout of puzzlement, swirled about as she recognised Marilyn as the driver.

'Hello,' Kathryn greeted as the Jeep rolled to a stop. Marilyn always looked so neat and pretty in her brown dress uniform with her hair pinned up beneath her little pointed hat that sat slightly off to one side. 'Thank you for the hand lotion. That was so thoughtful of you.'

'You're welcome,' Marilyn said quickly. 'I've come to give you a ride to the base.'

The urgency by which the other woman spoke made Kathryn's hands shake. 'What for? What's happened?'

'Dale's being shipped out. The papers came in last night. They're loading the plane as we speak.'

Kathryn pressed a hand to her chest as her heart leaped into her throat. 'Where to? For how long?'

'Thorpe Abbotts. The papers say it's temporary, but no one knows how long temporary may be.' With a gentle smile that held more compassion than happiness, Marilyn said, 'I thought you might like to say goodbye.'

'I do.' Which was a lie. She didn't want to say goodbye to him, not ever, but she did want to see him. Trying not to become too overwhelmed, she told herself that he'd still be in England, just further away. Turning about to shout for Charlotte, she found Norman standing a few feet behind her.

'Go,' Norman said. 'Give him our best. From all of us.'

She nodded and hurried around the Jeep to climb in. As Marilyn shifted into Reverse, Kathryn pulled off her gloves and brushed the dust from her skirt and blouse, then ran her hands over her hair.

'You look fine,' Marilyn said.

'Thank you for coming to get me. Did Dale send you?'

Marilyn shook her head. 'He's been too busy preparing his squad. Major Hilts just learned of the transfer last night and informed Dale this morning. I came here on my own, knowing you'd want to say goodbye to each other.'

Kathryn tried to steady her uneven breathing with a few deep breaths, but it wasn't helping. She was trembling inside and out. They'd both admitted this time would come, but she wasn't prepared for it to happen so soon. 'Thank you, I appreciate it.'

Little else was said during the drive to the base and Kathryn was glad of that because her mind was occupied with trying to convince herself to be brave and understanding. War was full of sacrifices and this was one of them. People around the world were making the same one, saying goodbye to friends and family. Even knowing all that wasn't making it easier.

As they turned on to the road that led to the base, Marilyn said, 'I don't know how long you'll have. The cargo plane is scheduled to depart in less than two hours.'

Kathryn managed a nod. Her eyes were stinging and a dull ache had already taken over her heart. The hurt she'd felt before, when he'd said they could no longer be friends, was gradually filling up her insides like rain did a bucket left out in the open.

Marilyn parked the Jeep behind the building, an area that Kathryn had never seen.

'You'll have to wait inside,' Marilyn said as they both climbed out. 'I'll show you where and send a message to Dale. It may take a while, depending on how far along they are in loading the cargo plane.'

Fully aware that there were areas of the base civilians were restricted from entering, Kathryn followed Marilyn up the steps. 'I understand.'

Within a few minutes, Kathryn was left in a small room containing a table and several chairs. A single window overlooked the garden, including the bench she and Dale had sat upon the evening he'd returned from the bombing mission that had damaged the plane so badly it had been put out of commission for the rest of the war. That had been the same day Phillip had left. Word had yet to arrive from Phillip's mum and, though everyone still missed him, the ache inside her had lessened. That's what had happened when she first moved here, too. The pain of living apart from her parents and friends had lessened and she'd grown to care more and more about the people she now lived with.

Time. That's what it took. However, living through that time wasn't easy. Doing that again, this time missing Dale was going to be difficult. Very difficult.

Still trembling, she pulled a chair away from the table and placed it near the window, hoping the garden might settle her nerves a small amount. She would need all her fortitude once Dale walked into the room.

* * *

It felt as if hours had passed before the door opened and, though she'd used that time to prepare herself, to rehearse the strength and understanding she needed to portray, the instant she saw Dale's face, her tears burst forward like a tidal wave.

The next instant, his arms were around her, hers around him, and her face was buried deep against the thick leather of his flight jacket.

When able, she whispered, 'I told myself I wasn't going to cry. That we both knew this was inevitable.'

His arms never loosened. 'I know, but it doesn't make it any easier.'

'No, it doesn't.' She willed for resolve, not wanting their parting to be so sorrow-filled. 'Do you have any idea how long you'll be gone?'

'No. Because of their location, planes are landing at that base faster than the mechanics can fix them. My entire squad is being sent up there.'

She was relieved to hear he would be performing mechanics' duties and not training flight engineers. 'Including Corporal Sanders?'

'Yes.'

She drew in another deep breath and then eased her hold on him enough to lean back and lift her head. 'I'm glad you'll be with people you know.'

'And I'm glad you have a houseful of people who will keep you busy.' He kissed her forehead. 'Tell the children not to worry, I've assigned the candy drops to another squadron.'

That was so like him. The way he cared about others was what had drawn her to him all those months ago. Meeting his gaze, she grinned. That and his handsomeness.

His smile, complete with dimples, made her heart thud harder than ever.

'I'm going to miss you,' he said softly.

'I'm going to miss you, too,' she answered.

The way his lips pressed against hers was the definition of perfect. The kiss didn't last nearly as long as some the other night had, but it filled her with just as much desire for more kisses. More of him.

As their lips parted, he placed a thumb beneath her chin to keep her looking up at him. 'If you need anything, Marilyn will always know where I'm stationed. Always be able to get a message to me.'

She nodded, but wanting as much as she could get, she asked, 'Will you have time to write?'

His grin was back. 'I'll make the time.'

He *would* make the time, that's how he did

things. No matter how busy he'd been, he'd made time to see her, including right now. 'I'll write, too.'

They stood in silence for several moments, looking at each other as if not sure what to say next. There were things she wanted to say, but nothing would form, perhaps because they weren't as important as just standing in his arms.

He spoke first. 'If I get a furlough, I'll come down to see you.'

Having learned furloughs depended greatly upon the transportation provided, she said, 'I could meet you in London.'

'I'll remember that.'

With her heart constricting painfully, because there was so much she wanted to say, but couldn't, she settled for, 'I'll remember you.' A sob bubbled in her throat. 'For ever.'

He pulled her into another hug and kissed the top of her head before saying, 'I have to get back to—'

'I know.' Hugging him a bit tighter, she repeated herself, 'I know.'

They kissed again, a long bittersweet kiss that left her breathless and forlorn. Which grew as he released her and walked across the room.

When he opened the door, Marilyn stood

there. 'I didn't want to interrupt.' She held up one hand. 'I have a camera. Could send you each a picture when they get developed.'

Kathryn stepped forward as Dale turned to look at her. 'I'd like that,' she said.

Marilyn hurried in the room. 'Stand by the window and smile.'

Kathryn didn't think she could find a smile, but when Dale wrapped an arm around her and pulled her tight against his side, she glanced up at him and the sparkle in his eyes did that thing it always did. Filled her with glee.

'Perfect,' Marilyn said. 'I'll send you each a copy.'

'Thanks, Marilyn,' Dale said, crossing the room. 'For everything.' He then gave Marilyn a quick hug before he turned back around.

Kathryn glided into his arms for a final hug, then stood next to Marilyn as he walked out the door.

'It's a hard thing,' Marilyn said quietly, 'to be separated from the man you love.'

That was the one thing Kathryn couldn't admit, not to him or herself. She couldn't love him, be in love with him, because that would make everything so much harder. It was as if something was squeezing her heart, making it hurt worse than any pain she'd ever known, and that made her wonder if loving him would make this harder. That seemed impossible. If something was harder than this, she didn't ever want to experience it.

'Thinking about when you'll see him again will make it a little easier,' Marilyn said.

Contemplating that, Kathryn asked, 'How long have you been separated from your husband?'

'Over a year, with only three furloughs,' Marilyn said. 'But our tours will both be over by the end of this year and then our life together will really start.'

'How long have you been married?'

Marilyn sighed. 'Over a year. We met on the bus on our way to boot camp. He's from western Nebraska, so he was already on the bus when I boarded it in Missouri. No one was sitting in the seat next to him, so I sat down and by the time we reached Georgia, we were head-over-heels in love. We got married the day before we each checked into our boot camps.'

'Camps? You weren't stationed together?'

'No, we weren't and we had no idea where either of us would be shipped to afterwards. All we knew for sure was the very real possibility of never returning. We both wanted to live as much as possible in case that happens.'

Kathryn's stomach sank. That did happen. Servicemen didn't return daily. All around the world.

'I can give you a ride home now,' Marilyn said. 'But Dale's plane will be leaving in less than half an hour if you want to stay and watch it leave.'

She wouldn't be able to see him, but knowing he'd be in the plane sealed her decision. 'I'll stay, if you don't mind.'

'Not at all,' Marilyn said. 'I was hoping that's what you'd choose. I want to wave goodbye. They'll turn around after take-off and fly right over the base.'

A short time later, that's exactly what happened. Kathryn stood among several others all dressed in uniforms and waving at the huge plane that, as it flew directly overhead, tipped its wings one way and then the other.

There were no windows in the plane, so Dale closed his eyes and imagined Kathryn standing below, waving as the plane tilted left, then right while flying over the base. Her image was embedded in his mind as deeply as she was embedded in his heart. Standing in that small room, looking deep into her glistening brown eyes, he'd almost confessed his love for her. He'd stopped short, though, because she'd admitted that she didn't know who she wanted to become and he couldn't, wouldn't, force becoming Mrs Dale Johnson on to her. No matter how much he wanted that.

He shouldn't, but he did.

Much like many of the experiments he and Ralph had embarked in over the years, everything was all fine and dandy in theory, but in reality it didn't always play out. He also knew second chances didn't always arise and wondered if he should have taken the opportunity to tell her that he loved her. She didn't have to love him back. No one could force that upon someone else. The other thing that he needed to bear in mind was that telling her he loved her wouldn't have changed a thing. He'd still be on this airplane and she'd still be standing below, waving goodbye.

Dale opened his eyes and glanced around at the men sitting across from him and next to him. All fourteen men in his squad counted on him to lead them wherever and in whatever situation they encountered. Telling Kathryn he loved her wouldn't change that either.

The only thing his words might have changed would have been expectations. Hers and his, and there were too many unknowns to be making any sort of promises right now.

The roar of the cargo plane was too loud to talk above and, as passengers, none of them had interphones, which left Dale with nothing to listen to but his own mind. That left him in a rather sorry state by the time the plane set down. He'd imagined everything from meeting up with her in London soon, to seeing her twenty years from now happily married to someone else.

High Wycombe's base had been large, but the one they stepped into was bigger and busier. And muddier, and foggier, and there wasn't a thing he saw that impressed him. The barracks were made of Nissen huts, with no insulation, windows or inner walls. Long and narrow beds formed two long rows, leaving nothing but a thin walkway in between. The dome-shaped roof was so low, the only place he could stand straight was in the centre aisle.

On one full side, the beds were nothing but a mattress on top of metal cots. Sets of bedding sat on each mattress. 'Looks like this is home sweet home, boys,' he said. 'Pick a bed and get it made.' There were exactly fifteen beds, including his, the last one in the row and closest to the door. He assumed the fifteen others across the aisle were the other mechanic squadron.

Beds made, he ordered his squad to follow him back outside. The air was so thick and grey it stung his eyes.

'Dang, Sarge,' David Brunswick said, 'No one told us we'd need a machete just to cut the air.'

'It's sea fog, mixed with a good portion of offshore battle flak,' Dale said. 'From my understanding, it won't get much better.'

'How can the planes even see the runways?' Sanders asked. 'I can't see three feet in front of me.'

'You'll get used to it,' Dale said. 'Just as the pilots have.'

More than once in the weeks that followed, he'd eaten those words. There was no getting used to fog that thick and the pilots flew mainly by navigation, which had them missing the runways on a regular basis. High Wycombe had been paradise compared to Thorpe Abbotts. His squad worked from morning to night, but the line of aircrafts to be repaired got longer rather than shorter. Getting the needed parts was a nightmare and they were for ever stealing parts from one plane to patch up another. Safety for the flight crew members and the ability for them to complete their missions was being compromised by the inability to have what was needed, but his reports and complaints seemed to fall on deaf ears.

Morale here was low, too low. Even if he could have seen through the fog, he wouldn't have found a smile. His men were working on planes that were still blood-splattered from former crew members and that was affecting them. Day and night.

Kathryn rarely left his mind and he'd penned her a letter late one night, but kept it brief, made it sound as though they were sunbathing on the beach, rather than choking on thick, dark, salt-filled air, and ended the letter by simply writing 'Yours truly.'

He'd yet to receive a response, but had received a letter from Marilyn, who he missed as well. He hadn't fully understood how much time and effort she'd put in to keeping High Wycombe running as smoothly as it had. No one at Thorpe Abbotts had skills even close to Marilyn's.

In her letter, she'd enclosed the picture of him and Kathryn. After staring at it for a length of time, fully studying how Kathryn was looking up at him and smiling, he'd tucked it inside his billfold and left it there. He didn't pull it out because even though it was just a picture, he didn't want to expose Kathryn to this place. There was a war going on here. Unlike High Wycombe, there were bloody and death-filled battles that overflowed on to the base and there was no end in sight. When thirty airplanes left at the crack of dawn, it was considered lucky if twenty-five returned before nightfall.

No one said if, they said when, and every Nissen hut had crates stacked up along the back wall, personal belongings of fallen soldiers that needed to be sent home. The number of men who rotated through the base was impossible to keep track of and that gave him a further understanding of and a more in-depth look at how easily Ralph had disappeared. Without the time or resources, looking for Ralph was little more than a thought that intercepted those of Kathryn right before he fell asleep.

Every day planes that had been headed to another base, but unable to make it that far, touched down and, once repaired, if those repairs were possible, it was hard saying where those men might touch down next, if they survived another flight.

Unable to sleep one night, Dale had added up the number of days he had until his tour was complete and shouldn't have. Days here seemed a lifetime long and knowing how many more laid before him held no comfort.

After one particularly gruelling morning of scrounging in order to have the basic supplies for planes to pass their preflight checks, Dale stormed into the supply clerk's office, demanding to speak to the commanding officer, Major Greenwald. In the weeks since his arrival, he'd only seen the Major once.

'Major Greenwald isn't here,' the bug-eyed clerk said.

'Where is he?' Dale asked.

The clerk shrugged. 'I'm not privy to that.'

'Well, who is?'

The clerk shrugged again. 'Captain Chambers went upstairs a short time ago. You could try him.'

Dale knew Chambers, he was a lead pilot in several bombing missions. 'Where upstairs?'

The clerk took off his glasses and wiped at the smudges with a handkerchief. 'Might try the third door on the right.'

Dale didn't bother to ask what might be behind the third door on the right, he'd find out soon enough. Taking the steps two at time, he was up the steps in no time and entering the third door on the right a few minutes later. It was a briefing room, full of tables and chairs, with a small side room off the far side. That's the direction he headed, due to the clank he'd heard.

Rounding the doorway, he paused, waiting for Chambers to finish pouring a cup of coffee.

'Want one?' Chambers asked. 'The stuff they serve in the mess hall isn't worth drinking.'

'Sure,' Dale answered, crossing the room. 'I'm looking for Major Greenwald, or someone I can talk to about supplies.' After pouring a cupful of coffee, he took a sip. 'Any ideas?'

Chambers was tall and lanky, with a lean and long face that held a permanent scowl. 'I have lots of them, but none that will help with those questions.' Having moved to the other side of the room, Chambers was peering out the window. 'See that?'

Dale crossed the room to look out the window. The haze had lifted somewhat, but a drizzling rain had replaced it. At one time, he'd told Kathryn he loved the rain and thought he always would, but since being stationed here, his love of rain had been challenged long and hard. 'See what?' Dale asked. 'Mud? Or mud?'

Chambers cracked a smile. 'That's why this place is unfinished. It hasn't stopped raining since they started building it six months ago. I'm sure Greenwald found a reason to travel further inland, away from the sea haze, the flak, the mud and mess.'

Dale could understand the building delays— the framing of a second hanger was rotting in place because the wood had been left exposed so long. 'We built the base I was at before this in the rain.'

'Because you had the right leader. Several have come and gone from this place. I'd bet that's what Greenwald is focused on, obtaining a transfer. That's what's happened to the other three stationed here.'

Four Commanders in less than six months. 'No wonder it's so unorganised,' Dale said. 'I don't even have the supplies to grease the axles of planes needing their preflight checks tomorrow morning.' After taking another sip of coffee, Dale continued, 'I've been reporting shortages and ordering supplies since I arrived, but have yet to see a full order arrive.'

'And you probably won't,' Chambers said as he turned about and rested his backside against the window. 'What did you do to end up here?'

'Do?' Dale shook his head. 'I didn't do anything. I was transferred here because of the planes needing work.'

Chambers nodded. 'So maybe the higher-ups are looking to do something with this place after all. The location is good. It's a straight shot into Germany and back out again. Under the right Commander, one who recognises the smuggling issue, this base could win the war.'

'What smuggling issue?'

'Your supplies,' Chambers said while taking a drink of coffee, 'have never arrived because they were most likely transferred elsewhere en route. There are ships crossing the Channel day and night, smuggling things into England as much as they are smuggling them out, and an army transporter, being driven by some young private who is now wishing he'd never signed up for job, is an easy target. Those drivers are more than happy to give away half his load in order to have a few more dollars in his pocket.'

Dale had never had a reason to even think about such possibilities.

'Can't blame them,' Chambers continued. 'There's no one, no one side or person, who's on the up and up when it comes to this war. Every one's looking for a back-door deal or to have their palm greased.' He crossed the room, rinsed out his cup and set it on the counter to dry. 'I have three missions left to fly and my tour is up. I'm heading back to the States then, to my wife and baby boy I haven't even seen yet.'

With his mind fluttering from smugglers to

the idea of having a wife, Dale walked over to rinse his cup.

'You know, Johnson, you look a lot like a tail gunner I had several months ago. I'd lost mine and this guy filled in.'

Even with all else going on, and thoughts of Kathryn front and centre, Dale still hadn't given up on finding Ralph. 'What was his name?'

'I never knew his full name. Everyone just called him Junior.'

Dale shrugged as the small light of hope that had flamed inside him went out. Ralph wasn't a junior and would never have been called that.

'If you want your supplies, you're going to have to find someone who knows how to work the channels and I don't mean the English one. You know how easy it is to tap a phone line? Make that call go somewhere else? There are more ways to fight a war than bombs.' Chamber's slapped Dale's shoulder. 'For the record, I have my own supply of axle grease and a few other spare parts.'

'Back-door deals?' Dale asked.

'We all have to look out for number one, because no one else cares if you make it home or not.'

Chambers left the room, but Dale remained. He walked back to the window, but not to see anything in particular. Chambers, along with being stationed here, had changed something inside him. His outlook. His perspective.

He pulled his billfold out of his pocket and took out Kathryn's picture. She cared. He did, too. Not only about himself, but every member of his squadron. If everyone only cared about themselves, this world would be worse than it was. It might mean a court-martial, but he was willing to risk it to make sure he and others had a fighting chance.

Slipping the picture back in his wallet, he headed back downstairs.

At the clerk's desk, he spun the phone around and picked up the receiver. 'What's the connection to High Wycombe?'

'I don't know, sir, and you can't use that phone. It's only for supplies.'

Setting the receiver back in place, he said, 'You're right, I can't.' Bugging that phone would have been easy. He needed a more secure line.

Back upstairs, he walked the empty hall, peeking into each room until he found the one he wanted. Major Greenwald's office. In the top drawer was a listing like the one he'd seen Marilyn refer to more than once. Scanning it, he found the number he wanted and then dialled it. One ring sounded before the other end was connected.

'Hilts here.'

'Major Hilts, it's Sergeant Dale Johnson.'

'Johnson?' The Major sounded confused. 'How'd you get this number?'

'I need your help, sir, will you hear me out?'

Chapter Nine

16th of November, 1942

Dear Diary,
Dale was shipped out over two months ago and every day seems to be longer than the one before. I never knew time could go so slow, or that I'd feel so low. Lack so much energy. It's simply not in me. I don't have the heart to do much of anything. I never knew a person could feel so rotten. I've been separated from others before, but can honestly say it was never this hard. Which is why I decided to do something to keep my mind off missing him so much. This week, I started helping Marilyn search for Ralph. She's collected numerous lists and documents about every soldier enlisted in the army. Now that the fields are all

ploughed, not needing attention until next spring, I'm spending every afternoon while the children are in school at the base, double-checking the lists and correlating them with each other. It's tedious work, but it makes me feel closer to Dale. I've written to him several times and his letters assure me he's doing well, but I've decided not to mention what I'm doing. He told me once that he didn't want me to help, but I don't think he'll mind, especially if I do discover Ralph's whereabouts. I know this sounds like a simple thing, but it makes me feel as though I'm doing something specifically for Dale and this is the only thing I can think of.

Kathryn flipped over another sheet of paper, adding it to the *read* pile. Before starting to study the new sheet, she leaned back and stretched her hands overhead. Sitting this much, day after day, was getting harder rather than easier. Used to being up and moving around, her muscles were growing stiff, so she stood and walked to the window. This was the same room she'd said goodbye to Dale in two months ago. They had stood before this window while Marilyn snapped their picture. The one that had been tucked inside her diary, until she'd taken it out and pinned it to the wall near her bed. She liked it there. Seeing him first thing in the morning and the last thing at night was comforting.

After stretching her arms and legs one final time, she walked back over to the table, sat back down and started scanning the list before her.

Several sheets of paper later, something caught her eye. Although she'd memorised the information she had on Ralph, she still reached across the table for the notepad on which she'd written his name, date of birth, place of birth, parents' names and address.

Her heart started thudding faster as the information on her notepad and the one on the roster started matching up. Running her finger across the line, she held it under the name. John R. Johansson. That wasn't right, but the rest of it was. Scooping up the piece of paper and her notes, she left the room.

She paused at the doorway to the room Marilyn sat in and waited until the other woman had hung up the phone. 'May I come in?'

'Of course.' Marilyn glanced at the papers and smiled before asking, 'You didn't find something, did you?'

'I'm not sure. I need a second opinion.'

Marilyn clapped her hands as she stood up. 'Let me see.'

Kathryn laid both pieces of paper on the desk. 'Look at this name right here. John R. Johansson.'

'Okay.'

'Now look at all of his information, including the names of his parents.' Pointing to her sheet of note paper, she said, 'See how it's all the same?'

'I do see that. And I know that Harold and Caroline are Dale's mother's and father's names,' Marilyn said, her voice growing higher. 'And Buchanan is the town he's from in North Dakota.'

Kathryn's insides started to bubble and she pressed a hand to her stomach. 'The name doesn't match up, but everything else does.'

'I see that.' Marilyn pointed to the top of the roster. 'This is where he went to boot camp.' Tapping the paper, she said, 'They made a clerical error.'

'A what?'

'A clerical error!' Marilyn threw both hands in the air. 'They're made all the time. People transpose letters and numbers constantly and it drives me crazy!' Pressing her hands to her head, she continued, 'Why didn't I think of a clerical error? It makes sense. Ralph's name is Ralph John Johnson, someone transposed that into John R. Johansson.'

'How? Why?'

'It could have been sloppy handwriting, or a clerical aid with poor hearing, who knows, it happens all the time.' Marilyn then jumped up and down. 'You found him, Kathryn, you found Ralph! Dale's going to be ecstatic.'

'I found a name. We haven't found him.'

'It'll be easy now. See this number?' Marilyn pointed to a set of numbers next to the name. 'This is his army serial number. That's all I need to find out where any serviceman is stationed at any time.'

'How?'

Marilyn sat down at her desk and pulled open a drawer. 'With this form right here.' Grabbing a pen, she pulled the roster closer and started filling out the form. 'I'll send it out in the evening mail and within two to three weeks, we'll have a report back telling us where he is.' She set the pen down and squealed while jumping to her feet.

The next moment they were hugging and laughing. Kathryn was so happy, because she knew how much this was going to mean to Dale.

'Are you going to write to Dale?' Marilyn asked.

Kathryn considered that for a moment. 'No, I'll wait until we have an exact location.'

'That's probably a good idea.' Marilyn sat back down and picked up the pen. 'This is so exciting. So very exciting.'

As her excitement waned slightly, because they hadn't found Ralph yet, Kathryn asked, 'Wouldn't someone have discovered the error before now? Wouldn't Ralph know they had his name wrong?'

'Probably, and he'd probably reported it and his superior probably submitted it, and they probably think it's been cleared up. But let me tell you what also probably happened. The correction order would have been passed along to someone assigned to correcting a thousand other clerical errors and that someone moves on to another job before they are all corrected, and a new person starts over on that pile that has now grown even larger.'

Marilyn licked the envelope she'd placed the folded order in and sealed it shut before continuing, 'Whoever finally gets around to making the change has to go back and change the name on every list. Every list. It won't be like it was for you, scanning list after list, they would now be able to use his number to find it, but it's time consuming and, with everything else going, an order to fix a clerical error sits in a to-do box for a long time. It'll get corrected some day, but no one should ever hold their breath.'

'It seems like so much for a simple misspelling,' Kathryn said. So much agony for Dale, too. Something else hit her then.

'It is,' Marilyn said. 'Which is why I wish people would pay more attention to what they are doing the first time.'

With dread creeping up her spine, Kathryn asked, 'Marilyn, will that report tell us if something has happened to Ralph?'

Marilyn grew sombre. 'Yes. It will tell us if he's lost his life, if he's a prisoner of war, missing in action or been discharged and why.'

Kathryn let out the breath she'd been holding.

'Dale needs to know whatever we learn.'

'Yes,' Kathryn agreed. 'He does.'

Dale couldn't believe his luck. Things had started to look up shortly after he'd called Major Hilts. Within weeks, Thorpe Abbotts had started to change. New Commanders arrived and stayed, hangers were built, gravel hauled in, supplies, including parts and oil and grease, arrived and an assortment of other things. The transformation had changed the men, too. Even though there were still days of grief and sadness when planes arrived damaged or didn't return at all, there were other days where smiles could be seen, joking and laughter could be heard, morale was lifted.

His morale was flying about as high as the plane that would soon be touching down at High Wycombe. Major Hilts had requested his presence and, even though he had no idea how long he'd be here, he was bound and determined to find enough time to visit Kathryn. Even if it was just a few minutes.

He was squashed between crates and barrels, and had no idea how close they were to the base, other than his own internal instincts, which said it wasn't much further, but he didn't care. When his new Commander, Major Eddy, told him yesterday that he was to board the cargo plane this morning for a trip to see Hilts, Dale didn't ask questions.

Hearing the engines pull back, his grin grew tenfold and he braced his feet against a crate for when the tyres hit the ground and started bouncing. That happened a moment later and he pressed his hands to the makeshift seat beneath him, holding on until the worse of it was over.

As soon as the rolling stopped, he jumped out of his seat and headed for the door.

The sun appeared brighter than it was because he'd been encrusted in darkness for just over an hour, but that didn't stop him from rushing forward. The base looked so familiar, a sense of homecoming that he hadn't expected washed over him, making him stop long enough to take a lengthy look around.

Familiar faces appeared, men he'd worked alongside for over nine months. He greeted them, shaking hands and slapping others on the backs, just as they did him. Major Hilts was at the side of the tarmac and Dale saluted.

Hilts returned the gesture, then held out his hand. 'Good to see you, Sergeant.'

'It's good to see you, Major,' Dale said, shaking the man's hand.

Hilts spun about on one heel and Dale stepped up beside him as the Major started walking towards the headquarters building.

'I hear Thorpe Abbotts has been brought up to code,' Hilts said.

'Yes, sir, it has.'

'That's why I've asked for your attendance. I'm travelling to London tomorrow, to attend a collective meeting concerning all the Army's Air Force bases and Bombing Command Stations, and may need your first-hand information about the transformation that took place at Thorpe Abbotts so it can happen elsewhere.'

For the chance to see Kathryn, he'd walk through fire. 'I'll be glad to answer any questions, sir,' Dale replied, 'though I must ask if a Commander wouldn't be more useful?'

'They'll be there, too, Sergeant,' Hilts said. 'Former and present.'

Dale had nothing to hide. 'Glad to hear that, sir.'

They were approaching the building from the back, which meant he wouldn't be walking past Marilyn's desk. He was hoping to ask her to go to Norman's and collect Kathryn.

'Our meeting shouldn't take long,' Hilts said. 'I'm sure there are plenty of people you'll want to say hello to.'

Dale bit the inside of his lip to keep from voicing his enthusiasm. 'Yes, sir,' he said while entering the building.

The meeting took less than an hour. After a series of questions concerning whether the overall operation of Thorpe Abbotts now compared more closely with this base, Hilts supplied him with a list of questions that might be asked tomorrow, none of which were out of the ordinary, and then said they would leave for London by 0800. The Major also said a room had been prepared for him in the visitor's wing of headquarters.

It took Dale less than five minutes to store his gear in the room and head for Marilyn's office. A Jeep hadn't been assigned to him for such a short visit, so he was hoping to borrow the one the clerical personnel used.

She was in her office and let out a squeal that echoed into the hallway when he knocked on the open door. With her arms spread wide, she raced across the room.

Rather than saying hello, or his name, she asked, 'Does Kathryn know you're here?'

He gave her a quick sisterly hug before answering, 'No, and I'm hoping to borrow your Jeep.'

'Of course, let me get the keys.' Hurrying back to her desk, she said, 'I wish I was a fly on the wall when she sees you.'

'I don't. I hope no one's around.'

She laughed. 'Men. I swear.' Glancing at the clock on the wall, she tossed him the keys. 'Actually, she should be on her way to the pub right about now.'

He hadn't checked the time, or thought about that. 'I gotta go.'

'Yes, you do!'

Before he made it to the door, she asked, 'How long are you here for?'

'I'm going to London with Major Hilts in the morning, so I believe it's just for the day.'

'Then go, you don't have much time!'

'I was going until you stopped me again,' he pointed out while making it through the doorway this time.

The quick snapping of heels echoed in the hallway and he paused, waiting for her to catch up to him.

Marilyn shrugged. 'Figured I'd walk you out to the Jeep. Might be all I see of you. How are you doing?'

'Might be,' he agreed, hopeful. 'And I'm doing fine. How about you? How's Bruce?'

'Fine and fine. Counting the days.'

'Still the first of the year?'

'Yes, by January we both should be home. I'll stay with my folks until he arrives and then we'll move in with his.'

'Take my address with you.' He held open the door for them both to walk outside. 'Nebraska isn't that far from North Dakota.'

'No, it isn't.' Her face lit up even brighter. 'That would be fun. Getting together back home.'

'Yes, it would be.' They'd arrived at the Jeep. He held up the key while climbing in. 'Thanks.'

'My pleasure. Just put the keys on my desk.' She shrugged. 'Or leave them in it.'

He waved while backing out of the parking space. 'Good seeing you!'

'You, too! Have fun!'

He nearly skipped first gear in his hurry to get off the base and on to the road Kathryn just might be pedalling down. This was almost too good to be true. The Jeep rattled and bounced as he dodged some of the deeper ruts while holding a speed that was probably as fast as the little vehicle had ever gone.

Hitting the brakes at the main road, he scanned for cars and any sign of a woman on a bike. Nothing in either direction. He was in a quandary as to which way to go. The pub was to the right, but she might not have pedalled as far as that yet, which meant she'd still be down the road to the left. If he went towards the pub, he could check for her bike and, if it wasn't there, turn around. If he went towards her house, he'd have to go all the way up the drive to see if her bike was home and be delayed by Norman and Charlotte.

Torn, he finally chose the pub, really hoping that was the right choice. Dropping the clutch as he took off, gravel spouted from beneath the wheels that spun as he shot up the road.

Less than half a mile later, excitement shot through him at having made the right decision. She was on the far side of the road, leisurely pedalling along. His grin doubled in size as he eased off the gas and downshifted in order to come upon her slowly.

The recognisable rattle of a Jeep didn't surprise Kathryn. One or more often passed her on the way to the pub. Since Dale had left, she hadn't bothered to turn around at the sound of them because she knew it couldn't be him. Today was no different, but that didn't stop her from wishing by some astronomical miracle that Dale was driving the Jeep coming up behind her. That he was still stationed at the base.

It had only been a week since Marilyn had sent off the form requesting Ralph's location, but since that day, Kathryn had been wondering if there might be a way, any feasible way, she'd be able to tell Dale in person the results.

Her thoughts shifted. The Jeep should have already passed her, yet it was rumbling behind her, slowly, and that was too odd not to investigate.

She applied the brakes and lowered her feet to the ground before turning about.

The leather bomber jacket made her heart skip a beat and she was in the process of telling herself that hundreds of men from the base wore those when her heart nearly leaped out of her chest.

She tried to tell herself it couldn't be, but her heart was as convinced as her eyes.

The Jeep stopped beside her and Kathryn was too stunned to move. She had to be seeing things. Imagining things. A shiver that had nothing to do with the cool air rippled over her. 'Dale?'

'Hello, Kathryn.'

Her heart leaped at the sound of his voice, so hard and fast she pressed a hand to her throat and stared harder, still not sure she was seeing what she thought she was seeing. Hearing what she thought she was hearing.

He was moving, climbing out of the Jeep.

'Is it really you?' It was a ridiculous question, but it was all she could think to ask.

'Yes, it's me.'

Elation filling her, she leaped off the bicycle to land in front of him and to wrap her arms around his neck. Their lips met at the same time their bodies collided. When their lips parted, it was to take a breath, a fast one. The kiss this time was slower, deeper, and one that left her clinging to him and gasping for air when Dale pulled his mouth away and held her tight. So tight she could barely get the air she needed, but she didn't mind. Not in the least.

She'd dreamed of the leather scent of his jacket, of having his arms around her, of kissing him.

'I can't believe you're here,' she said, finally able to breathe without gasping.

His hold tightened as he kissed the top of her head. 'I've missed you.'

'I've missed you, too.' Twisting enough look up at him, she said, 'So very, very much. I can't believe you've been transferred back here.'

The smile on his face slipped. 'I haven't been. I'm only here for the day.'

A large portion of her happiness disappeared. 'A day?'

'Yes, I have to attend a meeting in London tomorrow morning.' He kissed her forehead. 'Don't be sad. We have the entire afternoon and evening to spend together, that's more than we had yesterday.'

His optimism never seemed to dull. To him, there was always a bright side to everything. She needed to be more like that. And would be, at least for today. 'You're right. We do and it is.'

He kissed the tip of her nose. 'Let's get your supplies delivered to the pub so we can—'

She followed his gaze to her bicycle lying on its side and the food that had tumbled across the ground.

'I see a couple of eggs that aren't broken,' he said.

The last thing she wanted to do was let go of him, but his hold had already lessened. She gave him one final, hard squeeze and then stepped back. Suddenly filled with a sense of urgency, she hurried towards the bicycle. 'We'll salvage what we can and I'll replace the rest tomorrow.'

Side by side, they gathered the supplies and removed the basket from the bicycle. While she carried the basket to the Jeep, he carried the bike. Once all was in the back, she climbed in the passenger seat. The enthusiasm of spending the day with him grew inside her, as did the urgency. They didn't have much time and she wanted to live as much as she could during those few hours.

He started the Jeep and as his hand landed on the gear shifter, she laid a hand on his forearm. 'I can't believe you're here. Can't believe it.'

'Well, I am.' He winked one eye. 'And very glad about that.'

'Me, too!' She bit her lip at how she'd nearly shouted her answer. And then laughed.

He was laughing, too, and she leaned her head against the back of the seat, smiling at how wonderful that sound was. How wonderful it was to be sitting beside him. Even how wonderful it was to have the wind tugging at the scarf on her head.

'How are the children?' he asked. 'And Norman and Charlotte?'

'Fine,' she answered. 'Everyone is fine. How are the men? How's Corporal Sanders?'

'Good. Busy.'

He'd said as much in his letters and she referred to something else he often mentioned. 'I'm sure that does help the time go by faster.' Nothing had helped her in that aspect. Even though there had been all her usual chores, the days and nights had crawled by.

'It does in some ways, but it still seemed like years rather than weeks.'

'For me, too,' she admitted. Her thoughts had always been on him and she was curious about things he never mentioned in his letters. 'Have you met any of the locals?'

'Not really. A few make deliveries to the base, but that's about it.'

'Have you arranged for sweet drops to happen there?'

'No.' He glanced her way and his smile grew slightly. 'Have there been any more here?'

'No.' Although the children would have enjoyed them, she hadn't wanted there to be any more sweet drops. It might take away from just how special they'd been. He'd been the special part, not just because he'd created them, but because of how much he'd enjoyed them. How much she'd enjoyed them because of him. Life itself, even with the war raging on all around them, had been enjoyable because of him.

'So, what's new around here?' he asked, glancing towards her again with his smile still reflecting in his eyes. 'What have you been doing? I'm assuming the crops have all been harvested.'

Telling him about Ralph, what she'd discovered, shot across her mind. So did the fact she truly had no more idea as to where Ralph was, how he was, and wouldn't until the report returned. Still, the idea of how excited he'd been bubbled inside her. 'Yes,' she said, with more enthusiasm than harvesting crops had most likely ever instilled in anyone. 'They are all harvested.'

Then, because she needed to focus on something else or her happiness about how excited he'd be to know the small amount she did know about Ralph might win out and she'd spoil the surprise she'd one day be able to provide him, she said, 'Norman is on the ham radio every day, still hoping to break Hitler's Enigma code. He swears that will turn the tide of the war.'

The silence that ensued between them had a flash of guilt rising up inside her. Anything to do with decoding the German messages was top secret. She'd known that and had never mentioned that before, not even to Dale. When she'd first figured out that Norman was more than an amateur ham radio operator, shortly after coming to live with them, she'd also deduced that was why she'd been sent here. Her father and Norman maintained regular communications and not even Mum knew how little of that communication had to do with her.

'I shouldn't have said that.'

'Norman's secret is safe with me,' Dale said while keeping his gaze forward, as if concentrating on driving.

'I know.' She did trust him, which was the only reason she'd spoken without thought, mentioning Norman's tasks, but if it had been anyone but him, she could have just put everyone and all she knew in jeopardy. 'But loose lips sink ships,' she quoted one of the many posters that had been hung up across the nation far and wide encouraging the entire country to watch what they said and to whom.

Dale smile hadn't diminished, in fact, his dimples were showing. 'You do not have loose lips.'

Her cheeks burned slightly, mainly because if anyone knew her lips, other than herself, it was him.

'Actually, you have the most beautiful lips I've ever seen.'

The heat in her cheeks increased. Though she had a great desire to know what else he found beautiful about her, which would be very vain even though she hoped he found her as attractive as she found him, she couldn't bring herself to ask. Therefore, she skipped to another subject. 'Patricia finally lost a tooth. She was fretting that it would never happen and seeing Doreen walk around with four missing had become very upsetting.'

Dale chuckled before he turned a more serious look her way. 'What about Phillip? Have you heard how he and his mother are doing?'

'No, we haven't.' Then, using the same reassurances she told herself and the other children,

she said, 'I'm sure we'll hear once they are settled. Travelling to America is a long journey.'
She'd used the globe to show the children where
the state of Georgia was located and each time,
as well as numerous other times while looking
at the globe, her eyes had gone to North Dakota
and her mind had drifted to Dale.

'We're here,' he said.

They had indeed arrived at the pub. He retrieved the basket and carried it inside, holding
the door for her to enter first.

'Sergeant Johnson!' Oscar's shout nearly
rattled the roof as he hurried around the long
wooden counter. 'I'm happy to see you're back.'
Oscar's glance settled on her for a moment as
he said, 'As I'm sure others are.'

Kathryn couldn't hide the blush that crept
into her cheeks any more than she could hide the
shine she felt in her eyes every time she looked
at Dale. She was so glad he was back. So very,
very glad.

'It's good to see you, too, Oscar,' Dale replied,
setting the basket of food on the counter. The
inside of the pub had given him the same sense
of homecoming as he'd experienced back at the
base. But none of that had compared to how his
insides had nearly exploded when he'd pulled

up next to Kathryn and her bicycle. 'I'm afraid a small mishap caused a few eggs to break,' he said, gesturing to the basket.

'I'll replace them tomorrow,' Kathryn said. 'I hope that won't cause too much of an hindrance.'

'Oh, no, none at all,' Oscar said. 'Sit down. Let me get you a cup of coffee. Both of you.'

Dale would like to have refused, he wanted to spend every possible moment available during his short visit with Kathryn, preferably alone.

'That would be nice,' she said.

Still wishing otherwise, Dale gave in. 'I've missed your coffee.'

The old man nearly beamed as he spun around to shout into the backroom, ordering Ed to put on a pot of coffee. Just as Dale had known would happen, Ed blasted through the back door, as excited to see him as Oscar had been moments ago. The brothers had become as familiar to him as many of the people at the base. If his stay had been for a longer amount of time, he would have enjoyed spending this time with them more completely.

As it was, the two men planted themselves at the table along with him and Kathryn, chatting on about things Dale knew he wouldn't remember because his focus was on Kathryn. On how she sipped her coffee and nodded at Ed and

Oscar, but continuously provided him with an apologetic smile that said she knew he didn't want to be here.

Luckily, it didn't take long to drink their obligatory cups of coffee and they were able to take their leave. However, once at the Jeep, he was a bit dumbfounded as to where they could go next. He wanted time alone with her, which wouldn't happen at the farm, Norman and Charlotte would expect his company as much as Ed and Oscar had, and there was nowhere at the base he could take her. Although there was the small town up the road, where the children went to school, there wasn't any place for the two of them to spend time either. There was no cinema they could visit and, though there was a small café, they'd just had coffee with Ed and Oscar. Furthermore, they might encounter others one of them knew, or both, so they would not be alone there either.

'Norman took the boys fishing last week,' she said.

He'd started the Jeep, but had yet to shift into Reverse, and sensed she knew what he'd been thinking about. 'Should we go take a look at the creek?'

She shrugged as if it didn't matter, but the smirk on her face said more. 'If you'd like to.'

The idea appealed to him all right. He'd known he'd missed her, but hadn't expected to be this overwhelmed by the idea of leaving again. The few hours they would have together would pass swiftly and the same sense of urgency he'd had while leaving the base filled him.

He drove faster than he should have, causing the Jeep to bounce and rattle harder than ever, but Kathryn's laughter said she was enjoying the ride as much as he was enjoying her delight. Hardly a word was spoken, yet they were both joyous and in agreement when he parked the Jeep and hurried down the pathway.

The brook was flowing swifter than when they'd been there before. The sound of water rushing over the rocks mingled with the crunch and crinkle of the fallen dried leaves beneath their feet as they traversed to the log they'd sat upon before.

Upon arrival, Kathryn spun around and, with her eyes glowing, settled her hands on his shoulders and stretched upwards. Her lips landed on his as perfectly as a well-seasoned pilot lands a plane on the runway.

The rightness of the next few hours would live with him for ever. They kissed and talked of minor, inconsequential things that neither of them gave much thought to, but were only saying because neither of them wanted to talk about the things they should mention. The war. That he would soon be leaving again. The future, and how neither of them knew what that would look like. It also gave them time to catch their breath in order for another long bout of kissing.

His insides were on fire, wanting more than kisses, but Dale held rein over those wants, those needs. Simply kissing her, just being with her, was all he could ask for. Anything else could compromise her and he wouldn't, couldn't, do that to her. His conscience wouldn't let him forget that his time in England was limited and that, beyond that, his time on this earth could be limited. He witnessed that every day. Knew men who would never again see the light of day. Never again see their loved ones and homes.

After a very serious and heavy bout of kissing, he pulled her close to him and caressed the length of her hair, her shoulder, the trim curves of her side, before saying, 'We should leave. Norman and Charlotte will be worried about where you are.'

She sighed heavily. 'I was thinking the same thing, but I don't want to.'

'I don't either.' Then to himself only, he admitted that if they didn't, something more would happen between them. 'But we don't have a choice.'

She snuggled closer and her hand, inside his jacket, stroked his chest with a touch so close to heavenly that every ounce of his being ached with desire. If they were lying in a soft bed, with walls for privacy, he might have already taken things further.

Therefore, it was a very good thing that they were stretched out on the chilly ground with little more than bare trees surrounding them. 'Come on,' he said, bringing her with him as he sat up. 'Time to go.'

Her little groan of protest could have been his breaking point, but he didn't let it. He'd pushed himself hard since joining the army, giving his all no matter what the task, how much he agreed with the outcome or not, and had to use a good portion of that same willpower to get off the ground and pull her to her feet.

It also took a considerable amount of that same willpower to keep his true feelings hidden. If he admitted, revealed, that he'd fallen in love with her, he'd have to take action, but there was no suitable action for him to take. Yes, she was happy to see him, but that still didn't mean she wanted the for ever he was thinking about. And now wasn't the time to ask her either. He couldn't think about the for ever he wanted until he found Ralph. Made sure this war hadn't cost his parents the last of their children.

They walked back to the Jeep hand in hand. 'You will stay for supper,' she said.

'I was hoping for an invitation.'

She twisted and stretched on her tiptoes to kiss his cheek. 'You don't need an invitation. You're always welcome.'

The slow curl of her lips and the hint of promise in her eyes stretched his resistance to the brink. If he didn't get his mind to focus on something else, he might drag her back into the woods. 'Do you have any gooseberry pie?'

Her laughter tinkled in the air like chatter from songbirds. 'No, but we do have some gooseberry jam.' She curled up one shoulder and was biting her bottom lip.

He shook his head and tried his hardest not to smile. The food truly didn't matter. He doubted he'd remember what he ate tomorrow. Being with her, however, he'd never forget. Yet he had to tease her by saying, 'No pie, I don't know if I can—'

'Oh, stop.' She playfully slapped his chest. 'You aren't very convincing.'

She was right. He was not very convincing, even to himself. And tearing his lips off hers one more time was harder than ever. But he did it and drove her to Norman and Charlotte's, where he was welcomed as if he was the long-lost prodigal son.

The children's questions revolved around the sweet drops, Charlotte's covered his eating and health and Norman's were more war focused. Dale answered them all and asked about their well-being and thoughts, but his attention remained on Kathryn.

He was as bad as a pup, following her from room to room when possible and anxiously awaiting her return when she did get out of sight. The meal and evening were enjoyable, but not nearly as much as they would have been if they'd been alone. There had been so many times he'd wanted to catch her by the waist and spin around for a quick kiss—or a long one. The silent communication between them said she was thinking the same thing. Wishing for the same thing.

It wasn't to be, though. The weather had turned cold and damp. Not full-on raining, but misting enough that it was too cold for him to ask if she'd care to go for a walk after they'd finished the meal and Norman had switched on the radio. Furthermore, the time had passed as swiftly as he'd known it would.

Everyone had gathered in the front room,

listening to the broadcast. He hadn't heard a word said and knew Kathryn hadn't either. They were sitting side by side and kept looking at each other, knowing their time together was almost over. Her hand was beneath his, tucked between them, and he squeezed it, wishing with everything inside him he didn't have to leave her again. Not tonight. Not tomorrow. Not ever.

The way her smile trembled and moisture gathered on her lashes when she blinked said she fully understood his thoughts. And that made his throat thicken and his eyes sting like they never had before.

He wondered what she would say if he asked her to go to London tomorrow, meet him there and get married. Which was completely impossible. It took months to get permission to marry.

Knowing what he had to do, whether he liked it or not, as soon as Norman shut off the radio, Dale stood. The words stuck in his throat like concrete and he was thankful when the older man stood and extended a hand.

'We all hope to see you again, Dale,' Norman said. 'Very soon.'

Charlotte was next. She gave him a gentle hug while saying, 'We'll be praying for you.'

The children bid him farewell, too, and then climbed the stairs, followed by Charlotte and

Norman. Bracing himself, he turned to where Kathryn stood beside him. She'd wiped her cheeks, but they were still damp and tears remained welled in her eyes.

'I don't…' She shook her head and pinched her lips together.

He took her hands, one in each of his, and held on tight for a silent moment. Letting out a breath that snagged inside his chest, he said, 'All I need from you is a kiss goodbye.'

She landed in his arms and he could taste her tears that fell while kissing her. Her body was trembling, so was his, and in his heart of hearts, he knew this was by far the hardest goodbye he'd ever had. The need to say more was there, but so was the tenacity not to. The fact he'd fallen in love with her hadn't changed the war raging on around them. Hadn't changed the commitments he'd made, or the ones she had. Some day that would be over and then he'd vow his life and ask her to become tethered to him for evermore.

When the kiss ended and she parted her lips, as if to say something, he pressed a finger against them.

'I'll write,' he said, not removing his finger.

She nodded.

With his finger still against her lips, he kissed her forehead and let his lips linger there until his very soul shook so hard he was certain it would shatter, then he turned and walked out the door. Telling himself this was how things had to be. At least for now.

Chapter Ten

23rd of November, 1942

Dear Diary,
My hand is shaking as I write and my tears
have already smudged two of your pages
beyond use. I saw Dale today. It was the
most bittersweet day of my life. I loved seeing him, spending time with him, kissing
him. We kissed so many times I lost count,
but then I had to say goodbye to him again.
I'm afraid I'm going to miss him more than
I can manage. The moment I saw him
today, something happened, inside me. I
can't explain it, but I suddenly knew that
I love him more than anything else. Anyone else. I've been sitting here for hours
wondering what to do about that. I've even
thought about going to the base. The only

thing stopping me is that it's guarded and I know I'd be caught, which could put him in jeopardy, which I could never do. But I would do just about anything else to be with him if it was only for one more hour.

The pain inside me is so overwhelming, so hard to put into words. I have no way of knowing when I'll see him again, IF I'll see him again, and that hurts so badly. It feels as if someone is tearing my heart into little pieces. I don't know what to do, but there has to be something.

It is now morning and I've decided that I need to contact Father and have him transfer me closer to where Dale is stationed. I've never made such a request of Father, asked him to use his influence on my behalf, but I must, and although I know Mum will be extremely upset, it's what I have to do. She'll just have to understand that. I am worried about leaving Norman and Charlotte and the children. I do cherish each one of them and will miss them. I will ask that Father sends someone to replace me here and that he continues to provide them with funds.

Forgive me if I sound selfish, perhaps I am, but this is what I must do. This war overtaking the world may not end any time soon. Dale is in danger every single day and I have to find a way to be with him as much as possible. If anything were to happen to him and I hadn't tried, I would never forgive myself.

A noise coming from Charlotte and Norman's bedroom off the kitchen had Kathryn closing her diary and wiping the tears from her cheeks. None of this was easy, nor would it get any easier, but her mind was made up. She would continue to do what she could for her country, but this time she would also take into consideration what she wanted and needed, and ultimately, that was Dale.

She waited until both Charlotte and Norman arrived in the kitchen and then explained her decision forthrightly. Although neither seemed surprised, they both expressed how much they would miss her. Norman then offered to get a message to her father, and stated he would give her a ride to the rail station in High Wycombe.

Saying goodbye to the children was tearful, but Kathryn's resolve never waned. Dale was worth any sacrifice she had to make—in fact, compared to his, hers seemed small. He'd left

his family on the other side of the world in order
to put his life on the line to defend her country.

At the train station, she hugged Norman one
last time, saying she'd write to all of them as
soon as possible, and then boarded the train.
Her own tenacity surprised her a bit. She'd
never taken such a stand. Never been so stead-
fast when it came to herself. Never known she
had this much courage.

Then again, she'd never cared this much about
another person before either, and had to believe
there would never be another person she loved
as much as Dale.

She also hoped her courage would remain
intact. She'd need it when it came to Father and
Mum.

As the train pulled out of the station, she
looked out the window and her heart skipped
a beat at the sight of an army Jeep. A woman
was driving it and though the woman didn't re-
semble Marilyn, that's who Kathryn thought
of as a shimmer of guilt raised up inside her.
They'd become close the past couple of months
and she hadn't even said goodbye to her. With
her mind so focused on Dale, she hadn't even
thought of it.

She eased her mind by telling herself she
would call Marilyn from London and then

practised what she'd tell her father. Having not seen him for over two years, since the last time he'd travelled to Norman's to visit, she was a bit apprehensive about his reaction. Norman hadn't said if Father had been upset, only that she would be met at the station and taken to his office.

Which is precisely what happened. Because her decision had been made and acted upon early in the morning, it was still well before lunchtime when she arrived in London. Several of the streets that she'd known for so many years were unrecognisable. Buildings gone, empty spaces and, in some areas, rubble had passed the windows of the car that delivered her to Leconfield House, where a uniformed officer escorted her down long and empty hallways to the headquarters section. The officer knocked once on the door and then nodded his head before spinning around and staunchly marching back down the hallway.

The click of the door opening had her turning back around.

As a child she'd run into his arms upon his arrival at home, as she'd got older, it had become a peck on his cheek and today, standing before him as a woman who'd matured a great deal since they'd last seen each other, she was unsure how to react upon seeing her father. He looked the same, except like her, a bit older. There were more wrinkles between his eyebrows and his hair had turned completely grey, but his brown eyes held a shine she remembered. That made her heart thud and she smiled in return.

'Ah, Kathryn, my dear, it is good to see you,' he said, holding out a hand.

She laid her fingers in his palm. 'Hello, Father, it's good to see you, too.'

His fingers encircled hers as he pulled her closer and kissed her cheek before gesturing for her to enter. 'I thought it best for us to meet here, to discuss your wishes.'

'I appreciate that,' she said, squeezing his hand as they crossed the room. 'I'm afraid Mum isn't going to be very happy with me.'

His raised brows and slight nod were reminiscent. The two of them had had conversations before concerning Mum not being happy with her. Although it had been years and those events had all been trivial compared to this one.

'Only because she loves you,' he said, guiding her on to stiff back wooden chair. 'You're no longer happy with the Harrises?'

Her heart took a tumble. 'I do hope that is not how Charlotte or Norman feel. They have been truly wonderful and I've enjoyed staying with them, and would continue to if things were different.'

'How different? What's changed?'

He'd taken a seat beside her in an identical chair. Built for brief visits, not long conversations, the chairs were not comfortable, but his ease, his genuine tenderness, said he'd sit there as long as it took. His reputation of being a hard, stern man when needed had rarely ventured home and she hoped that would be the case today.

Taking a deep breath, she set into her silently rehearsed speech before giving herself time to worry overly much about his reaction. 'I've fallen in love, Father, with an American soldier. He's now stationed at the Thorpe Abbotts base and I'd like to be stationed in that vicinity as well. I've gained many skills while staying with Charlotte and Norman, so any agricultural position, or assisting with billeted children, would serve me well.' Her steam was running out and her nerves were jumping. 'And you. Serve you well, I'm mean England. Serve—'

'I know what you mean, Kathryn.'

She closed her eyes and took another deep breath, blowing it out before opening her eyes again.

'Tell me about him…' he sat back in his chair '…this American.'

Her insides melted at the thought of Dale. 'Oh, Father, he's so amazing and nothing like Mum always claimed Americans were like.' She started prattling then, telling him about the first time she'd seen Dale, how he'd tried to pay for the damaged supplies, and then about the sweet drops and how he always brought the children treats whenever he came to visit. She went on about his mechanical skills and how he'd trained engineers for flight squads, and how he'd put out the barn fire.

Nearly breathless and full of a soft and genuine adoration for Dale, she laid a hand over her heart while finishing, 'You would like him, I know you would.'

'He sounds like a man I'd like to meet.'

Remembering one thing she'd forgotten to mention, she then told him about how Dale was searching for Ralph and how she'd assisted in that, without his knowledge, and was still waiting for the report to be returned.

'This is the same man your mum went to see you about.'

It wasn't a question, merely a statement, yet she nodded and went on to explain, 'But she doesn't know him. Dale is not like Aunt Melody's—'

He held up a hand. 'I have remained neutral in all of Melody's affairs and will continue to do so.' Using the arms of his chair, he stood. 'No good comes from getting in the middle of someone else's romance, except,' he said, holding up a finger, 'when it's your daughter.'

The steam she'd been running on seeped out like a teapot boiled dry. 'He's not like Andrew either, Father. I offered to ask you to help in his search for Ralph, but he refused. He said he didn't expect that of me, or want it.'

He nodded and smiled briefly. 'Everything you mentioned are things I already know about Sergeant Dale Johnson,' he said. 'As you very well know, I converse with Norman regularly.'

She did know that, but had tried to tell herself their conversation wouldn't have included her private life, except for the fact she didn't have a private life. No one did right now.

'I'd like to know something else about Sergeant Johnson.'

She wet her lips before asking, 'What would that be?'

'You say you love him,' Father said, crossing the room to gaze out the window. 'Why do you say that?'

'Because I do.'

He turned around and the way he looked at her reminded her of when she'd needed to be scolded for misbehaviour. 'You said the same thing about Andrew, did you not?'

She stood and held her chin up. 'Yes, but I was young and didn't know any better. I've grown up, in many ways. No one has ever made me feel so wonderful, and...' The lump in her throat made it impossible to swallow. There wasn't anything she could do about the tears either. 'Nothing has ever hurt as bad as thinking I may never see him again.' She had to swallow before she could continue. 'But my feelings are only a piece of the reason I'm here. He means more to me than my feelings. It's hard for me to explain, but I want him to be happy. I want him to know that he's not alone over here. That I'm here and that I will do anything I can to...' Suddenly, she felt six years old again. 'I don't know, Papa, except that I don't want to live without him.'

The tears fell in earnest as her father's arms wrapped around her.

Dale had sat in the long and empty hallway most of the day. The meeting he'd been requested to attend had started at noon. By one, he'd answered all the questions he'd needed to and been asked to wait in the hall. He understood things were different in headquarters than what he was used to. Nothing happened quickly here. He also told himself there was nothing to worry about. He'd chosen his answers carefully, making sure not to point blame for the conditions of Thorpe Abbotts upon his arrival. However, he made sure to thank those in attendance for how the base functioned now.

Furthermore, his mind was too wrought with other worries. Kathryn worries. He'd barely slept last night, thinking about her and being haunted by the sadness in her eyes as they'd said goodbye. He'd put that sadness there and hated himself for doing so.

The opening of the door snapped his attention and he rose to his feet to assume the salute position as American officials filed out the door.

'At ease, Sergeant Johnson.'

Dropping his hand from a salute, Dale stood straight with both hands behind his back as Major Hilts walked over to him.

'You've been requested at another meeting, Sergeant,' Hilts said. 'Third door up on the right. Your transportation back to Thorpe Abbotts will be arranged afterwards.'

'Yes, sir,' Dale answered as an eerie sensation rippled his spine due to the request and the unusual smile on the Major's face.

'Third door on the right,' Hilts repeated before he spun around and walked down the hallway.

Really ready to have the day over and head back to Thorpe Abbotts, where he could wallow in his self-imposed misery over Kathryn, Dale walked down that hallway.

At the third door, he knocked and entered upon request.

'Sergeant Johnson, do come in,' a man standing near the table said. 'I'm Brigadier Hubbel Winslow.'

'Sir,' Dale replied, trying not to reveal the shock of standing face-to-face with Kathryn's father. He stood stiff, with his chin up, all the while imagining that as a Brigadier in the intelligence division, Winslow probably knew more about the time he and Kathryn had spent together than he did himself.

'Shut the door, Sergeant,' Winslow said. 'As you can imagine, this concerns my daughter.'

Dale closed the door and, unable to stop it, his mind went to the worst. Although she'd been fine, health wise, when he'd left last night, a number of things could have happened. 'Has something happened to Miss Winslow, sir?'

'No, nothing has happened to her, thank you for your concern,' Winslow said, gesturing towards a chair near the only table in the room. 'It's my understanding the two of you have become friends.'

Dale waited until the other man sat in the chair across the table before following suit, but answered, prior to sitting, 'Yes, sir, we have.'

'I'd like to know what you think about that, Sergeant Johnson. What your intentions are.'

Laying both hands on the table, a gesture to show he was not trying to hide anything, Dale replied, 'I've given that considerable thought, sir, and once the war ends, I intend to ask your permission to request her hand in marriage.' A sense of relief at admitting his plans aloud washed over him.

Winslow's eyebrows rose. 'Once the war ends?'

'Yes, sir.'

'That could be years from now.'

'I realise that, sir, and I intend to do my part to shorten it as much as possible.'

Winslow quirked a smile while asking, 'Have you asked Kathryn if she's interested in waiting that long?'

'No, I have not. I have not suggested marriage between the two of us at any time.' Just talking about her warmed his insides, but thinking about being parted from her for so long emptied him just as thoroughly. 'Kathryn is a very strong-willed woman and she's deeply committed to the children in her care, the family she lives with and her duties to do her part in the war efforts.'

'She is strong-willed,' Winslow agreed. 'Like her mother in that sense. Once she's set her mind to something, there's no changing it.'

'I discovered that upon meeting her, sir,' Dale replied. 'When some of her food supplies were accidentally damaged and I tried paying her for the damages.'

'She refused payment?'

'Yes, she did, several times,' Dale said, keeping his smile hidden. Thinking about how fiercely she'd denied his payments always made him grin. 'I ended up buying candy from other GIs with the money and distributed it to the local children.'

'That's how those sweet drops originated?'

Dale nodded. 'If she'd taken my money, that would have been the end of it. There would have been no candy drops.'

Winslow rested an elbow on the table while grasping his chin with his thumb and forefinger. 'I've heard a lot about you, Sergeant Johnson, from several people, including how you once told Kathryn the two of you could no longer be friends. Why was that?'

Dale stopped himself from blinking or sighing. 'Just following orders, sir.'

Winslow's brows lifted again. 'Someone ordered you to do that?'

'Yes, sir.'

'Who?'

Not one to rat on anyone, Dale simply said, 'A superior who was transferred afterwards.'

'Lieutenant Banks, I believe was the name.'

'Yes, sir.' He should have expected that. 'In his defence, the army has continuously warned all GIs about becoming too involved with the locals.'

'Norman disliked Lieutenant Banks, probably as much as you did.'

Dale chose only to nod and waited for the next question, the one that would ask why he hadn't maintained his distance.

Winslow leaned back in his chair and rested both hands on his lap. 'I like the things I've heard about you, Sergeant Johnson, of how you commanded your squadron to succeed at all times and of how you took it upon yourself to have Thorpe Abbotts turned around.'

Waiting for the proverbial other shoe to drop,

for he sensed it was coming, Dale remained stock-still.

With a slight nod, as if he knew Dale's thoughts, Winslow said, 'Now, I'd like you to tell me the real reason why you once no longer wanted to be Kathryn's friend and now you want to marry her after the war ends.'

'The truth behind both of those, sir, is because I love her.' Dale took a deep breath then, knowing that even though it weighed heavy inside him, that explanation didn't hold enough weight to sink fishing line. 'And my mother.'

'Your mother?'

The grimace on Winslow's face could have made Dale smile, if the matter wasn't so serious. The tighter in knots he'd become over Kathryn, the deeper the words he'd heard his mother say had taken root. 'My older brother left for the war several months before I did,' Dale said, 'and was set upon marrying the girl he was seeing before leaving. My mother told him not to do that, for the girl's sake. Mother said it wouldn't be fair for Ralph to expect Deloris to sit at home waiting for word if he's dead or alive and then miss him even more when his letters would arrive. Mother has friends, family, who lost husbands and sons in the first war and had referred to Mrs Shakes, the local librarian, and how the woman has blamed her lonely lot in life on the fact her husband died in the war after only two months of marriage.'

Dale had known Mrs Shakes, or Shakes-a-Lot as the kids had deemed her because she shook when she was mad, his entire life and had never seen the woman smile or be nice to anyone. That was precisely what he didn't want to happen to Kathryn. For her to become a Mrs Shakes.

'Did your mother give you that same advice?'

'No,' Dale said, letting his first grin show. 'She told me not to bring home an Italian girl. Her brother did that.' Dale lifted both brows at how heated family dinners could become when his aunt and uncle came over.

Winslow smiled. 'Given the renowned fiery temperament of some Italian women, she did offer some sound advice there.' He leaned forward and placed both hands on the table, fingers entwined. 'Tell me a bit more about your family. I understand you have a brother you've been looking for.'

'Yes, sir. Ralph John Johnson. The army seems to have lost all record of him.'

'Why is it so important that you find him?'

'Because he is my brother, and again for my family. I had a sister who died at the age of thirteen and, having witnessed the pain of my parents and experiencing my own over the loss, I don't want anyone in my family to go through that again. I don't want anyone I love to go through that again.' As his heart constricted, he added, 'Which also contributes to why I haven't spoken of marriage, of love, with Kathryn. I would never want her to experience that pain.'

'But it will be easier once the war is over? People still die.'

'I understand that, sir, it wasn't during a war that my sister died, leaving my parents with just us two boys.' Dale let that settle for a moment. 'Therein lies the truth, doesn't it, sir? I've never spoken of marriage to Kathryn because I'm afraid. Afraid of hurting her.'

'You are a wise man, Sergeant Johnson. I consider myself a seasoned man, both in war and in life, and I've been enlightened by our conversation. Though I've experienced loss, that of a child…? The pain that must ensue is incomprehensible to me. I have no idea how I might react in that situation and hope I don't ever experience it.' After a time of silence, the Brigadier said, 'I would like to invite you to my home this evening, Sergeant Johnson.'

'I appreciate the offer, Brigadier Winslow, but I am due back at my base today.'

'I've taken it upon myself to request your furlough lengthened and it has been granted. You're not due back until Saturday, at which time I've arranged transportation for you.'

Dale's mind instantly went to Kathryn, how fast he could make it to Norman's and spending the next two days with her. His hopes died, realising that would be impossible.

'I have a car waiting for us,' Winslow said.

Dutifully, Dale stood and followed the man out the door. They paused long enough for Dale to collect his jacket and duffel bag from the chair in the hallway, then proceeded onwards. After a maze of hallways, they exited the building and climbed into a large black Hillman Minx, most likely the exact one Kathryn's mother had travelled out to see her in.

'It's my understanding, sir, that your wife does not think very highly of Americans,' Dale said, once seated in the back alongside the Brigadier while another man started the car.

Winslow nodded. 'Pauline believes she has her reasons due to her sister Melody.'

'Kathryn mentioned her aunt Melody and cousin Allen,' Dale stated.

'I'm sure she did,' Winslow answered. 'And I'm sure she believes what she told you. I, on the other hand, would caution you to remember there are two sides to every story and those who play with fire shouldn't complain about getting burned.' Winslow then gave the driver instructions on a route to take.

Other than today, Dale had only been in London once before, on the day he'd arrived in England. He recalled a few things from that time, but as the car travelled along, the carnage he saw on both sides of the street staggered him. The rubble, massive piles of bricks and mortar, mounds of splintered wood and glass, along with huge buildings half blown away and hosting ghostly empty spaces, and people. The streets were full of people. Some workers were clearing away the debris, but others appeared to be just standing around and watching, like buzzards on a freshly killed carcase.

'London's in the midst of two wars,' Winslow said. 'The one you and our other allies are helping us fight and this internal one against the gangsters. The professional criminals. Even before the first bomb dropped, we knew what was to come and knew we needed all the able bodies possible. The prison doors were swung open, letting free anyone who'd almost completed their sentences and, to our misfortune, others took advantage of the confusion. Crime in the city has more than doubled and continues to. Every time a blackout is issued, the streets

come alive. Thieves wearing warden helmets
and armbands break in windows and doors and
walk away with whatever they want. The black
market has never been so successful and will
only continue to rise. You name it, they have it
and are happy to sell it. The average man doesn't
blink an eye at buying a few more ration tickets
for his family.'

Dale couldn't pull his eyes off the streets as
his thoughts centred around Kathryn. Grateful-
ness that her father had had the foresight to send
her away from all this filled him.

'It's nothing new,' Winslow continued, 'this
robbing from the rich to give to the poor reasoning has been around since the days of King
Richard, before then even. Our police force is diminished and our courts are overloaded. People
are not only taking shelter in the underground,
they're squatting and selling prime spots to the
highest bidder. It'll be years after the war before
we truly start to come around.'

Winslow let out a heavy sigh and, as compassion rose inside him, Dale turned and met the
other man's gaze.

'My family has served this country for generations,' Winslow said. 'I suspect if I had a son,
I would feel differently than I do.'

'About what?'

'I knew what was coming and I wanted Kathryn as far away from it as possible. Her mum wanted to keep her home, thinking that would be safer. She finally agreed to let Kathryn go as far as High Wycombe.'

Recalling all Kathryn had said, Dale felt inclined to admit, 'Kathryn feels part of the reason you sent her there was because of Andrew, the boy who asked to marry her.'

Winslow let out a low chuckle. 'There wasn't a chance in hell that would ever happen.' With a nod, he then said, 'But I'm glad she told you about Andrew. He may have contributed to the timing, but I'd already chosen her destination.'

Winslow was a formidable man and Dale could believe few ever questioned his decisions. 'It was a good choice, sir. Safe. Liveable.' Knowing there was a chance that could change, he added, 'A place she can survive.'

Winslow nodded, then shook his head. 'If she'd have stayed there.'

A chill shot through Dale so deeply his shoulders quivered. 'What do you mean, stayed there?'

'She's insisting I have her transferred,' Winslow said.

'Where to?' Dale shook his head. Where

didn't matter. 'You can't,' he said. 'She needs to stay right where she's at.'

'That's easier said than done,' Winslow said, never pulling his gaze aside. 'Which is why I requested your furlough. You have two days to convince Kathryn of that.'

Her parents' home, the very one that had housed the Winslows for generations, was relatively the same as when she'd left. *She* was the one who'd changed, which was why Kathryn was in the kitchen, assisting Annie with the meal that would soon be served to her family and the guest her father was bringing home. That hadn't changed, he often brought guests home. Kathryn was disappointed. Company would mean she wouldn't learn the details of her transfer for hours.

James's entrance into the kitchen confirmed Father was home and his expression confirmed his surprise to see her clad in an apron. With a sly grin, he asked, 'Does your mum know where you are?'

Despite her visit to Norman's a short time ago, Mum was not happy she was in London, or that she'd requested a transfer. Kathryn smiled at James. 'Yes, and, yes, she's not happy I'm in the kitchen, but I am.'

'I can tell,' he replied.

She untied the apron and hung it over the back of a chair. 'I suspect I'm expected in the front room?'

He nodded. 'I suspect so.'

As she walked towards the door, she whispered to Annie, 'I'll be back to help with the dishes.'

'Oh, no, you won't,' Annie replied. 'I won't have your mum mad at me.'

Kathryn left the kitchen with a smile on her face. Annie was one of the few people mum was never upset with and everyone knew it.

As she entered the front hall her smile slipped. Whoever Father had brought home was getting an earful from Mum. The next sound, that of a man's voice, sent her heart racing. And her feet. Kathryn raced across the marbled hall and entered the front room through the wide arched doorway. Her first impulse was to run across the room and jump into Dale's arms. Controlling herself was hard, but she managed to cross the room at a relatively normal speed.

She went straight to Dale's side, where she hooked an arm around his elbow.

'What are you doing here?'

'That was exactly what I wanted to know. What are *you* doing here?'

'I had to come here, to be transferred—'

'No.' He shook his head. 'No.'

She pulled her arm out of his and pressed a hand to the cramp-like pain in her stomach.

'I'm here to escort you back to Norman's,' he said sternly.

This wasn't how she'd expected him to respond. She'd done all this in order to be closer to him, but his expression said he wasn't about to listen to her reasoning. And she wasn't about to argue with him in front of her parents. She'd spent the day convincing them she had to be closer to Dale, and if he…

The hint of empathy in her father's eyes, and the triumph in Mum's, had Kathryn stopping her thoughts right there. 'Dinner will be served shortly.'

She couldn't recall a time when she'd run away from a scolding or argument, but right now, she needed to gather her wits. Her wherewithal. And gather the pieces breaking inside her before they shattered on to the floor. Therefore, she merely said, 'I'll go see to the place settings.'

She didn't go to the kitchen, Annie already knew how many would be eating. Instead, she went straight across the wide span of the hallway and into her father's study. There she shut the door hard enough that the books on the shelves, some of them as old as the house itself, shook so that their pages probably wrinkled. She truly didn't care. It had been her decision to leave Charlotte and Norman's and she hadn't come by that decision lightly. Nor would she change her mind. She'd been honest with everyone, had made a request that her father use his officer status for her, something she'd never done before, *and* stood up to her mum, proclaiming she knew what she was doing. And this is what she got for it? To be told she'd be escorted back?

Not on her life.

The knock on the door sent her anger to a boil. Hot enough that she could have spit in old Hitler's face right now.

She didn't turn around at the sound of the door opening, but did say, 'I don't want to talk to you right now.' It didn't matter who it was. She didn't want to talk to anyone.

The door shut, much quieter than she'd closed it.

'Well, you don't have much of choice.'

As much as she didn't want it to at this particular moment, the softness of Dale's voice sent ripples over her.

'Because I'm not staying out there with your mother any longer.'

Despite all the fury inside her, a smile pulled too hard on her lips to deny it completion. Drawing it back by pinching her lips together hard for a moment, she said, 'That's your fault for coming here.'

'You think that was on my own?'

A quiver coiled around her spine. Slowly, she turned about. 'How did you get here?'

'Your father requested a meeting with me after the one I'd been sent here to attend ended.' He moved closer, his feet quiet on the thick rug that covered the hardwood floors from corner to corner. 'That's where he told me that you'd requested a transfer and that it was my job to change your mind.'

'Father said that?' Disappointment shrouded her. She'd truly thought he understood and agreed with her request.

'Yes.'

Dale stopped less than a yard away and his nearness was already playing with her insides, including her ability to think. Twisting, she crossed the room to where the ladder on wheels rolled over the floor and along the top of the wall full of bookshelves. 'I'm not going back and you aren't going to change my mind.'

A frown, one that said he couldn't fathom her

reasoning, took over his face as he asked, 'Why do you want to leave? What's happened?'

She had to close her eyes as a curl of unexpected warmth coiled in the pit of her stomach. Focusing on how familiar it was, how real and complete it made her feel as it slowly spun upwards, she opened her eyes as it entered her heart. 'You,' she whispered. 'You happened.'

Dale smiled as he walked towards her and his eyes took on *that* shimmer when he held out a hand. 'Come here.'

She took a step forward, restraining the urge to hook her arms around his neck rather than take his hand. His fingers wrapped around hers and were the only thing touching her when his lips met hers. The kiss was so soft and gentle, it took her breath away like none of his other kisses had.

'We happened,' he said quietly, his lips brushing hers as he spoke. 'We happened.'

Her restraint was gone, leaving her with no limits when it came to the desires that threatened to completely overwhelm her. Throwing her arms around his neck, she held on as their lips met again, and again, and then pressed her entire length against his when their lips parted, taking the kiss as deep as it could become. The swirl of his tongue against hers was like a surge of electricity that made her feel more alive than imaginable.

Dale ended the kiss, long after it had left her body surging with an indescribable but extremely explicit desire, and held her close, giving them both a moment of reprieve.

When her breathing became as close to normal as it might ever be, she snuggled closer. 'Yes, we happened.'

Her eyes were closed and he did little more than place a soft kiss on the top of her head, so she couldn't see his smile, but knew it was there, dimples and all.

Who would have guessed a person's heart could be so full? So happy? Not her. He'd made that happen and she didn't ever want it to end.

Growing so content surrounded by his arms, she could have easily dozed off, considering she hadn't slept a wink the night before, but Kathryn drew in a breath and lifted her head. 'I left in order to ask my father to transfer me closer to where you are stationed. So we can see each other more often.'

The grief that overtook his face as he shook his head had her stepping backwards.

'I know it can't be every day, or even every week, but—'

'No, Kathryn. The base I'm at isn't like the

other one. It's busy, demanding. We barely have time to sleep and eat, and the countryside around it isn't safe. Not safe at all. It's not safe here in London either. You have to go back to Norman's.'

She shook her head. 'It's not safe anywhere.'

'But some are safer than others.' He took her hand, held it tight. 'Please, for me, will you consider going back? Where I know I don't have to worry about you.'

Chapter Eleven

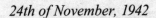

24th of November, 1942

Dear Diary,
I'm here in London. I was so certain this was what I needed to do and that Dale would be happy. Now I'm not so sure. Dale asked me to return to Norman's. I want to make him happy. I shouldn't be so selfish, but something inside me screams out that I can't return. I've come to trust my instincts, that sixth sense that I'd only ever heard about, but never experienced, and it tells me not to return.

I know Dale is worried for my safety, just as I am worried about his. There is nothing I can do back at Norman's, except for worry more. However, Dale's request for me to return was so sincere, I *told him I would think about it and that we could discuss it tomorrow. He agreed, so now I just need to figure out a way to convince him why I can't return. I have no idea how and hope writing about it will help me figure that out. You've done that before. More than once, while writing my thoughts between your pages, significant thoughts have formed. Things I may not have thought of otherwise and I'm counting on that happening again.*

Despite all the urgency inside me, the realisation we could all die tomorrow, we did have a lovely dinner this evening. Father thanked Dale for his service, saying that without men like him, without American support, we would not have fared as well as we have. To my surprise, Mum agreed and was more than pleasant to Dale. I understand some of that might be because she believes he'll convince me to return to Norman's, but I can't help but hope that she might also see why I love him like I do. I can't imagine life without him. I just can't.

It had been so long since she slept in a bed alone, Kathryn had a hard time falling asleep and staying that way. She kept reaching over to make sure that Patricia or Doreen hadn't fallen out of bed. Her thoughts would shift to Dale then, of him sleeping just down the hall, and she'd doze off, only to repeat the entire process over again.

After the fourth or fifth time, she gave up trying to sleep and merely stared at the darkness filling the room. Even if the sun was rising, she couldn't see it.

Her bedroom was not exactly as she'd left it, there had been no blackout curtains covering the windows. Those had come about after she'd been sent to the country. Other things had come about, too. Changed. During their row yesterday, Mum had made a show of telling her what had happened to many of the friends she'd had, back before the war had started. Several had perished, some had simply disappeared and a large number of them were either serving in one of the many auxiliary branches or had entered the workforce, replacing the men who were serving in the armed forces.

It had been clear that Mum wanted her to realise how lucky she was that Father had sent her away when he had, to where he had. Kathryn did realise that and was thankful for it, but what Mum didn't understand was that the war *had* changed her life. Changed who she was. She was no longer the young girl they'd sent away. She was a woman ready to live her own life.

She was still grateful for being who she was. The loss of so many saddened her and she held great empathy for their families. She even felt a form of remorse for having been privileged enough to have been sheltered from so much. Along with that shelter had come a sense of immunity. It was hard to explain. Although she fully understood there was a war happening, her family's social status had shielded her from the worst of it because they'd been able to afford to send her away.

When she'd arrived in London yesterday, her mind had been too focused on herself, on what she needed to do, to really notice the devastation, but she had afterwards, and now, and it had made her understand how precious life was, love was, with a new perspective.

No one knew what tomorrow might bring, nor would they ever. Life was like that. No one knew how long they had on this earth and the reality of the war raging on around them heightened that. However, what she now fully understood was that even if the world wasn't at war, she'd want to spend the rest of her life with Dale.

He wanted that, too. She just had to make him admit it.

Walking down the stairs a short time later, the rich aroma of coffee made her smile. Annie must have made some for Dale, which meant he was already up, too.

'Good morning,' she said while entering the dining room, her heart skipping every other beat.

Dale's grin was quick and charming. 'What are you doing up so early?'

'I'm not used to sleeping alone,' she answered honestly. 'How did you sleep?'

He lifted one brow and set aside the paper he'd been reading. 'Fine.'

'I explained to Annie how Oscar made coffee. How is it?'

'Good,' he said, lifting his cup to his lips. 'Real good.'

'I'm glad.' The ringing of the telephone didn't surprise her, it had rung a few minutes ago, too, and explained Father's empty chair.

Dale set his cup down and gestured towards the side table ladled with more breakfast options than she'd seen in years. 'James will drive us to High Wycombe after breakfast.'

The food suddenly turned unappetising. She shook her head. 'I'm not going back.'

He nodded slightly. 'I thought you'd given in too easy, but had also hoped you had come to your senses.'

'I have, that's why I'm not—'

'I don't need one more person to worry about,' he said. 'I have a crew, pilots, an entire base, not to mention a brother I'm still searching for and a family back home. I don't want to have to worry about one more person.'

She understood all that. 'That's why I want to be closer to you, so you won't have to worry and I can help—'

'I don't need your help. I never have. Not in finding Ralph or anything else.'

Having already determined convincing him wouldn't be easy, she quelled a bout of hurt and anger. 'You're just trying to be mean. Trying to make me—'

'See the truth,' he interrupted. 'The world is at war, Kathryn. If you won't go back for my sake, or for your parents, then do it for yourself. Do you have any idea how many people wish they could have been sent someplace safe?'

'Of course I do!' Anger boiled inside her. 'But I'm no longer a child who needs to be sent to safety. I'm a woman who knows what she wants.'

'What if what you want isn't what anyone else

wants?' He stood and shook his head. 'Your father should have let you marry Andrew.'

A chill overtook her and she was still contemplating a response when her father appeared in the doorway.

'Sergeant Johnson, I need to speak to you.'

The glance Dale sent her way was cold. Or maybe just her insides were. He was acting so differently. So unlike the person she knew him to be. She sank into the chair, trying not to accept the idea that Dale didn't want her. Not just near, but at all. Had she fallen in love with someone who would never love her in return? She couldn't believe that. Wouldn't believe that. It was just this war. This damnable war.

At the sound of feet running up the stairs, she jumped up and rushed into the front hall.

Seeing Dale disappear at the top of the stairs, she asked her father. 'What's happened?'

'The Germans are making a push to break up the beachhead,' he answered. 'A maximum-effort retaliation has been called.'

As her heart dropped to her feet, she asked, 'What's Dale doing?'

'Getting his things, he's been called back to the base.'

The front door opened and James appeared. 'The car's ready, sir.'

She spun back towards the stairway, Dale was running down them, carrying his duffel bag. Hurrying that way, she searched for something to say. Nothing formed by the time he arrived at the bottom step so she just wrapped her arms around his waist and held on.

He hugged her in return and then kissed the top of her head before he let her loose. 'I can't make you any promises, Kathryn. I can't. There's no future for us.'

He was gone then. Out the door.

The desperation she'd heard in his voice hung inside her, making her shiver and leaving her numb at the same time.

Mum's arm settled around her and squeezed softly before she said, 'Go get your things. We'll leave as soon as James returns.'

Numbness still enveloped her, but Kathryn shook her head. 'I'm not going back. I can't.' The tears came then, there was no holding them back. 'I love him, Mum. Love him more than I ever thought possible.'

Mum twisted about and folded both arms around her. 'Hush now, darling,' she whispered. 'Hush.'

They stood there for some time, Kathryn trembling and crying on her mum's shoulder in a way she hadn't done in years. When the worst of it passed—the tears, that is, the ache inside her wouldn't dull until she saw Dale again—she lifted her head and blew out a long and shaky breath. 'I do love him, Mum. It's not like before. Like Andrew.'

Mum was silent and still for so long Kathryn started to tremble all over again. Dale was wrong. There was a future for them. There had to be.

'Come,' Mum said quietly.

They walked into the study and Mum shut the door behind them.

Kathryn sat as Mother gestured to the sofa, where they'd spent hours reading the books on the shelves when she'd been little. Classic tales of long, long ago and places far, far away. That, too, seemed long, long ago, reading those books, snuggled in Mum's lap and imagining all those beautiful places the books described. And the heroes. Those stories were filled with so many wonderful heroes.

Mum sat down beside her and let out a heavy sigh. 'I should have told you all of this years ago. Your aunt Melody was never in love with a man named Doug Ralston. I don't even know if there is a man with that name. American or not.'

With her mind on Dale, the hero of her story, Kathryn shook her head, trying to clear it enough to grasp what Mum had said. 'Then who is Allen's father?'

'I don't know, but there was an American by the name of Leroy Wilson.' Mum drew in an audible breath before saying, 'Who both Melody and I thought we were in love with. It was before I'd met your father, before I understood true love. Leroy was extremely handsome and so full of himself he stood out in a crowd. We both were captivated by him, but, ultimately, to my dismay, he chose Melody over me. After Leroy shipped out, Melody discovered she was pregnant. My parents were beside themselves and eventually discovered Leroy's whereabouts, but he claimed there was no possible way he was the father of Melody's baby. So the story was invented that Melody and a man named Doug Ralston had been wed while he was stationed here and that he'd deserted her, went back to America without her.'

Shocked and confused, Kathryn asked, 'So is Leroy Allen's father or not?'

'Only your aunt Melody knows that,' Mum said, rising to her feet and walking over to desk. 'And if not for her and the story we all had to stick to for so many years, I would have sent you to America when this war started. That's what your father wanted, but I had to stick to the story I'd half started to believe myself and insist you stay here. Your father conceded because he loves me.'

'America? You would have sent me that far away just to keep me from marrying Andrew?'

'Andrew had nothing to do with it, you didn't love him and he didn't love you. We would have sent you to America to keep you safe. Now you're stuck here in the war-ravaged country.'

'How do you know I didn't love Andrew?'

'Oh, darling, there are things a mother just knows.' Mum sighed heavily. 'And as much as I don't want to admit it, I know that you do love Dale.'

'I do, Mum, so very much.'

Mum nodded. 'He loves you, too, but he's afraid. Afraid of what his love might do to you.'

'What do you mean?'

'There is no pain greater than losing someone we love. Dale understands that and he doesn't want you to experience it.' The strength in Mum's hands as they squeezed hers was solid. 'I don't want you to either, and, for your sake, I have to prepare you. The war hit a new level this morning. Maximum effort means every plane that's capable of flying will be and any man with any flying experience will be in them. What you need to be prepared for are the ones that won't come back.'

Kathryn's heart leapt into her throat.

Every plane capable of taking off had, loaded with anti-personnel bombs to be dropped simultaneously over the German concentration of troops behind the line. Because of the thick and heavy fog, they were having to circle around and around, trying to break out of the cloud cover, and to Dale that put nerve-racking at a new level. He kept his concentration on the gauges, reporting the engine performance and fuel consumption to the pilot at regular intervals, while also assessing, determining and reporting the distance between them and the planes circling with them.

He would have let out a sigh of relief once they broke the cloud cover, but there was no time, no relief either as other squadrons joined them, creating traffic in the sky that stretched out for over fifty miles, more maybe, as he calculated the numbers quickly. Collectively, the massive group made up of several squadrons flew over the North Sea, then turned slightly, angling their way towards Hamburg.

In the engineer's seat, with his back to the pilots, Dale continued his reporting over the interphone, including their speed and altitude, but his thoughts were on other things. The fact that there was only one-sixteenth of an inch of aluminium between him and all the fire power the Germans would soon be blasting their way. And Kathryn. She was front and centre in his mind, making him wish things were different. But they weren't. He'd done what he had to. British or American, a superior officer had given him an order and he'd followed it. He'd hurt her, saying the things he had, but he hadn't had a choice. She should never have left Norman's. She wasn't all to blame. He was just as guilty. He should never have fallen in love with her.

He was in no position to love anyone. In no position for someone to love him either.

He tried to clear his mind, knew he needed to concentrate on the tasks at hand. The Germans had been building their eighty-eight anti-aircraft guns since the first war had ended and thousands upon thousands of them pointed up at the sky, ready and able to take down aircrafts like duck hunters in October. Those eighty-eights weren't just guns, they were cannons. He'd seen planes return shot so full of holes they should never have made it back to England.

His only hope was that this plane, *The Belle of the Ball*, had the stamina to stay in the air despite it all. The Germans knew they were coming. Intelligence had cracked that code, which didn't make it any better or worse. It just was.

'Lock and load,' came over the interphone, and Dale sucked in a breath of icy air before making a destination report that gave them mere minutes before they'd be over their target.

The flak from the eighty-eights came first, shells bursting in the air all around them. Dale's gut sank. They'd be hit, there was no if, buts or maybes. The German planes came next, filling the air like a swarm of hornets stirred from their nest.

Orville Orson was in the pilot's seat and did a hell of a job manoeuvring the big and heavy *Belle* close enough to let the bombs fall in a rush that had them all sweating and swearing at the cold air that rushed in.

It was the turn around that got them. Rather than heading south, they'd been instructed to head back towards the North Sea.

The centre of that turn brought fighter planes so close Dale could see the German pilots. The sky was rumbling with them and they were having a field day taking down American planes. One after the other, American bombers, ablaze and falling apart, spiralled to the ground.

A couple of hits rattled the *Belle*, then a direct blow struck her hard. Dale knew even before checking the panel that the number four engine had been hit. Oil poured out of the right wing and the engine started to run wild, vibrating the entire plane.

Dale tried, but nothing worked. 'Number four's mechanism was shot apart,' he shouted into the interphone. 'I can't shut the engine down!'

'Hold on, boys,' Orville responded. 'It's going to get rougher.'

Just then number three engine took a hit, on the same wing, and the disproportion of power made the plane shake and rattle so hard things started to break. Power lines and hoses, bolts and flaps, let go, whipping around like debris in a windstorm.

Another shell hit the ball turret, sending shrapnel in all directions. Kale Jones was in the hole and scrambled up into the belly of the *Belle*. About that same time, Hank Whipper climbed down out of the top turret, knowing like the rest of them the *Belle* didn't stand a chance. She was going down.

Calculating quick, Dale gave an ETA of when they'd reach the North Sea. If they had any hope of parachuting out it should be over land, not sea, but at the same time, with the German planes surrounding them, jumping wouldn't give them much hope of survival. They'd be shot before they ever hit the ground or water.

Orville probably understood that as well, but he still ordered the radio operator Wayne Austin to send out a SOS and told everyone to grab their chutes.

The *Belle* took another direct hit, one that felt as if it pushed her backwards in the sky. Dale checked his panel, reporting the damage was useless, even if the gauges hadn't quit working, there was nothing that could be done.

Through the haze of flak, the ocean appeared beneath them, white caps foaming atop rolling waves, and his hopes, his dreams, seemed to flash before his eyes, each one unfulfilled. He saw Kathryn, his mother, his father and sister, Ralph and an assortment of others before Kathryn appeared again, calling his name, rushing towards him.

'There's nothing left for us to do, boys. Gotta ditch *Belle*!'

The pilot's shout brought Dale around and he scrambled off the seat, across the bomb base and through the radio operator's room to the waist of the plane, where others were gathering.

'Get ready to start pitching,' Dale instructed as he reached for the emergency door pull. As engineer that was his job. Nothing happened, so he pulled on it again. Then kicked at it, which was useless. 'Get me a screwdriver!' he shouted. When one appeared, he took it and pried on the emergency release until it broke loose.

Anything not bolted down was tossed out: guns, ammunition, armour plates. Next went the heavy parachutes and, finally, everyone pulled off their heavy flight boots and tossed them out, knowing the boots would weigh them down when they hit the water.

They all ran back to the radio room, sat on the floor, knees bent in front of them and leaning against the man behind them. Dale was the last one to sit down and cupped the back of Wayne Austin's head, a drilled precaution to keep the other's man neck from snapping when they hit the water.

Time seemed to slow to a snail's crawl and, though the plane was still vibrating and making more noise than a runaway freight train, an eerie silence echoed inside Dale's head. They were still travelling over a hundred miles an hour and would come to a dead stop upon hitting the water. The impact would shatter the plane, she'd fill with icy water immediately and, in less than a minute, completely sink below the water.

Dale reached into his pants pocket, pulled out

his knife, then stuck it in his flight jacket pocket for easy access. He'd need it to cut the ropes holding the life rafts on the sides of the plane.

They were still going down, fast, flak was still exploding around them and all Dale could think of was the picture of Kathryn in his wallet and how it was going to get wet. Get ruined.

His eyes burned as he silently said, 'I'm sorry, Kathryn. So, so sorry.'

Chapter Twelve

2nd of December, 1942

Dear Diary,
It's been a week and, though Father has tried, I have tried and even Mum has tried, we can't find where Dale is. All we do know is that he wasn't on one of the planes that returned from the blitz. Dozens upon dozens were shot down. Father says it will be weeks, months, before every man is accounted for. I have to believe that Dale survived. That his plane went down, but that he survived. If I don't, I will die myself. I can't believe how foolish I was. Why I waited so long to admit my love.

From the moment we met, I knew Dale was special. He made me feel special. He made me forget there was a war. Made me happy when nothing had for months. He did that for others, too. The children with his sweet drops. I never even got the chance to tell him about Ralph. He's here. In England. Only a hundred miles from Thorpe Abbotts. At least he was, until the blitz. If I could live the past seven months over again, there are so many things I'd do differently. I'd allow myself to fall in love with Dale the minute I'd met him and ask him to marry me. Yes, I'd ask him to marry me.

The idea of that almost makes me smile despite the tears that haven't stopped falling. I can almost see the look on Dale's face. Of course he would have rattled off some nonsense about there not being a future for us, but I'd have told him that was hogwash. We happened, he said to me the other evening, and that's just what happened. We. We fell in love. How wonderful the following months would have been being married to him. How truly wonderful.

I know that wouldn't have made sitting here any less painful, not knowing any easier, but I would have been Mrs Dale Johnson, the person I believe I was destined to become.

Kathryn's heart was racing so fast she couldn't breathe and tremors had her entire body shaking, even as Mum held her hands tight as they sat side by side on the sofa.

'Dale was on a B-17 known as *The Belle of the Ball*,' Father said. 'She crash-landed in the North Sea. The entire crew managed to get in the life rafts and were picked up by a naval ship.'

'Oh, thank God,' Mum whispered.

Tears were again rolling down Kathryn's face. 'Where is he? Where's Dale?'

'Well, darling, the intel I received said that a pilot was trapped in the cockpit and Dale went in to save him. A fighter plane dropped a bomb just then and though all the men, including Dale, did manage to get in the lifeboats and on to the naval ship, Dale was severely injured.'

'H-how severe?' Kathryn forced herself to ask through her burning throat.

'He was stabilised and then put on a hospital ship bound for the United States. I'm waiting to hear more, but for now, that's all I know.'

'Stabilised,' Kathryn said, trying to get control of her racing mind. 'So he's alive.' She jumped to her feet. 'I have to go to him. I have to go to America.'

'I knew you'd say that,' Father said. 'But you can't. There is no way for you to get there.'

Mum grasped one of her hands. 'Your father's right, darling.'

Kathryn shook her head. The past few days had been nightmarish, but they had brought her closer to her mother than they'd been in years. 'Mum, what if that was Father? What would you do?'

Mum's lips, pinched tight, trembled as she closed her eyes.

'Mum?'

Opening her eyes, Mum smiled slightly before turning to Father. 'There has to be a way, Hubbel.'

'Pauline.' Father shook his head. 'Air service is strictly regulated to the war effort and transoceanic travel is too dangerous. German U-boats are everywhere.'

'Dale's on a ship,' Kathryn said, fear overcoming her again.

'Hospital ships are protected by the Geneva Convention,' Father replied.

'Then put her on a hospital ship,' Mum said.

Kathryn nodded in agreement as Mum stood and wrapped an arm around her.

'Pauline—'

'Hubbel, there is a way and you will find it.' Hugging her closer, Mum then said, 'Come along, Kathryn, and don't worry, your father will find a way to get you to America.'

Kathryn went along with her mum, out of the room and up the stairs, and surprisingly, every step became easier to take. She'd find a way to get to Dale's side. War efforts and U-boats be damned.

As her mind travelled down several routes, little Phillip and his mother came to mind, making her stop in her tracks.

'Mother, a child who lived with Charlotte and Norman, his name was Phillip Newman. His mother had married an American and she said the army was transporting her and Phillip to America, that they do that regularly.'

'I'll check into that,' Mother said.

'I don't know what her name is. Newman was Phillip's name, so it must be something different now, but she—'

'Don't worry, we'll look into it first thing in the morning.'

Anticipation grew too strong inside her. 'I can't wait until morning. We have to go now.'

'Darling, it's not safe to go out after dark. London is not the town it used to be. As soon as the sun goes down, evildoers fill the streets.' Pulling her towards her bedroom door, Mum said, 'You try to get some sleep and I promise, we'll check into it first thing in the morning.'

Grateful for all her mother had done for her the past weeks, Kathryn turned to say, 'Thank you, Mum, I don't know what I would have done these past few weeks without you.'

Mum opened the bedroom door and took a step into it. 'After I returned from seeing you at High Wycombe, I came home and entered this room, and sat on that bed and cried.'

'Why?'

'Because you'd made me see the truth. You can't be my little girl for ever. As much as I wish you could, you can't.' Mum then kissed her cheek. 'But I can be just as proud of the woman you've become as I was the little girl you were and I will always want you to be happy and safe and well cared for. I trusted Charlotte and Norman to do that when I couldn't and now I'll trust Dale to do it.'

'He will,' Kathryn said, hugging her mum close. 'He will.'

'I know he will, or I wouldn't be helping you find him.' After another gentle kiss on her cheek, Mum said, 'Now, to bed with you. We'll check on things first thing in the morning.'

Mum did more than check. As soon as James returned from taking Father to his office the next morning, Mum had James drive them to the docks. A uniformed man met them at the car.

'Mrs Winslow, I've found the woman you are looking for,' the man said. 'Right this way.'

Although unsure exactly who they were meeting, Kathryn followed beside her mother, their arms locked at the elbows. They were taken into a small, sparkling clean room, with a small table and two chairs. The man left, but returned a moment later, with a woman and small child.

'Kathryn!'

Her heart flipped so fast and hard it nearly choked her. She wouldn't have recognised Phillip if she hadn't known his voice. His was thinner and pale. Kneeling down to enclose him in her arms, Kathryn looked up at Phillip's mother, who was almost as unrecognisable as her son. 'You're still here?'

'Yes,' his mum replied. 'The process is much longer than we anticipated, but I can't send Phillip back, we are hoping to be on the next ship.'

'I'm not here to—' Kathryn stopped. Phillip, still in her arms, had slumped, as if sad that she wasn't here to take him back.

'What's taking so long?' Mum asked, then held out a hand. 'I'm Pauline Winslow, Kathryn's mother.

'Joyce Fredrickson,' the woman said while shaking Mother's hand. 'The paperwork for one.

It's much more complicated than I expected. Mounds of forms to fill out, in triplicate, and more documents that you have to read and sign off that you did. Both of us had to have physicals.' Her face turned beet red. 'Stripped down to nothing. But it's all in order now and we are hoping to be on the next ship. The last one only had room for ten women. There are hundreds of us waiting, but several are too far along now.'

'Too far along?' Kathryn asked.

'Yes, a woman can't be more than six months pregnant and babies have to be at least three months old.'

Kathryn's hopes of seeing Dale any time soon were sinking.

'Well, Kathryn was curious about how Phillip was faring,' Mum said. 'Would you mind if we sent a care package for you? Things you can use here and take with you when you sail?'

'I couldn't ask—'

'You aren't asking,' Mum said. 'I am. Would that be all right?'

'I can't even begin to say how much we'd appreciate it,' Mrs Fredrickson said, bowing her head slightly.

Mum and Mrs Fredrickson visited for a short time, talking about things they could use, and Kathryn used the time to tell Phillip about the other children, how Patricia had finally lost a tooth after Doreen had lost four, and other things she thought he might like to hear. Then, she hugged him soundly and kissed him goodbye, telling him a surprise would arrive soon.

Once in the car, Kathryn said, 'Thank you. That was very kind of you.'

Mum nodded while taking her gloves off and sliding them into her pockets. 'Nonsense. I'll have James deliver the things this afternoon. While we figure out something else.' Pointing out the window, she added, 'That will not do.'

Kathryn readily agreed. 'She's been waiting four months.'

'Precisely.'

To their surprise, Father was home when they arrived. 'We don't have much time,' he said as they walked through the door. 'If this is truly what you want, we have to hurry.'

'You've found passage?' Kathryn asked.

'Yes, on a hospital ship. You'll be expected to work, help out.'

'I'll do anything. Anything.'

Her father's eyes were on her mum. 'Is this what you want?'

Kathryn's insides hiccupped. She hadn't thought about this piece, not in its entirety. She'd be leaving her parents, her family, possibly for ever. Tears came to her eyes as a sob bubbled up her throat.

'Nurse!' Dale shouted. His throat was raw from all his shouting, all his complaining, but he wasn't about to stop.

'There's no need to shout, Mr Johnson,' a female voice said. 'I'm right here.'

Although her voice was kind, it didn't change any of the feelings inside him. 'How the hell was I supposed to know that? I can't see a damn thing. When can these bandages come off?'

'Not until we arrive in America.'

He'd been told that. Told how glass had been embedded in both eyes. He'd also been told that his left arm was broken and the weight said it was casted. The other hand was bandaged, as were both legs. Only his mind was working and his voice. 'Did you deliver my message?'

Her sigh was soft. 'I will send it as soon as we arrive.'

'You can't wait that long,' he argued. 'Use the ship-to-shore radio.'

'I would if I could,' she said. 'Now just relax.'

But he couldn't relax. Not being able to open his eyes, not being able to see, messed with all his senses. He didn't even know how long it had been since the *Belle* had gone down.

Didn't know how long it had been since he'd seen Kathryn.

See Kathryn. He needed to get over the idea of ever seeing her again. Her smile, her emotion-filled eyes, her sweet, perfect body? Although one arm was kept motionless by the cast and the other hand bandaged, the doctors and nurses had warned him not to try to take the eye patches off. That he could cause more harm.

Disgust filled him.

He could be permanently blind. The doctors had said as much. Going stateside, going home, was the best thing. He'd told her there was no future for them. And there wasn't. He wasn't worthy of her. He'd let his own family down. His mother. Father. Ralph. And Kathryn. She'd left Norman's because of him. Put herself in harm's way because of him.

'Nurse!'

'I'm right here.'

'I need something to help me sleep,' he said. 'Sleep until I get home.'

Sleep didn't help. Nothing did. He was in sorry shape. A sorry man. Not at all what any woman needed.

He wasn't any more used to not seeing when he arrived in America than when he'd left Europe. The movement, being transferred from the bed to wheelchair and then being pushed around, made him more seasick than the ship had. Then there was the lack of control. Of not seeing where he was going and being solely dependent upon someone else.

As unimaginable as it was, he was happy to finally be settled on to a bed, where nothing was moving, nothing made his head spin.

'Sergeant Johnson?'

Recognising the voice, he said, 'I thought you'd have stayed on the ship.'

'Not until I see you settled,' she said.

Her name was Suzie Crompton. And he imagined she was tiny. Had to be with how soft and gentle her touch was. She also had tenacity. Considering she hadn't smothered him with a pillow during their long journey. 'I'm settled.' Feeling a bit guilty over how he'd treated her, he added, 'But thanks for all you've done.'

'You're welcome,' she replied, straightening his pillow. 'I also mailed your letter.'

A knot formed in his stomach. 'Just the one?'

'Yes, just the one.'

He drew a breath and nodded. He'd dictated several letters, but had her destroy all but the last one. That one was to Norman, asking to let the children know he was on his way to North Dakota and to give Kathryn his best wishes for her future. The Brigadier was a smart man and would have sent her back to Norman's.

Dale swallowed hard. He'd been right when he told her they didn't have a future together, now he just had to get used to it.

'Do you need something for the pain?'

'No,' he said. He could no longer sleep through life. He had to face it. Face whatever came to be.

'The doctors will be making their rounds first thing in the morning.'

'Is it day or night?'

'It's seven thirty in the evening,' she said. 'They'll be bringing food soon. I'll help you eat and then let you sleep.'

For the first time, he was curious to know a touch more about her. 'Are you married?'

'I don't know.'

'How can you not know?'

'I haven't heard from my husband in four months.'

His throat swelled. 'You'll hear from him soon.'

'I hope so.' She patted his hand. 'I'm going to go get you some water.'

She did so, which he drank, then she fed him.

To his surprise, hers was the first voice he heard in the morning. Telling him it was time to wake up.

The patches had gone beyond irritating. Every time he woke up, he tried opening his eyes, and not being able to hadn't got any easier.

'Good morning, Sergeant Johnson,' a male voice said. 'How are you this morning?'

Blind. Irritated. Lovesick considering the dreams full of Kathryn last night. Dale settled for, 'Fine.'

'I'm Dr Stark. Nurse Crompton has filled me in on your injuries and will help me remove your bandages and patches, but don't open your eyes until I tell you to.'

Dale mentally braced himself. The time was here. The result of the patches being removed would determine if he would ever see again. Half of him didn't care. He would never see Kathryn again either way. 'All right.' Then a fear overcame him and he reached blindly to stop anyone from touching him. 'What day is it? What's the date?'

A gentle touch grasped his hand and lowered it to the bed. 'It's Thursday, December twenty-fourth,' Nurse Suzie said.

A month. It'd been a full month since he'd seen Kathryn. The date settled deeper into his mind. 'Christmas Eve?'

'Yes,' Suzie whispered, squeezing his hand. 'A time of miracles.'

* * *

Kathryn washed her hands in the sink of the narrow galley and then made her way towards the nurses' quarters where she shared a small berth with five other women. Overall the accommodations were far better than what she'd expected. Actually, she hadn't had time to expect anything. Within twelve hours of arriving home with Mum that morning, she'd flown from London to Liverpool aboard a large British plane. Mum and Father had flown with her and saw her aboard the large hospital ship. It had been a tearful farewell, but also a joyous one, knowing what was on the other end of her voyage. Dale.

She hadn't been allowed to bring much with her, only a few clothes. Mum had said they'd ship anything else she needed once she was settled, but Father had said that might be impossible for months yet, so he'd handed over an envelope thickly stuffed with money already converted into American dollars. Because of that, and because of who he was, he'd then escorted her to the officers' quarters, where he'd insisted her personal belongings, including the money and important papers, be safely stored.

She was to retrieve everything upon arriving in America. Where she'd also be reunited with Dale.

He filled her mind day and night. Even while completing her twelve-hour shifts of stripping beds, washing sheets and remaking beds. It wasn't strenuous work, merely busy, and she didn't mind that. Every day got her one day closer to America. She refused to believe Dale wouldn't be happy to see her.

The ship had made several stops, picking up injured soldiers until all the one hundred beds had been full, before heading out to sea. It was all new to her, but she hadn't minded a single thing and eagerly awaited reaching port.

A smile tugged on her lips. Two more days and that would happen. They were scheduled to arrive in the port of New York City on December 26th.

'That's an awfully big smile.' Beverly Roseau was another laundry volunteer. 'Is it because your shift is over?'

Kathryn shook her head, but then nodded. 'Only two more.'

Beverly was a thin woman, with a head full of black curls that bobbed as she nodded. 'Still counting the days.'

'Yes, I am,' Kathryn didn't mind admitting. 'I'm anxious to see America.'

'And that handsome husband of yours.'

The thrill that raced through her nearly stole her breath. 'Yes,' Kathryn said. In order for her to stay in America upon arrival, she had to have an apt reason. Father had taken care of that by forging a stack of papers. Marriage documents. They were indeed forged because Dale knew nothing about their false marriage. They had never talked of marriage, and though that worried her slightly, she had readily become accustomed to being called Kathryn Johnson or Mrs Johnson.

With a half-grimace, half-smile, Beverly asked, 'Would you mind helping me with a patient? He's too large for me to roll and change his bedding by myself.'

'Of course,' Kathryn agreed, following Beverly down the hallway. Each volunteer was assigned a specific area, specific beds to change, and she was lucky that the patients in her unit were mobile enough they didn't mind getting out of bed while she changed their bedding.

'Thanks,' Beverly said. 'He's on the end and bandaged from head to toe.'

They'd entered the area lined with sets of bunk beds on both sides of the room. Everything was stark white. The metal beds, the walls, the floors and the patients themselves, clothed in their white gowns.

Kathryn had quickly gotten used to the strong smell of bleach and no longer noticed it, just as she'd gotten used to seeing so many partially clothed men.

They arrived at the man's bed, who was indeed covered with bandages and sleeping soundly. That had been hard to get used to, waking them to change their bedding, but it had to be done, as the charge nurse had insisted the very first day.

'I haven't seen him awake in three weeks,' Beverly said.

'Me either.'

A man's voice made Kathryn's heart stop. Dale was always on her mind and every so often a tall man with dark hair would cause her to take a second look, but this was the first time a voice had done that. She glanced at the upper bunk, but saw nothing except an arm.

'And I've never seen you asleep,' Beverly said to the man who was in the upper bunk, her cheeks turning pink. 'Don't worry about him,' Beverly continued while removing the top sheet from the bandaged man's bed. 'He's a rounder if you've ever met one.'

The man in the upper bunk laughed and that

was enough to assure Kathryn it wasn't Dale.
That would have been impossible, which meant
her mind was playing tricks on her.

Having helped others with the task, she and
Beverly made quick work of rolling the sleeping and bandaged man, slipping the clean sheet
beneath him, rolling him again to tuck in the
other side, then repositioning him to gently pull
the old sheet out from beneath him and finally
covering him with a clean one.

'You two sure are quiet down there,' the man
on the top bunk said.

Better prepared this time, Kathryn's heart
only fluttered slightly. It must be because he
was an American. She'd heard other Americans
speak, though, and they hadn't reminded her so
much of Dale.

'Because we know you're listening.' Beverly
said.

The metal braces of the bunk rattled as his
legs dropped over the side. 'Got secrets, do you?'

Kathryn kept gathering up the used sheets
while Beverly laughed, telling the man he'd
never know her secrets.

He dropped to the floor and the sheets in
Kathryn's arms fell to the floor. The resem-
blance was too uncanny for it to be anyone else.
Excitement raced through her, but quickly ebbed

as she thought about how hard Dale had looked for his brother.

Without further thought, Kathryn stomped around the end of the bed. 'Ralph Johnson, do you have any idea how worried people have been about you?'

He shook his head. 'How do you know—?'

'His name's not Ralph,' Beverly said.

'Yes, it is.' Kathryn kept her gaze on Ralph. 'Isn't it?'

His grin alone said he was a relative of Dale's and the likeness of it sent her heart thudding. Ralph was alive. Dale would be so happy.

'Yes, it is. My name's Ralph Johnson.' Ralph grinned. 'Damn, it even feels good to say it.'

Beverly eyed him critically. 'Then why—?'

'There was a clerical error.' Ralph shrugged. 'When I arrived at boot camp, they'd had me down as John Ralph instead of Ralph John and, while telling them they had that wrong, I made a joke about my last name being Johansson instead of Johnson. My best bud started calling me Junior Johansson and somehow it stuck.' He frowned as he turned from Beverly to her. 'Who are you? How do you know who I am?'

In the split-second Kathryn found herself tongue-tied, Beverly answered, 'This is Kathryn Johnson.'

'Johnson?' Ralph said. 'Are we related?'

Kathryn nodded.

'How?'

She shrugged. Her plan had been for Dale to know about their false marriage before anyone else.

'You don't know how we're related?' he asked.

Beverly was frowning, and staring at her oddly.

Drawing in a breath, Kathryn nodded. 'I'm married to your brother, Dale.'

Beverly gasped while Ralph said, 'No.'

'Yes,' Kathryn said, swallowing hard.

'Dale?' He shook his head. 'My brother, Dale?'

She nodded. 'Yes, your brother, Dale.'

'That's impossible.'

'No, it's not.' A flash of fury had her adding, 'I have the paperwork to prove it.'

Running a hand through his hair, Ralph shook his head. 'You could never have met my brother. He's in Buchanan, North Dakota.'

Understanding rushed over Kathryn, yet it was his fault that he didn't know where Dale was. 'No, he's not,' Kathryn said. 'He enlisted after you did. Something you'd have known if you'd ever written a letter home.'

Ralph turned visibly white. 'He did?'

She nodded.

'And he's here?' He shook his head. 'I mean, in England? Where?'

Keeping her voice from cracking was difficult, but Kathryn explained how Dale had been stationed at High Wycombe, and then Thorpe Abbotts, and then about his plane going down. Refusing to believe otherwise, she insisted he was doing fine now and should have already arrived in America and that she was on her way to meet him.

The colour had returned to Ralph's face and, with a wide smile, he grabbed her waist with both hands and lifted her off the floor. 'Just when was thinking I be spending another Christmas alone, I get a sister!'

Chapter Thirteen

25th of December, 1942

Dear Diary,
It has been an entire month since I've seen
Dale, and I miss him as much as ever.
Perhaps more. It's Christmas Day and a
miracle has happened. Ralph is here on
the ship. Been here the entire time. I had
never been to the lower deck, where he is,
so hadn't realised he was on board. He'd
been hit by shrapnel and because that had
happened on his twenty-fifth flight, after
having surgery to remove the shrapnel,
he's being sent home. We spent hours talk-
ing about things last night, mainly Dale
and their family. Ralph's a lot like Dale,
but even more of a jokester, and is nearly

as excited to see Dale as I am. We will arrive tomorrow.

Tomorrow!! I simply can't stop smiling. However, I am nervous. Especially now that Ralph believes Dale and I are married. I find myself worried over my deception. It was necessary, but, it could put Dale in a precarious position and me if I'm caught. And Father. All of that makes me nervous. I've never done anything like this and wonder if I should allow it to continue.

Kathryn's head was pounding. She'd never experienced anything like this before in her life. The papers, giving her permission to remain in America as Dale's wife, had all been in order, so that process had gone swiftly—due to an officer from the ship. It was what came next. The waiting. She had expected to arrive, go to the hospital and find Dale.

That wasn't to be. After escorting her to a military headquarters building, where he stayed with her until her papers were all processed, the ship's officer had delivered her to another area of the large building, telling her that someone would soon collect her and then left. She'd now been here for hours and hours. Her, her suitcase holding her clothes and a stack of papers including her marriage papers and birth certificate, and her purse stuffed with money, sitting on a hard metal chair, watching people walk by.

Her stomach was growling and her eyes burned as she tried to keep them open. It had to be late. Very late.

'You're still here?'

Kathryn lifted her gaze and recognised one of the women she'd spoken to hours ago. An older woman with grey hair and brilliant green eyes.

'Yes,' she replied.

'Come with me,' the woman said.

As tired as she was, Kathryn still jumped to her feet. 'Have you found my husband? Know where he is?'

'No, but I'll take you to a hotel so you can get some rest.'

'I can't leave, I have—'

'Honey,' the woman said softly. 'It's after eight o'clock at night and you're exhausted.' The woman waved to a man sitting at a desk near the door. 'Corporal, come collect this woman's luggage.'

As the man hurried across the room, the woman said, 'I'll find out what's going on and send word to the hotel. You might as well wait in comfort and get some sleep…'

Too tired to think clearly, Kathryn agreed, but

as they followed the Corporal, she said, 'There's another soldier, one who was on the ship with me, his name is Ralph Johnson, he's looking for my husband, too. They're brothers.'

'You mentioned that earlier,' the woman said. 'My name is Edith Price. There's a hotel a few streets from here, but we'll take my car. Do you have a heavier coat?'

Kathryn shook her head. The jacket she was wearing, the one she'd worn to Liverpool, was the only one she'd brought along. Surely it would do for now.

The moment she'd stepped outside, she discovered her jacket wouldn't do at all. She'd never breathed air so cold. So cold it struck her clear to her bones.

'I have a blanket in my car,' Edith said. 'And the hotel isn't far.'

'Thank you,' Kathryn said, her teeth chattering. 'I appreciate your help.'

She did appreciate the help and appreciated it even more when Edith helped her acquire a hotel room.

After showing her how the lights and plumbing in the small, but clean, room worked, Edith walked back to the door. 'Lock the door, take a bath and crawl into bed. I'll contact you as soon as I have any information.'

It might have been exhaustion, or worry, or frustration, or a number of other things that brought tears to Kathryn's eyes. 'Thank you.'

'Lock the door behind me,' Edith reminded her.

Following Edith's advice, Kathryn locked the door, but, too worn out to take a bath, she climbed on to the bed.

What felt like mere minutes later, her eyes, sore and feeling sand-filled, snapped open again at the sound of a knock.

Jumping off the bed, she twisted an ankle, not realising she still had her shoes on. Without asking who might be on the other side, she unlocked the door and pulled it open.

'What were you doing? I've been knocking for half an hour.'

She blinked twice before able to completely focus. 'Ralph?'

'Yes, it's me.' He stepped into the room and shut the door. 'I have good news and bad news, which do you want first?'

Dale had never been so frustrated in his life. Or mad. Madder than mad. He was downright furious. The army refused to let him sign up for a second tour.

'There's no sense in getting yourself so worked up,' Suzie said while neatly folding and packing his clothes into the army-issued duffel bag.

It wasn't his bag, his was still in England. Where *he* should be.

'I can see just fine,' he answered. 'And by the time I get to England, this cast will be ready to be taken off and I will no longer need this damn thing.' He slapped the arm of the wheelchair. 'Don't need it now.' His leg wasn't broken, but shrapnel had sliced his calf open and the damaged muscles and ligaments still wouldn't let him put much weight on his right leg.

'I know you can see and you should be thankful for that.'

Suzie was as no-nonsense as ever. She'd been the first thing he'd laid eyes on once the patches had been removed. As plump as a pumpkin with a mass of fuzzy red hair, she wasn't the prettiest woman he'd ever seen, certainly not compared to Kathryn, but Suzie had been downright beautiful to him three days ago when he'd realised he could see again.

'I am thankful for that,' he said, not feeling overly thankful.

'And you should be thankful for going home,' she said.

Home. That's where the army was sending
him. A set of army-green clothes and a train
ticket to North Dakota was what he was getting
for his service and there was no negotiating.
Most men, and women, didn't want to negotiate
a free trip home. He just wasn't most people. He
was going home empty-handed. He had no news
to tell his parents about Ralph. He was empty-
hearted, too. His heart was back in England.

'There,' Suzie said, 'everything's packed.'
Reaching down, she pulled something out of a
bag she'd set down earlier. 'You'll want to wear
this. It's cold out.'

An odd sensation rippled across his chest at
the sight of his flight jacket. 'Where'd you get
that?'

'You've had it with you the entire time,' she
said. 'Your billfold is in the pocket.'

Dale grabbed the coat and dug in the pocket,
pulling out the wallet.

'I hope you don't mind,' Suzie said. 'It was
still damp, so I took everything out and dried
them out.'

His heart skipped a beat as he pulled out the
picture of him and Kathryn and his eyes stung
as he examined it closely.

'It faded a bit, but you can still see how beautiful she is,' Suzie said.

His throat swelled. 'Yes, I can. She is.' The bout of emotion that rippled through him had him looking up at Suzie. 'Thank you. I don't know why you stuck beside me this entire time, but thank you for all you've done.'

'You're welcome.'

'Why have you?' He shook his head, not sure how to say it, 'Taken such good care of me?'

'Because I like you. You remind me of my husband and I hope that, if he's hurt, there's someone looking out for him.'

He took her hand and squeezed it. 'You'll hear from him soon. I know you will.'

She nodded and then leaned down and kissed his cheek. 'Thank you. And despite how ornery you've been, I'm going to miss you.'

'I'm going to miss you, too,' he admitted. 'Despite how ornery you've been.'

They both laughed, which felt good.

'Stand up, I'll help you get your coat on,' she said. 'The bus is out front to take a good dozen of you to the train station.'

'Where will you go?' he asked while shrugging into the coat.

Her smile wasn't as genuine as she tried to pretend it was. 'I'll ship out again soon. Back to pick up another boatload of those needing nursing care on their trip home.'

Dale nodded. 'If you ever get as far west as North Dakota, you have my address.'

'I do.' Suzie laid a hand on his arm. 'Be patient, you'll heal faster.'

'I'll try,' he said. He'd never been patient, he'd never been this frustrated either. The war was still raging on overseas, any number of things could happen to Kathryn. Might already have. He had no way of knowing, but unable to do anything besides think during the long voyage home, he'd had plenty of time to think. Hubbel Winslow had said there was no chance he'd have let Kathryn marry Andrew and, though Winslow hadn't said it, Dale didn't have much hope that the Brigadier would have let Kathryn marry him either.

Suzie handed him a pair of crutches, the other thing the army was giving him. 'You'll need these.'

Dale shook his head and took off towards the doorway, but halfway down the long corridor, when the pain was too much, he grabbed the crutch Suzie held out. 'I only need one.'

'That's good,' she said. 'Considering you only have one arm that's not in a cast.'

'Maybe I'm not going to miss you.' He would miss her, but not nearly as much as he missed Kathryn. If he had it to do over again, he'd have married Kathryn as soon as his stubborn mind had realised he was in love with her and sent her home. Not her home. His. North Dakota. If he had, she'd be there now, safe and sound and waiting for him. But none of that had happened. Nor would it. Furthermore, considering how he'd left her, she probably hated him and he couldn't blame her.

Suzie walked with him all the way to the bus. While they were waiting to board, with the cold wind chilling him to the bone and his leg aching, an army delivery boy arrived, asking if he was Dale Johnson. When he confirmed he was and the boy handed him an official envelope, Dale shoved it in his pocket, because it was his turn to board, to try to manoeuvre the steps while carrying a crutch and a green duffel bag with one arm.

He was winded by the time he found a window seat and sat down. Suzie was waving both hands. The bus was closing the door by the time he finally managed to make the window drop low enough he could hear her.

'You dropped this!' she shouted, holding up the letter he'd just be given.

'It's just the final report saying they don't want me,' he said. There was no other reason the army would be giving him a letter. 'Burn it.'

'Behave yourself!' she answered in reply.

The bus was already pulling away from the curb as he shouted, 'I'll try!'

'I can't believe you managed this,' Kathryn shouted above the roar of the airplane.

Ralph, sitting across from her, stuck one thumb up in the air. 'It pays to know retired army pilots! This is your last chance to say no.'

Kathryn shook her head. 'You aren't getting rid of me that easily!'

'All right, then, snuggle down in that new coat and enjoy the ride. We'll be in Minnesota before you know it.'

That was a bit impossible with the way her heart thudded, mostly from fear. She'd only flown in an airplane once before and wasn't sure she was going to like it any more than she did then. Ralph's good news this morning had been that Dale had been released from the hospital with a broken arm and injured leg. His eyes had been injured, too, but the report said they were fine now.

The bad news had been that Dale had already left for North Dakota. On a train. But Ralph's last piece of good news was that he knew a pilot who flew mail to Minnesota and had agreed to let them sneak aboard.

If things were different, she would never have agreed. As it was, she was sitting on a wooden box, in the belly—as Ralph called it— of a plane surrounded by huge crates of letters and packages. It was a good thing that before they'd boarded the plane, he'd taken her to a store where she bought some warmer clothes, including a heavy coat, mittens, thick socks and a pair of boots.

She was also wearing trousers. Ralph said she'd freeze in a dress. Though she'd already discovered that just walking from the hotel to the store.

They'd also bought food to bring along. Ralph said the flight would take about eight hours and that they'd get on a train from there. Not that she'd be able to eat. The plane rumbled and shook so hard it took all she had just to stay atop the box. Still, she was thankful for all Ralph was doing. Without him, she had no idea where she'd be right now. She hadn't considered just how much of a foreigner she'd be, or how strange everything about America would be to her. Things were different here, very different, but Ralph insisted she'd get used to it.

He'd been right about other things, so she suspected he'd be right about that, too.

* * *

When the plane landed, her legs wobbled, but she didn't have time to worry about that. The air here was even colder and, though it was dark, snow glistened in the light cast by huge bulbs attached to the building.

Just as he had all day, Ralph quickly acquired what they needed. This time it was a ride to the train station.

'You sure are a trooper, Kathryn. Made of tough stuff,' he said with a voice that faded as the wind whipped around them as they trudged through snow that was a foot deep in places and still falling from the black night sky. 'No wonder Dale married you.'

Too cold to pull down the scarf wrapped around her head and mouth and nose, she merely nodded. The plane ride had given her plenty of time to think and some of those thoughts were not welcome ones. Several had to do with the plane going down. Thank goodness it hadn't, but that didn't solve everything. While shopping with Ralph, he'd made mention that there would be broken hearts all over North Dakota when women heard Dale had got married.

Was that why Dale had insisted they had no future? Because he'd already been in love with one of the girls back home? She'd never asked him that. Maybe he didn't love her as much as she loved him. What would she do then?

The car, driven by a man who'd been at the airport to give the pilot a ride, had dropped them off several streets away from the train station due to the snow. By the time they finally walked through the door and into the warm building, Kathryn was questioning if she should even go on to North Dakota. She was also wondering if her toes were frozen.

Ralph told her to sit down on one of the long benches while he enquired about the next train. She sat down, once again grateful not to be making this journey on her own, and then used her stiff fingers to open her purse. 'Here,' she said, handing him several bills. 'I have more if that's not enough.'

Ralph looked at the bills in her hand before he took the money. He didn't have any. The army had offered him a ride home on the train, but that wouldn't have included her, so he'd denied it, and every time he used some of her money, he promised to repay her.

He did that again, left and then returned a short time later. 'We're in luck. The train will be here in about four hours.'

Kathryn glanced at the clock on the wall. The time itself didn't mean much, her body was confused, not knowing when it was time to sleep or be awake. 'At midnight?' she asked.

'Yes, we'll be home around eight tomorrow morning,' Ralph said. 'It won't be overly comfortable, but you'll be able to sleep on the train.'

Warming, inside and out, she looked around the large station, at the other travellers who looked as worn out and weary as she must.

'Come on,' Ralph said, encouraging her to get up.

'Where are we going?'

He gestured towards a wall lined with wooden and glass phone booths. 'I need to call home so someone meets us at the station in Jamestown.'

Following him across the open space, she asked, 'How long will it be from there? To your home?'

'Only ten miles.' He sighed wistfully. 'Only ten miles.'

At one of the empty booths—others had people inside them, the glass smothering their conversations—Ralph reached into his pocket and pulled out a handful of coins. Picking through them, he shook his head. 'We'll need change. Most of these won't work.'

She dug in her purse and handed him several bills. Without the time to fully examine the currency, the denominations were still strange to her. 'Is this enough?'

'Yes, I'll be right back,' he said. 'Save this booth for us.'

As she'd done several times since their travels had started, she watched him walk away. Her heart thudded as her mind once again tried to trick her. It almost made her feel guilty. Ralph was being so kind, so helpful, yet every time she saw his back, clothed in his flight jacket, he reminded her so much of his brother she found herself wishing he was Dale. Then, fear would set in and she'd remember how he'd said they didn't have a future.

Ralph returned shortly and insisted she crowd into the small booth alongside him. Once they were inside, he told her to hold her hands out. When she did, he filled them with coins. As he dropped coins in the slot, spoke to someone and then deposited more coins, she realised even this, making a phone call, would have been nearly impossible without him.

'Hello? Ma? Ma? It's me, Ralph.'

The excited squeal coming through the telephone made Kathryn smile, or maybe it was the smile on Ralph's face that created hers.

'Yes, yes, it's me. I'm in Minneapolis, on my way home. I need someone to pick us up at the train station in Jamestown tomorrow morning at eight.'

After a long amount of talking on the other end, words Kathryn couldn't make out, Ralph spoke again.

'No, no, Dale's not with me, but Kathryn is.' After more questions she couldn't make out, he said, 'Yes, he's on his way, too, but Kathryn, his wife, is with me.' His response to additional questions was, 'Yes, you heard right. Dale's wife.'

Kathryn's stomach dropped slightly. The truth was bound to catch up with her eventually.

After saying he'd see them tomorrow, Ralph hung up, then scooped the coins out of her hands. 'Your turn,' he said, handing her the receiver. 'Time to call your parents.' He dropped in a coin. 'Give the operator the number.'

Kathryn barely had time to contemplate anything before a voice asked for a number. She rattled it off by rote, but looking at the coins in Ralph's hand, she shook her head at the amount the woman on the phone had told her to deposit. Ralph must had heard, because he started sorting coins and dropping them in the slots.

Along with static and crackling, she heard faint ringing sounds. Her heart flew into her throat when she heard her father's voice. He sounded so far away. 'Father! It's me, Kathryn!'

The static made it difficult to hear every word, but she answered what she'd heard, said that she was fine and almost to North Dakota. She was in the midst of saying that Dale wasn't with her, but Ralph was, when a voice broke in, asking for more money.

She waved a frantic hand to Ralph, who deposited the rest of the coins in his hand. When the line connected again, Mum was on the other end. Assuring Mum that she was indeed fine and not certain how much time she had, Kathryn talked almost as fast as a true American. She said she loved them and missed them, and was in the middle of promising to write a long letter with all the details as soon as possible, when the voice broke in, asking for more money.

Ralph grimaced, holding up his empty hands, and Kathryn hung the phone up.

'I can go get more change,' he said.

Turning, and noting the others waiting for the phone, she let out a sigh that was as full of satisfaction as it was longing. 'No, that's okay. It was good to hear their voices and enough to let them know I'm fine.'

He opened the door and they walked towards

the bench seat, where they'd left her two suit-
cases and his large green bag.

'Why didn't you write home while you were
gone?' she asked.

'Because of a girl named Deloris,' he said
once they'd sat down. 'Mother told me every
letter I wrote would only make Deloris miss
me more and how that wouldn't be fair to her. I
hoped she'd write to me, but then, after the clerical error, I knew her letters would never reach
me, so figured there was no use writing.'

She nodded and glanced around the room,
once again wondering if there was a girl that
Dale had written to. All this time she'd thought
she knew everything about him, but now, she
was questioning if she knew him as well as she
thought she did.

'Your turn,' Ralph said.

'My turn for what?'

'The truth.' He lifted a brow much like
Dale often had. 'Are you really married to my
brother?'

Snow was falling as the train pulled into the
station. That was nothing new for North Dakota.
It was the end of December. If he hadn't been
so despondent, Dale might have been excited
about being home. He just didn't seem to have

it in him. The three days it had taken the train to travel across the nation had made it that much longer since he'd seen Kathryn. And it made her that much further away. With no hope of the army giving him a second tour, getting back to England was little more than a pipe dream.

The train ride had also given him time to contemplate other possibilities, which were few. If he'd have married Kathryn, he could petition for the army to have her transported to America. But he hadn't. He'd been too big of a fool and had made it worse. That was for damn sure. Falling in love with an English girl. A Brigadier's daughter. He could never give her the life she'd known in England. For sure not the one she'd known before the war. A man who couldn't even fulfil a simple promise to his mother about finding one of her children had no business making other promises. Especially lifelong ones.

'Need help, soldier?'

Dale used his crutch to help him stand, then flung his duffel bag over his good shoulder. 'Thanks, but no,' he told the train porter. 'I got it.'

The air was cold enough to freeze his eyeballs open when he stepped off the train, but that didn't stop him from taking a deep breath of air. He was home, or almost, and needed to be thankful for that much. He'd get over Kathryn in time.

As much as he hated it, he was glad to have the crutch to steady his steps on the icy platform as he made his way towards the depot. There would be a payphone inside he could use to call his folks for a ride home. Dad would have to put the chains on the truck to make it to town, so his waiting wasn't over. Rather than stewing over Kathryn, he should have used the time figuring out a way to tell his mother he'd never found Ralph. He'd failed at everything he'd set out to do. Failed at finding Ralph. Failed at saving his mother from more pain. Failed with Kathryn. That hurt the most, because of all the women he'd ever known, she would be the only one to understand what he was feeling right now, his failures, and still love him. That's the kind of person she was. And another reason he'd miss her for ever.

The wind was blowing hard, yet a frown formed as he stopped walking in order to turn around. He could have sworn he'd heard someone shout his name.

The crutch slipped from his hold when he saw a man walking towards him. 'Ralph?' He questioned his sight. 'Ralph, is that you?'

'It sure is, little brother!'

The next moment he was hugging his brother in a way he'd never imagined he would. Not after years and years of living together and trying to beat up each other on a weekly basis. Questions formed faster than he could ask them.

'What are you doing here? Why didn't you write? How'd—?'

'I'll explain it all on the ride home,' Ralph said, grabbing the duffel bag that had also dropped to the ground. 'The truck's right over here. I had a friend in New York find out what train you were on, but I'm the only one who knows.' Ralph's grin grew even wider. 'Everyone's going to be excited to see you. Every. One.'

The ride home was slow-going, but the time was well used to catch up on where Ralph had been—in England, not fifty miles from Thorpe Abbotts—the clerical error, his trip across the ocean on a floating hospital and an amazing volunteer he'd met, his airplane ride home and of course how well all the family was doing. Dale told him about the plane going down and his injuries. The rest, the parts he'd enjoyed—and Kathryn—he didn't mention. No use rubbing salt in wounds.

It was still snowing and whatever sunlight there had been filtering through the clouds had faded, so when the house came into the view, the glow of lights in the windows filled him with a unique warmth. There was also plenty of emptiness. He felt torn, obligated to be happy and excited about coming home, while knowing deep inside he'd never be truly happy again. Not with the way things had ended with Kathryn. With her living on the other side of the world.

Ralph parked the truck as close to the front door as possible, then grabbed the duffel bag while jumping out the driver's door. Dale, using the crutch, was slower. He walked up the shovelled pathway and then up the steps on to the porch, where Ralph was waiting to open the door.

Dale moved forward to walk in first. The idea of surprising everyone had grown on him during the ride. Had to with the way Ralph kept insisting everyone was going to be happy to see him.

Ralph pulled open the screen door and Dale pushed open the solid front door he'd ran through a million times. The rush of warmth, the smells of supper cooking and the familiar sights that he hadn't even realised he'd missed, filled him as he stepped inside the house.

His mother was in the dining room, looked at him and her mouth dropped in astonishment before she let out a squeal that would have woken the dead.

'Dale! Dale!' she shouted, running across the room.

Dale let go of his crutch and caught her, giving her a solid hug, but his head had snapped towards the kitchen door, where a clatter and crash had sounded.

'I hope that wasn't one of your good dishes,' he said jokingly.

'I don't care if it was.'

'Neither do I.'

He spun around as his father walked out of the living room. They hadn't changed. Not a bit. His mother, with her curly dark hair, still looked young enough to be his sister and his father, wearing his bib overalls, still looked as though he could toss bales of hay, one in each hand. Which he probably still did.

Dale hugged each of them and agreed it was good to see them, too. As they stepped back, looking around him oddly, he shifted to glance over his shoulder. If they were both here, who had broken the dish in the kitchen?

The woman standing in the doorway shocked him so soundly he couldn't move. Couldn't think. Other than to admit what he already knew. That she was the most beautiful woman on earth. Her dark hair was tumbling over her shoulders and the blue dress fit her perfect curves like a glove.

Was he seeing things? 'Kathryn?'

She nodded and, though she was smiling, he heard the sob she tried to contain, saw the tears burst from her eyes. Tears smarted in his eyes, too, and he'd never crossed ten feet of space so fast in his life. Ten feet had never seemed so far either.

They met midway between the front door and the kitchen. He caught her around the waist as she threw her arms around his neck. He lifted her off the ground and kissed her, kissed her as though he hadn't seen her in years. Which was exactly how it felt.

She was kissing him, too, and laughing and crying, and kissing him again.

He'd never been so full of love, of happiness. The only frustration he had was the cast preventing him from holding her with both arms. 'I can't believe you're here,' he said between kissing her eyes, her forehead, her lips. 'How?'

'Let me take this off for you,' Ma said, pulling on the flight jacket that his good arm was still through while the rest of the coat hung to the floor.

He let go of Kathryn long enough for his mother to pull off his coat.

'Why didn't you tell us you got married?' Ma asked.

Dale froze, so did Kathryn, and the mischief in her eyes said there was a whole lot she wasn't telling him.

Ralph slapped him on the back right then. 'Don't try to deny it. She's got the papers to prove it.' Then, still walking, Ralph said, 'Something sure smells good in the kitchen.'

The happiness shining inside her was brighter than ever, yet Kathryn couldn't deny the splattering of fear bubbling in her stomach. 'Are you mad?' she whispered.

Dale frowned and quietly asked, 'Does your father know you're here?'

'Yes.'

'And your mother?'

The way his blue eyes started to twinkle made her toes curl. 'Yes. They helped me.'

'They did?'

He was as handsome as ever in his green uniform, with his dark hair waving across his forehead. 'Yes, they did. Please say that's all right. Please say you're not mad.'

Pulling her forward, he hugged her tight. 'I'm not mad. Not mad at all.'

She hugged him tighter and, while doing

so, frowned. 'You've lost weight. Good thing I baked a pie today.'

'Gooseberry?'

She laughed. 'No, blueberry. We figured you'd arrive today or tomorrow.'

He shook his head, but was grinning. 'How long have you been here?'

'Two days.' She kissed his lips quickly. 'I'll explain later. Supper is ready.'

The meal was the most wonderful one she'd ever eaten, even though she barely tasted anything. Barely ate. She couldn't take her eyes off Dale long enough to eat. But there was laughter. So much laughter. And happiness. The entire house bubbled with it.

That happiness continued long after the meal had ended.

They entered his bedroom, the one she'd been staying in since arriving, together. As soon as the door was shut, he grasped her hand and spun her around, kissing her until she was completely breathless.

Then, while still holding her, while they were both catching their breath, he asked, 'Married?'

Although she'd hoped otherwise, convinced herself otherwise, there was a chance he didn't want that. He also could be very upset she'd lied to his parents. They believed her completely and the way they'd welcomed her into their family had planted a good supply of guilt inside her. She'd never lied to anyone before and this lie was so large, she wasn't sure she'd ever be able to correct it.

She stepped out of his arms. 'It was the only way I could come to America. Stay here.'

He ran a hand through his freshly washed hair. 'And if it's ever discovered, you could be in very serious trouble.' Letting out a groan, he said, 'Your father, your mother—'

'Helped me,' she interjected. 'Father had the papers written up, they are as real as they can be.'

Her heart skipped a beat at the way he shook his head. 'Except we aren't married.'

'I know.' She shrugged while adding, 'But I was hoping you might want to be.'

He took her hand, rubbed the back of it while saying, 'More than anything on earth or in heaven.'

She hadn't realised how much anxiety had been inside her until that moment. 'I want that more than anything, too.' Stepping close enough to wrap both arms around him, she said, 'When I heard you'd been injured, that they were sending you home, I had to come. I love you more than anything, anyone, and you are more important to me than…' she couldn't think of a suitable comparison, other than '…my own life.'

'Don't say that,' he whispered.

Leaning back, she said, 'It's the truth. I met Ralph on the ship and wouldn't be here today without his help, but I would have eventually got here. Someway, somehow, I would have gotten here.'

'I believe that,' he said, kissing the tip of her nose. 'I almost didn't come home. I tried to get a second deployment so I could return to England. Return to you.'

She'd never thought of that. 'Thank goodness you didn't.'

'Thank goodness the army said no.' His hand ran up and down her side, as he asked, 'So when did we supposedly get married?'

'June twelfth.' She'd chosen the date, telling her father she and Dale had been together that day and that others could prove it.

He grinned. 'The day you dropped your scarf in the pub.'

Her heartbeat increased, both because he remembered the date and because his hand was still caressing her side. 'The day you came up with the parachute idea.'

'And the day I fell in love with you.'

Her insides nearly melted. 'That's the day I

fell in love with you, too.' Which had been the reason she'd chosen that date. But he was right. They really hadn't been married that day. 'I thought I'd find you in New York. Never imagined that it would go this far. Lying to your family.' She let out a heavy sigh. 'What are we going to do?'

His kissed her soundly before whispering, 'We're going to do what every married couple would do upon seeing each other again after months, Mrs Johnson.'

Happiness nearly bubbled out of her as she glanced towards the bed. 'We are?'

'Yes, we are. We'll figure out how to make you an honest woman tomorrow, but I know it won't be too difficult. Not too difficult at all.'

Epilogue

❦

1st of January, 1943

Dearest Diary,
Little did I know how important you would
become when Charlotte gave you to me.
You've been my confidant in what has
proven to be the greatest journey of my
life, and though I'm saddened that our time
together has come to an end and I shall
never forget the people I wrote about be-
tween your pages, it's a new year and I'm
embarking on a new journey, one of being
a married woman. An honestly married
woman! Dale and I were married yester-
day, at the courthouse in Bismarck. Ralph
and Deloris stood up for us and then we
stood up for them. Of course, other than
the four of us, everyone believes just Ralph

and Deloris got married. Dale says that's just fine and will be for ever. I agree. I wish I could put into words how extremely happy I am. After our wedding, we spent the night in a hotel where everyone was celebrating the new year. The festivities were so much fun! I called Mum and Father, and they, too, were excited. Mum says Dale and I are special, because no other married couple will get to celebrate their anniversary twice every year, she also says they'll come see us as soon as possible.

The day after he arrived home, Dale received a letter from Father, asking him, if possible, to stay in New York because I was on my way there. Dale said the letter was given to him as he was boarding the bus, but fell out of his pocket and the nurse who took care of him found it and forwarded it on to him. He received another letter, it was from Marilyn, who had heard of his accident. She and her husband are both in Nebraska and they, too, plan on visiting once the weather allows.

It snows here a lot, which is amazing. I've written the children and Charlotte and Norman all about it. And about marrying Dale, and my new family here, and so many other things. I could fill a book with stories about every wonderful thing that happens to me each day, but that would take too much time. This will be the last note I write because this is your last page, but I will tuck you safely away and keep you for ever. You have been a very special part of my life this past year. The memories between your pages will always be some of the most wonderful, and perhaps harrowing, of how I went from being Kathryn Rose Winslow to Mrs Dale Johnson.

* * * * *

COMING SOON!

We really hope you enjoyed reading this book. If you're looking for more romance, be sure to head to the shops when new books are available on

Thursday
26th July

To see which titles are coming soon, please visit
millsandboon.co.uk

MILLS & BOON

Coming next month

THE CAPTAIN CLAIMS HIS LADY
Annie Burrows

Lizzie felt her cheeks heating as her thoughts, and her tongue, became hopelessly tangled. How she wished she had more experience of talking to men. Well, single men, who'd asked her to dance with them, that was. Then she might not be making quite such a fool of herself with this one.

'I will make a confession,' Harry said, leaning close to her ear so that his voice rippled all the way down her spine in a caressing manner.

'Will you?' She lost her ability to breathe properly. It felt as if her lungs, now, were as tangled as her thoughts.

'When I looked in upon the ballroom, earlier, and saw how few people were actually dancing, and how many were watching, my nerve almost failed.'

'Well, it is just that there are not that many people here who are fit enough to dance. But they do enjoy watching others. And then…'

'Giving them marks out of ten, I dare say,' he finished for her.

'Yes, that's about it. And I'm terribly sorry, but—'

'Oh, no,' he said sternly. 'You cannot retreat now. We are almost at the dance floor. Can you imagine what people will say if you turn and run from me?'

'That you've had a narrow escape?'

'That I've had…' He turned, and took both her hands in his. 'Miss Hutton, are you trying to warn me that you are not a good dancer?'

She nodded. Then hung her head.

She felt a gloved hand slide under her chin and lift her face. And saw him smiling down at her. Beaming, in fact. As though she'd just told him something wonderful.

'I have no…' she tried to wave her hands to demonstrate her lack of co-ordination, only to find them still firmly clasped between his own. 'And people do try to get out of my way, but…'

'I can see that this is going to be an interesting experience for both of us,' he put in.

'And for the spectators.'

'Yes,' he said, turning and leading her on to the dance floor where she could see the dim outlines of other people forming a set. 'Let us give them something worth watching.'

Continue reading
THE CAPTAIN CLAIMS HIS LADY
Annie Burrows

Available next month
www.millsandboon.co.uk

LET'S TALK
Romance

For exclusive extracts, competitions
and special offers, find us online:

- **f** facebook.com/millsandboon
- **⦿** @millsandboonuk
- **🐦** @millsandboon

Or get in touch on 0844 844 1351*

For all the latest titles coming soon, visit
millsandboon.co.uk/nextmonth